Praise for *USA Today* bestseller
A SEAL in Wolf's Clothing

"A delightful and tantalizing read. The characters are spirited and realistic… You'll be captivated."

— *Thoughts in Progress*

"I have a thing for wolves and Navy SEALs…put them together and I'm in HEAVEN."

— *Book Lovin' Mamas*

"Another riveting, fun, and sexy read by Terry Spear. If you love werewolf books, you don't want to miss this one."

— *Star-Crossed Romance*

"Excitement, hot and sexy love scenes, and situational humor that has me laughing out loud."

— *Fresh Fiction*

"Navy SEALs are the bomb to start with, and the one in this book is a shapeshifter to boot. Very sexy!"

— *Debbie's Book Bag*

"Spear, you did it to me again. I am in love with the wolf world you created and wouldn't mind an alpha SEAL wolf of my own."

— *United by Books*

"Tantalizing and suspenseful…Terry Spear is an alpha in her own right."

— *Anna's Book Blog*

Praise for *A SEAL Wolf Christmas*

"Spear's wonderful gifts as a writer [are] on clear display…the story is thrilling, containing edge-of-your-seat action."

—RT Book Reviews

"A complete, adventure-filled romance overflowing with the best of what keeps me addicted to books by Ms. Spear."

—Long and Short Reviews

"Terry Spear once again delivers… Well written, entertaining, and all around an incredible read."

—BTS Reviews

"A masterful storyteller, Ms. Spear brings her sexy wolves to life."

—Romance Junkies

"Escape to a world of amazing characters and intriguing adventure… Spear's extensive research and eye for detail brings this tantalizing tale to life."

—Thoughts in Progress

"Delicious, intense, and charming."

—Anna's Book Blog

"This book is a roller-coaster ride of mystery, intrigue, and wolfy love… Terry Spear is a masterful storyteller."

—HEAs Are Us

Also by Terry Spear

Heart of the Wolf

Heart of the Wolf
Destiny of the Wolf
To Tempt the Wolf
Legend of the White Wolf
Seduced by the Wolf
Wolf Fever
Heart of the Highland Wolf
Dreaming of the Wolf
A SEAL in Wolf's Clothing
A Howl for a Highlander
A Highland Werewolf Wedding
A SEAL Wolf Christmas
Silence of the Wolf
Hero of a Highland Wolf
A Highland Wolf Christmas

Heart of the Jaguar

Savage Hunger
Jaguar Fever
Jaguar Hunt
Jaguar Pride

SEAL WOLF HUNTING

TERRY SPEAR

sourcebooks
casablanca

Published by Sourcebooks Casablanca, an imprint of Sourcebooks, Inc.
P.O. Box 4410, Naperville, Illinois 60567-4410
(630) 961-3900
Fax: (630) 961-2168
www.sourcebooks.com

Printed and bound in Canada.
MBP 10 9 8 7 6 5 4 3 2 1

To my good friend Loretta Melvin, who fell in love with the SEALs and claimed Paul Cunningham for her own. He is yours, pink palm trees and green flamingos and all, as long as you promise to share him a little. But he will always be yours. Thanks for being a good friend!

Chapter 1

"Damn it, Paul. You couldn't help what happened," Allan Rappaport said as they unloaded their bags from the SUV. The two men had taken a red-eye and arrived at Allan's family's mountain cabin in northern Montana in the predawn darkness.

Paul Cunningham and Allan, his U.S. Navy SEAL buddy, had just returned from one hell of a mission in the Ecuadorian Amazon, where they'd tracked down four college students on a field trip who'd been taken hostage for ransom. Paul and Allan had managed to rescue the three young men. But not the woman.

Paul couldn't quit envisioning the woman pleading with him to hold on to her as she dangled in a harness off the cliff the rest of them had just climbed. The humidity and stress had made her hand sweaty, but he wouldn't let go of her for anything. Then the gunfire had erupted. Paul knew before it happened that he was going to lose her.

From across the stream that Paul and the others had so recently forded, the kidnappers had shot her three times in the back. A fourth round had slammed into Paul's arm. Yet he still hadn't let her go. Not even after he felt her hand release his.

"Thanks for helping with the woman," Paul said to Allan, looking around the cabin's familiar, rustic living room and trying to shake the images that haunted him.

He'd been so wrapped up in chastising himself that he had never even thanked Allan for taking out the men who had been shooting at them.

"Hell, I owe you for all the times you've saved my ass. I was only too glad to shoot the two bastards who killed the girl. Besides, you think I could have gotten the others to safety without you?"

Yeah, Paul knew Allan would have. He was good at his job. All of their SEAL wolf team were. But he also knew that Allan would never have left him behind.

Because of their high success rate on extractions and other jobs like this, they were often hired to do special contract work—though only the wolves on Hunter Greymere's team knew their wolf senses gave them the edge. They no longer served with the U.S. Navy because they didn't want to raise suspicions due to their longevity because of slower-than-human aging. Even so, they still considered themselves a SEAL team. They had met and operated that way for years, usually under Hunter's leadership.

In this case, no one else had been free to conduct the mission. When an undercover operative called Hunter with the job of extracting the students, he'd relayed the information to Paul and Allan. They had been the students' only real hope of being rescued without suffering for months in the hostage-takers' care—or dying at their hands.

With his added wolf's strength, Allan had carried the dead woman at a grueling run through the steamy jungle, insisting that Paul lead the way, as he always did when they were on a mission without Hunter. But Paul suspected Allan also knew he would have had a rougher time carrying the woman, wounded as he was. The burning pain in his arm, combined with the heat of the jungle, made him woozy, and he'd had a hell of a time keeping a clear head for some of the trek. His driving concern had been to save the rest of the students as quickly as possible and ensure he didn't lose his partner. And to take the woman's body home to her family.

"You did everything you could to save her life. We got the others out. We saved their lives. Sometimes we have losses. You know that."

Paul knew how hard it had been on Allan also. The two men just dealt with losing a hostage in different ways.

Thanks to their wolf's fast-healing genetics, Paul had only needed a short stay with Hunter and his pack to recover from his injury. He was glad he hadn't returned here first. Allan's mother would have fawned over him and his injury ten times worse than Hunter's pack mates had. That was also why he wasn't about to tell Catherine Rappaport what had gone down.

"Better call your mother. You know she'll have a fit if she learns we didn't contact her as soon as we got here. I swear she has spies in the area watching for our arrival," Paul said, trying to get off the subject of the mission.

"Old Man Stokes at the gas station. I bet you anything he's the one who calls her. We always stop there and fill up the tank before we come out here for our vacations. And he knows we're usually here for the last two weeks in July, unless we're held up for some reason."

Northern Montana was the perfect place for hiking, fishing in the streams, and running through the woods as wolves. But as Paul sorted out his gear, he still couldn't sort out his feelings about this last mission. *He* was on vacation. And the third-year botany student, Mary Ellen Wister, was *dead*.

Paul let out his breath in exasperation, recalling the way the woman's parents had dissolved into tears when he and Allan gave them the news. He'd tried to give up the ghost and quit rethinking the Ecuador mission. But he couldn't hide his feelings from Allan, who had been like a brother to him since Allan's mother had raised the pair of them.

"I'm fine. I'm not thinking about it."

Allan grunted and headed into the kitchen. "If you're not thinking about it, why are you mentioning it again?" He opened the refrigerator door. "No food in the fridge. We need to go into town and get some things."

"I'm not thinking about it. Okay?" And yet Paul was. He had nightmares every time he drifted off to sleep. In those dreams, he was staring down into the woman's frantic gray-green eyes, hearing the barrage of gunfire popping, feeling her jerk with the bullets' impact against her back, and seeing her mouth open and her eyes widen.

The last words she gritted out were "Thank you"— not for saving her, because she knew in that instant he couldn't, but for trying. Then she had closed her eyes and released his hand. He wouldn't leave her in the jungle. He'd had to get her home—to her family.

"We did the best we could," Allan said, returning to the living room, his dark hair tousled, his green eyes stern. "Her family was grateful we brought her home. Can you imagine what a nightmare that would have been for them? Envisioning her left behind in the jungle? You have to accept it and move on."

"Right." Paul still wondered if they shouldn't have taken a different path. One that would have ensured they all had made it out alive. Which was the problem with being the leader. Any mistake was his responsibility. He couldn't be like some men, who considered casualties a part of doing a mission. No one was ever expendable as far as he was concerned, and he was having a hard time letting go of the tragedy. She hadn't been just a casualty. She had been a flesh-and-blood woman with a boyfriend back home, parents and a sister, and tons of friends. He would have done anything to change the outcome and bring her home alive.

"I know what you're thinking. And no. They were coming at us from all directions. The only way out of there was to climb the cliffs. If she'd been stronger, like the men, she would have made it. But we had no other choice. You made the right decision. For all of us. Listen, feel free to talk about this anytime, but we've also got to take the time to let it go and enjoy our time off, to decompress. All right?"

"Yeah. Right."

"Did you get hold of Emma and check about her cabin?" Allan asked, stowing his scuba gear.

"Yeah, she said we can use it any time we want. I told her we'd stay there near the end of our two weeks here. I don't know why we've never done it before."

The Greypaws' lakeside cabin was on the opposite side of Flathead Lake from the Rappaports' property. The Cunningham family originally bought the cabin for the Greypaws to live in, since the Greypaws were Native Americans and not permitted to purchase the land at the time. Later, when the Cunninghams could gift it to the

Greypaws, they did. Allan's family's place was on the mountain and didn't have ready access to Flathead Lake, so his family was really looking forward to the change of pace. Being right on the water would be great for fishing, boating, and diving.

Paul started to haul the bags down the hall to the bedroom he always used. "I agree that we need the time to move forward and not constantly rehash what went down in the Amazon jungle."

"Good. Let me call Mom and—" Allan's phone rang.

Paul paused in the hallway. There was only a short list of people who might be calling this early. If Hunter, their SEAL team leader, had a job for them...

Allan put the phone on speaker, and Paul figured that meant business until he heard Allan's mother's worried voice. "I didn't know you were arriving this early. I just heard that you're at the cabin. *Don't* come by the house yet. Later. I'll call you and let you know when you can drop by."

Allan wore a worried frown as big as the Grand Canyon.

A chill crawled up Paul's spine.

He'd never known Catherine to be that flustered when they arrived home. Usually she gushed over her son and Paul's visit—and wanted to see them the minute they arrived. He thought of her fondly as a second mother, his own mother having died along with his father when Paul was eleven.

Allan said casually, "We'll have to run into town to get some groceries. I thought we'd drop by and say hi. Just for a minute."

"No, we're busy. I've got to go. Talk to you later."

She would never turn down the opportunity to see them right away, no matter how early it was. They'd been on missions for the last five months and hadn't had any time to return and visit with her. And every mission could have been the death of them. Right before she hung up on him, they heard a woman shriek and then another woman yell out, sounding just as frightened.

Paul and Allan only needed a second to grab their emergency mission gear and head out the door, hauling ass.

For a few minutes, they didn't speak as they jumped into Paul's SUV and roared down the dirt road.

"Probably nothing," Paul finally reasoned, hoping that was so, but he couldn't help worrying that the women were in real trouble.

"Right." Allan was wired tightly, clenching his hands and grinding his teeth. He was ready to spring into action as a wolf. They both were.

"Hostage situation?"

The vision of the half-starved college men and woman crouching near a swamp in the jungle—grungy and so grateful to be rescued—flashed through Paul's mind right before he imagined Catherine and Allan's sister, Rose, and her best friend, Lori Greypaw, at gunpoint in Catherine's home.

"Could be. Mom must have known we would realize something was wrong. She was trying to warn us not to come, which meant she wanted us to come."

Paul wondered why anyone in their right mind would want to take Catherine Rappaport hostage in vintage Cottage Grove. All that existed there were a small community of humans and the remnants of the Cunningham

wolf pack. Those left in the pack—Lori, her grandma,
Allan, his mother and sister, and Paul—still referred
to the pack that way. Though Paul had often said they
should rename it the Rappaport pack, because there
were more of that family left. Still, his mother and father
had been the leaders until their untimely demise, and in
memory of their leadership, those left behind still faith-
fully called it the Cunningham pack.

Thankfully, it was early enough in the morning that
he and Allan had the cover of darkness on their side. He
couldn't believe they'd risked their necks in the jungle
only to return to their hometown—where everything was
usually so quiet—and run into real trouble. He'd never
known Cottage Grove to have problems more serious
than the usual small-town drama—a drunk standing in
the road, not sure where he was; minor thefts, usually by
out-of-towners; and once, a newly married woman who
claimed her husband had fallen off the mountain cliffs
"accidentally." But now he and Allan sensed a new kind
of danger in their hometown.

Any rescue operation involved a huge risk—for
everyone. But this time, it was personal and hit way too
close to home.

"Rose." Paul thought that one of the screams had
come from Allan's twin sister, Rose, who had been like
a sister to Paul as well. She'd been a pain-in-the-butt
tagalong when he and Allan had wanted to do guy things
or spend time with girlfriends. And yet they were close,
and Paul would do anything for her—or take care of
anyone who had any intention of hurting her.

"Yeah." Allan's expression was hard and worried,
but he looked ready to kick ass.

"And the other? Lori Greypaw?" It was hard to tell. Paul had recognized Rose's shriek because he'd heard it often enough—like when Allan had dumped a cooler filled with crushed ice in the lake where she had been swimming. Or the time they caught her kissing a guy in the woods when she was fifteen. Allan had sworn he was going to kill the human male and taken off after him. But Paul didn't recall ever having heard Lori scream or shriek in all the years he'd known her while growing up.

Allan glanced at Paul. "I'm sure of it."

They reached the area where Catherine lived, with sparsely scattered homes surrounded by harvested alfalfa crops with rolled bales of hay scattered about, and cows grazing in some fields and horses in others. Most of the houses had lights on inside. Bordering the edge of Catherine's lawn, balsam fir trees reached a hundred and fifty feet into the sky and provided perfect cover for Paul and Allan. Paul pulled onto a dirt parking spot where farm equipment was off-loaded to sow and harvest the fields.

He and Allan quickly stripped out of their blue jeans and shirts and yanked on black pants and T-shirts to blend in with the darkness. They applied face paint, armed themselves with guns and knives, and headed through the dry fields to reach the fir trees, then crossed the grassy lawn to the part of Catherine's house that was dark.

They had done this kind of mission so many times that they didn't have to think twice about what they would do. Lights were on in the living room and kitchen only. Lori's bright red Pinto was sitting in the gravel driveway. Rose's pickup truck was parked next to the

Pinto, and a black sedan neither Paul nor Allan recognized was behind that.

Paul moved in behind the shrubs hugging the foundation to reach Allan's sister's bedroom, but the window was locked. They headed around to the back patio. Allan pulled out his spare key and unlocked the door as carefully and quietly as he could, then gently opened the door.

It made only a slight squeaking sound, and Paul hoped that whoever was there hadn't heard them enter. Only wolves—like their family—would be able to hear it.

"No!" Lori said from the kitchen. "I won't do it!"

Chapter 2

ADRENALINE SURGING, PAUL AND ALLAN RACED across the family room and down the carpeted floor of the hallway between two of the bedrooms. From there, they crept toward the kitchen, where they'd heard Lori speaking.

The living room was all clear. Paul and Allan silently passed the guest bathroom and neared the entrance to the kitchen and breakfast nook, where they heard the clinking of silverware and dishes.

In place, Paul was about to peek around the doorjamb to determine the extent of the threat when Catherine shouted, "No, watch out!"

The crashing of porcelain against the tile floor spurred the men on. Paul's heart was pounding triple time when he appeared in the doorway to the kitchen, materializing out of the darkness in black clothes and black face paint, gun in hand.

Rose saw Paul first. She screamed and dropped the coffee mug she was holding. It crashed on the floor, splattering coffee everywhere.

Lori swung the broom she was holding and whacked Paul in the head with it while Catherine yelled in fright. Confused, Paul assessed the situation in the kitchen and found only the four women there. One broken plate. One broken coffee mug and coffee splashed everywhere. The delightful aroma of huckleberries and blackberries

cooking and the scent of the spices Catherine was adding
to jars for Rose's gift shop filled the room. No armed
hostage-takers anywhere.

Overwhelmed with relief, Paul quickly holstered
his gun and tried to wrench the broom away from Lori
before she could hit him again. This time she looked
like she was dying to, just on principle for scaring her.
When he couldn't wrest the broom from her, he grabbed
her shoulders instead, pressed her hard against the wall,
and kissed her.

He'd been wanting to do that forever—since the last
time they'd resolved an issue in this manner.

His chest pressed against her breasts. She wasn't
wearing a bra under the slinky tank top—and his internal
thermostat turned even hotter. Her shorts were…short,
showing off her shapely tanned legs, and her feet were
bare. One scorching, sexy she-wolf package.

Unexpectedly, Lori twisted her body and swept her
leg behind him, tripping him and effectively knocking
him off balance. He pulled her down with him as he
fell on his backside, and she landed on top, dropping
the broom. He grinned at the way she'd outmaneuvered
him. He'd forgotten about her martial-arts training.

"It's me," he said, just in case she hadn't realized it.

"Jeez, Paul, you look like a bank robber!"

Lori was lying on top of him, not making a move to
get up. His body immediately responded with ravenous
hunger. He took advantage of the moment by flipping
her onto her back and kissing her again. She smelled of
lilacs, woman, and she-wolf, and tasted of honey as he
licked the sticky sweetness off her lips.

She finally smiled a little against his mouth, about

the same time as Catherine cleared her throat. As much as Paul didn't want to move from their stimulating pose—and hoping he could quickly get his body under control—he eased off Lori and pulled her to her feet.

This was how he wanted to see her when he came home from missions.

Brows raised, Allan put his weapons away. "I was going to ask if the two of you needed my help…"

"This is why I didn't want you and Paul to run with those boys any longer," Catherine scolded, picking the broom up off the floor so she could sweep up the broken dishes, while Rose cleaned up the coffee splattered on the floor.

"The boys" Catherine was referring to were their wolf Navy SEAL teammates, none of whom had been boys for a very long time.

Frowning at them, Catherine tucked a dark blond curl behind her ear. Dressed in her favorite apron—lavender with "Hot and Spicy" embroidered on it, a gift from Paul and Allan for Mother's Day this year—she was also wearing her mother-of-two-wayward-wolf-cubs look. "I told you I was busy and would see you later," Catherine said reproachfully.

Lori's gray-haired grandma, Emma, was sitting at the kitchen table, sipping tea and smiling. "Now, Catherine, don't scold. Allan and Paul are such good boys."

Still cleaning up the mess, Catherine snorted. "Running around in the jungle like that…" She turned to eye them. "Still practicing your stealth moves? You're *supposed* to be on vacation."

Paul had almost forgotten how he and Allan had taken a few years off Catherine's life when they were young by practicing sneaking up on her, either as wolves or as future SEALs. The whole point was for her never to see them. Only she always did—because of her wolf senses—and they'd gotten scolded back then too.

Paul glanced around the kitchen, trying to figure out what the women were up to. They'd had buttermilk biscuits and honey… He licked his lips, still tasting the sweetness on his mouth after kissing Lori. A stack of paper was sitting on the table. It looked to be some project Catherine was in charge of, as usual. And she'd been making jams and the like for Rose's shop.

Movement behind them in the dim hallway made Paul and Allan whip around to see Michael Anderson wearing only jeans as he strolled into the kitchen, his red hair mussed and his hazel-green eyes wide at seeing Paul and Allan. "When did you two get in?"

Michael was the brother-in-law of their SEAL team leader, Hunter Greymere. Neither Michael nor his sister, Tessa, had been born as *lupus garous*. Yet they both had been drawn to seek out wolves—Michael painting them, Tessa photographing them. Then Hunter had gotten involved with Tessa, and everything had changed.

"We got in just a little bit ago. Hell, we didn't know you were going to be here. Didn't you hear all the racket in here?" Paul stepped forward and shook Michael's hand.

"Heavy sleeper," Michael said, looking a little sheepish.

Paul remembered that the Bigfork Festival of the Arts had been last weekend on the shore of Flathead Lake. "Was your work at the art festival?"

"Yeah. Catherine and Rose had a booth showcasing

their homemade salsas and jellies. Emma displayed a lot of her Native American beaded jewelry, belts, and moccasins. And they invited me to showcase my artwork too. I stayed the week and painted a new picture for the…" Michael glanced at the women, then cleared his throat.

"For a special auction for a charitable cause. Then at the festival, one of the galleries put some of my paintings on display. I also brought some new paintings for Rose's gift shop. I've got a flight out to Portland this afternoon. I'm going to drop by and see Tessa and Hunter first, then I'm leaving for Brazil for another showing."

"Brazil." Paul was a little surprised that Michael would be leaving the States, but figured he would have someone from Hunter's pack watching over him. Newly turned wolves always had a shadow from the pack. "Are you doing well with your paintings?"

"Can't complain. They're still winning awards and selling well," Michael said. "Get lots of dates." He grinned.

Same old Michael. Charming. Talented.

"Doing all right controlling your wolf half?" Paul asked. This was the first time he'd seen Michael on his own, without a wolf chaperoning him—one who had either been born a wolf or who had been turned years earlier. For newer wolves, the call of the full moon could still wreak havoc with their control.

"Been doing great. Thanks for asking," Michael said, sounding proud of the fact.

Still, Paul thought it was way too soon to let Michael out on his own. Paul was just glad everyone in his wolf pack had been born that way. New wolves could be real trouble.

"If we don't see you before you leave, give Tessa a hug for us, will you?" Paul asked.

Allan said, "Yeah, and good luck with your exhibits."

"Thanks. Who would ever have thought I'd have the opportunity to paint wolves that weren't exactly all wolf? Hey, would you be up to shifting so that I can catch you on canvas?"

Paul smiled and shook his head. "Not this time." The thought of lying around for hours while Michael painted him didn't appeal.

Michael looked inquiringly at Allan.

"Not me," Allan quickly said.

Diversion over, Paul thought Allan would explain to his mother why they'd donned face paint, armed themselves to the max, and silently slipped into her home, ready for a fight. Instead, Allan said, "Come on, Paul. We'll come back later when the situation is less...hostile." He glanced at Lori. "Or...something."

Lori was wearing a small smirk, her dark hair curling about her shoulders, her dark brown eyes smiling at Paul, and he sure got the impression that she would hang around during his visit this time. He hoped he'd helped to change her mind if she had any notion of leaving again.

He and Allan had left the house and were making their way along the road to Paul's SUV when Paul asked, "So what was *that* all about?"

"I could ask you the same question. I...didn't know you had a thing for Lori. I mean, I used to think you were interested in her, but the two of you never went anywhere with it." Allan waited for an explanation, but Paul didn't offer one. "Did it seem to you that the ladies were hiding something?" Allan asked.

"Yeah, it did." They climbed into the SUV and drove off.

"They were being secretive," Allan said.

"Yeah, I agree." Paul recalled the guilty look Catherine had worn, which was why she'd turned her expression into a frown and immediately begun scolding them. Not that they hadn't frightened her and the other women, but he was certain something more was going on. Rose's mischievous expression indicated she knew what it was all about. He suspected it had something to do with Allan and him. Lori had worn a similar expression, once they were done kissing. Even Michael had seemed a little apprehensive—he had glanced at the women as if to get his cues.

"The last time they looked that guilty, they were contemplating marrying me off to Tara Baxter," Allan said. "Mom thought if she could entice me to settle down with a mate, I wouldn't want to tear off on these high-risk jobs any longer." Allan glanced at Paul. "Maybe Mom is working on a mate prospect for *you* this time."

That would be the day. Not only were there no other she-wolves their age in town besides Lori and Rose—well, and Tara—but Paul loved his job. Every assignment was completely different from the last, offering exhilarating, fulfilling, heart-thumping excitement. And it meant saving people who might not have a prayer otherwise.

"This place isn't known to have a big wolf population—as in our *lupus garou* kind—female or otherwise. So who would she try to set me up with?" Paul asked, figuring Catherine *wouldn't* attempt that with him.

"I was thinking of Lori, and then you went and kissed

her." Allan grinned at him. "Hell, I thought she would have used one of her more lethal martial-arts maneuvers on you, not taken you down and kissed you back. Have you been keeping in touch with her on the sly?"

"Me? Hell, no."

Since she taught martial arts to the local kids and had a fourth-degree black belt in jujitsu, Paul wondered how Lori would fare if he and she were to do a little workout—when he was better prepared for her takedown maneuvers. Paul had to admit that even though he loved his job, he had wanted to see Lori again. Especially since for the last two years, she had been conspicuously absent whenever he was around. He told himself it was just because she was part of his pack and he wanted to know what was going on, but that wasn't true. He had wanted to see *her*.

"So why *did* you kiss her?" Allan asked.

"To keep her from smacking me in the head with the broom for a second time. I couldn't get it away from her without too much of a struggle. I figured a more subtle and different approach might work."

Allan chuckled. "Subtle?"

Paul smiled.

"I don't think I've ever seen Lori scared like that before. When she hit you, I was glad you led the way. I wouldn't have thought to kiss her, though. Maybe we should add that to our tactical maneuvers training."

Paul chuckled as he pulled into the grocery store and parked. "What do you think about Michael coming here without a wolf chaperone?"

"Not something I would allow. Not yet. But Hunter must have trusted him."

"I can just imagine all the trouble Michael could get into." Paul considered Allan's black face paint, the whites of his eyes bright in contrast. "I don't know about me, but *you* sure as hell look scary."

"We apply it so much on missions that I had forgotten we were wearing it in the civilized public."

Darkness still enveloped the area, but the sun was just beginning to appear orange and gold behind the store.

They scrubbed off the face paint with wet wipes Paul kept in the backseat, then headed inside.

"You didn't just kiss her because of the broom incident," Allan said, not about to give up on the notion. "Just like she didn't kiss you back to say she was sorry for smacking you."

Amused that Allan was so curious, Paul grabbed a basket and began picking out some chicken and whatever else they needed for their stay. A couple of men nodded at them in greeting, seized a few snacks and a couple of bags of ice, paid, and headed out to a truck hauling a boat for early-morning fishing.

Paul was considering some choice cuts of steaks when a middle-aged man with longish sandy hair and a goatee stepped closer, eyeing the same ones. Paul grabbed a couple, then moved out of the man's way.

A brunette and a blond smiled at Allan and Paul as they loaded up their grocery carts. He wondered if they thought he and Allan were someone else. He didn't know the women, and they weren't wolves.

Three guys dressed in jeans, Western shirts, cowboy hats, and boots immediately caught Paul's attention. Damn it to hell. When did those wolves end up back in the area? Dusty Cooper peeled off to talk to one of the

women, his brother, Howard, and their constant companion, Jerome Huffman, observing. Omega wolves.
Losers. Troublemakers. So much so that their own pack
had chased them off, which essentially had saved their
miserable hides.

Allan moved closer to Paul and said under his breath,
"When the hell did they come back into the area?"

"Must have been recent or your mom would have told
us." Paul hadn't seen the men in eons and was glad of
it—the last time having been before their pack and an
all-wolf pack contracted rabies and killed most of the
members of the Cunningham pack.

"Dusty Cooper, I told you I'm not going out with
you. So get it through your thick head," the shorter of
the two women said.

Paul and Allan watched the situation, both ready
to defend the woman if she needed them to. It was a
hazard of being SEALs and protective wolves, even if
the woman was human and not part of their pack.

"You only say that because you've got your girlfriend
with you and she doesn't like me," Dusty said, casting
an irritated look at the other woman.

"Yeah." The brunette folded her arms. "Because you
can't take no for an answer. Why don't you go back to
Somerville's ranch and poke a cow. Leave Ellie alone."

"Why don't you mind your own business?" Dusty
said, using more of a growl now.

"Come on, Dusty. We're attracting a crowd." Howard
jerked a thumb in Paul and Allan's direction.

Dusty turned to look at them. Neither of them would
hesitate to put the man in his place.

"What the hell are you looking at?" Dusty's

expression declared he was ready for a fight, either to impress his friends or to show the women he wouldn't be pushed around.

"Nothing much," Paul said.

Eyes narrowed, Dusty made a move toward him, but his brother seized his arm and said again, "Come on, Bro. We've got business to attend to, and you know Somerville will dock our pay if we get involved in another fight."

Dusty turned back to the blond and said, "Later."

Then the men headed to the checkout counter, where Jerome pointed to a poster. Both Dusty and his brother glanced at it. All three men turned to stare at Paul and Allan. "Hell," Dusty said, then he and his buddies paid for their things and headed out of the store.

"Them being here doesn't bode well," Paul said to Allan as they finished getting their groceries. The cowboys were in great shape, but the SEALs had combat training the ranch hands wouldn't see coming if they got into a fight.

"I agree," Allan said. "I really thought they'd left the area for good."

When Paul and Allan reached the checkout counter, the pretty redheaded cashier smiled brightly at them. "My, my, everyone said the Somervilles' ranch hands would have the SEALs eating their dust at the auction because they'd be bought up so fast, but..." The woman looked them up and down, appraising them both. "I'd say they'll have a run for the money. I've never seen Dusty turn tail and leave when he's hitting on a woman before either. He's ticked off, to be certain."

"Auction...?" Paul asked. He wondered how she

even knew he was a SEAL. He didn't remember this woman either. Lots of people moved in and out of the community all the time.

"Sure." She motioned to a poster in the window featuring a lineup of ten men, including photos of Paul and Allan that Rose had taken when they were at the lake last year. They were wearing swimming trunks, their arms folded across their tan chests, their expressions gruff because Rose had insisted on taking the pictures. They hadn't wanted her to, but Catherine had interceded to get them to agree. Neither could say no to Allan's mother.

Now Paul realized they should have ensured that Rose didn't take the pictures.

"It's for a good cause. When Mike O'Keefe came home after losing both his legs to an IED explosion in the last conflict, the town went all out in refitting his home so that he can get in and out easier. He's got a wife, a toddler, and a kindergartner, and they can use all the help they can get. Since you're SEALs, I'm sure you understand. Anyway, the three guys on Somerville's ranch were the top contenders for getting the biggest bids. Even I'll be at the bidding. We sure hoped we could get that artist friend of yours to sign up too. But he said he had to fly off to a new exhibit."

"Michael Anderson? How do you know he's a friend?" Paul asked. Michael had only visited here a couple of times, and Paul didn't remember ever going anywhere with him in town where the connection would have been made.

"He was with Rose when they came in to get groceries yesterday. She's Allan's sister, right? And Michael was bragging to me about how those SEALs on the poster are his good friends." She pointed to a poster to the left of the other. "He's donating that beautiful painting of a wolf sitting at the river. That's just a small poster of it—he's actually donating the oil painting."

Paul gaped at it. Hell, it was Lori in her wolf form sitting beside Flint Creek. Then he grinned. He was bidding on it, and come hell or high water, he was buying it.

The clerk smiled sweetly at Allan, then finished ringing up the total. "That will be sixty-five dollars and seventy-five cents."

Neither Paul nor Allan moved to pay for the items. They both were still stunned to learn that they were on a honey-do bachelor auction block—two SEAL wolves for sale—even if no one else knew about the wolf part of the equation. And so were three troublesome cowboy wolves. Paul wondered just how long they'd been here and why no one had said anything to Allan and him.

Chapter 3

"OHMIGOD," ROSE SAID TO LORI AS THEY WALKED TO their cars, "I can't believe Paul kissed you! And not just...*kissed* you. I swore he and Allan had brought the jungle heat back with them, as steamy as it was in the kitchen with all the time Paul took to lock lips with you. No sweet little peck on the lips or anything."

Lori felt her cheeks flame hot—*again*. Though her grandma and Catherine hadn't said a word about it, Lori knew they were thinking plenty. Tessa's brother, Michael, was all grins, wanting to know everything he had missed and wishing he hadn't been such a heavy sleeper. But after he'd played role-playing games half the night on the computer in Allan's old room, she could see why he was having a time waking this morning. He was cute, but definitely not SEAL material.

A red hawk flew overhead, making a shrill *chwirk* several times in a row.

Rose glanced heavenward at the soaring hawk. "Even your spirit guide is telling you so."

"The hawk is calling a female in courtship."

"We've only seen the one hawk around Mom's place. He's telling you to get with the program where Paul is concerned."

Lori, Paul, and Rose had embraced their spirit guides, the animal spirits having come into their lives at a time when they'd needed them most—offering insight and guidance when most of their pack was being killed off by rabid wolves. In each case, the animal had come to them, connected with them, and guided them to safety. And from that day forth, their spirit animals had remained a part of their lives in mysterious ways. Allan continued to deny he had one, and Paul had been reluctant to believe a cougar was his. Which had to do with being a wolf and not an ally of the cougars.

"I didn't mean to clobber Paul. I didn't recognize him coming out of the dark, dressed in black, his face all blackened in guerrilla-warfare paint. All I could really see were the whites of his eyes. I couldn't even smell him yet. I thought he was that bank robber or something. So I hit him with the broom. When he kissed me, I—"

"Kissed him back?"

"That just sort of happened. Then I was annoyed that he had scared me and took him down."

"And kissed him again." Then Rose frowned. "Why did you think he was the bank robber? Why would he come here?"

Lori rolled her eyes. "He wouldn't. It was just on my mind because the robber hit another bank yesterday in the next county over. So that's who I thought of immediately. Who else would it have been?"

"Okay, got the connection."

God, every time Lori saw Paul, her darn heart rate sped up, which is why she'd been avoiding him every time he returned to the area for the last couple of years. She didn't want to be gloomy for days on end when he went on another of his missions that sometimes lasted months. She didn't believe she would ever have made a good military wife. Even though he was no longer on active duty with the Navy, his schedule was just as bad as far as not staying at home for any reasonable length of time.

So this was the first time in two years that she'd even seen him. He'd been near enough to hear and feel her heart thumping and know how much he affected her too. Which further annoyed her.

"So...do you suppose this means Paul might finally be thinking seriously about settling down?" Rose asked. "You know...after that kiss?"

"Certainly not because of the kiss. Who knows whether he will or won't be?" Lori shrugged as nonchalantly as she could. "Maybe." She had secretly hoped so for years. Not that he would mate her or anything. But... they needed a cohesive pack, and everyone had agreed that Paul should take charge in his parents' place.

"What if he decided to take over the pack? Would you consider mating him?" Rose persisted.

Lori's cheeks grew hot again. "Rose, how many years have we hoped he'd decide his home is here? Same with your brother. When they're ready, they'll settle down. But in the meantime, if either of us finds a suitable wolf mate and we decide to take over the pack, so be it."

"You don't really mean that," Rose said. "Paul's it. We've always known it. But I have to admit, I loved it when you smacked him in the head with the broom. You ought to do that more often. See what it got you this time?"

Lori chuckled. "A lot more than I expected." Then she sighed. She knew something was going on with Rose, but though they were best friends and had been forever, Rose wouldn't tell her what was wrong. "Are you sure nothing's the matter?"

Rose's expression turned from lighthearted and amused to worried in a flash. She shook her head adamantly. "No, I'm fine." She shrugged. "Why do you keep asking?"

"You've canceled on me for lunch and movie dates when you never do. You seem…well, on edge. Not yourself. Your…anxiousness started after the Cooper brothers were up at the lake with us last week. Are you still bothered about that?"

"No, of course not. They were being jerks. I doubt Dusty will hassle you any further. Or that Howard will bother me."

"You haven't wanted to go to the lake with me since then."

"I've been busy with the Howling Wolf. I've gotten a whole new shipment of art and gifts made by local artists, and you know how it is. Making room for them, changing displays, pricing everything. Even Michael brought in four new paintings. His wolves really sell well. And your grandmother has been sewing up a storm. The beaded moccasins, belts, and boots she creates are great sellers. And Mom's been having me help her design labels for the new line of salsa, spice rubs, and vinaigrettes she's started making in addition to the huckleberry jam."

"Okay." Lori had scrutinized every excuse Rose had given her, and they all held up. Yet the fact her friend was giving them made Lori suspicious. "You know you can talk to me about anything."

"Yeah, of course. Well, I've got to go and get ready to open my shop soon. And you've got martial-arts classes to give."

"Right." Lori loved her dojo and was glad she'd

finally opened it three years ago. She had a steady clientele and made enough money to support herself and her grandmother, if her grandmother had needed supporting. All the training Lori had taken in Bigfork had prepared her for having her own place, and she couldn't have been happier. Well, she'd be even happier if Paul would decide to settle down.

"See you at the auction tomorrow night," Rose said, smiling and looking her usual happy self.

Lori could see through the deception. She had every intention of discovering what was truly going on.

—∿∿—

The clerk repeated the checkout price for Paul and Allan's groceries as Paul was trying to figure out this business with the auction.

"When…" Then Paul saw the date on the poster. "Tomorrow night," he said, answering his own question.

"Yep, six sharp, Town Hall," the clerk said, smiling.

"Thanks." Paul paid for the groceries, the clerk promised to see them there, and he and Allan hauled the bags out to his car.

"Your mom," Paul said.

Allan shook his head. "She's just as much your mom as she's mine. I bet you anything that was why Mom was so reluctant to let us know what they'd been discussing before we barged in on them."

They finished loading the groceries and drove back to the mountain cabin.

"Not to mention that Michael nearly spilled the beans by mentioning a painting for the auction, don't you think?"

"Yeah, it clears up the whole mystery." Allan made a call and put it on speaker. "Mom, when were you going to tell us about the auction? What if we had hot dates for tomorrow night?"

Paul smiled at that—thinking he wouldn't mind one with Lori.

"Who told you... Oh, you stopped by the grocery store. You don't have hot dates for the night. You never have hot dates when you come here. Besides, it's for a good cause. You know Mike O'Keefe. He's a nice boy and he's got two little ones to take care of. So he and his wife need all the help they can get. Besides, he's a military man like the two of you."

Allan frowned. "You could have asked."

"You would have said yes anyway."

Paul believed she must have had some doubts, or she would have asked them before they arrived home.

"That's what you were discussing with the other ladies this morning in private?"

"I was going to have you come by for lunch and discuss it," she said.

"How long have the wolves been in town?" Paul abruptly asked, not liking that the troublesome men were hanging around the area. He wanted the situation addressed right away.

"The Cooper brothers? And their friend? They showed up a couple of days after the two of you went into the jungle. Though we didn't really know about it for about a month. They were hired at the Somervilles' ranch and stayed there the whole time, I suspect. Anyway, I couldn't get hold of you while you were on this last assignment or I would have let you know right away. After that…" Catherine paused. "You would be home and could deal with it. I wasn't thinking about them when you came here this morning—not when you charged in, looking ready to terrorize someone."

Paul was about to say something about being there to protect and save, not to terrorize anyone, but Catherine spoke again.

"There wasn't anything we could do about them coming here, and they haven't…" Catherine hesitated to speak. "Well, I'm certain they've grown up now and aren't causing the kind of trouble they did for their pack in the old days."

She was always willing to give others a chance and had a gentle spirit, which had earned her the name Running Deer as a term of endearment by Emma's husband, Lee Greypaw. Catherine didn't believe she was all that sweet and innocent—which was the deer spirit guide's message—but she was constantly looking for causes and helping others.

Paul had always thought Lee was right. He wasn't certain about the men not causing trouble for the pack though. Some people did grow up. Others were problems no matter how many years they lived. It just seemed to be their nature. "What time is lunch?"

"Make it noon. The auction is tomorrow night, and whoever buys your services has you for four to five hours over the weekend, depending on how much they pay for you. You still have two full weeks to spend on your vacation having fun, longer if you don't pick up another assignment right away. Isn't that so?"

"True," Paul said. They had purposely not put their

names in the pool for any assignment so their vacation wouldn't be cut short.

"What exactly are we required to do?" Allan asked.

"Odd jobs. Whatever your buyer needs you to do."

Allan grinned. "Hope she's my age and…"

"Oh, honestly, Allan. *I* plan to buy your services."

Paul laughed.

"Or Paul's. Depending on how high the bidding goes."

Paul truly wouldn't mind. Allan's mother was easy to get along with, and she wasn't picky about things, so he was more than willing to work for her if she needed a bunch of jobs done around the place.

"So it's not really a bachelor auction," Allan said.

"It's a honey-do bachelor auction. Whoever buys you will take you out for a night on the town after you finish your work."

"In *this* small place?"

"Oh, Allan, there are a number of places you can go. I've got to run some errands now so I'll let you go."

Paul interjected, "Is anyone looking out for Michael while he's in town?"

"All of us have been taking turns watching him," Catherine said. "The full moon won't be out for another week, and he seems to be doing just fine. But one of us has been either with him at the art exhibit or taking him around where he needs to go. Other than that, he's been having a good time playing some of Allan's games at the house. Tessa has called every day to check up on him. But she doesn't want him to know about it."

That made Paul feel a little better about Michael being on his own. Since he wasn't exactly on his own. "Good to know."

"All right. See you later." Allan ended the call with his mother.

Paul was shaking his head. "I can see if they had some local people who could do odd jobs around the place — carpenters, painters, plumbers, electricians, whatever someone might need to have fixed up. But *us*?"

"Hey, we can do anything the experts can do. Or... we can call the proper professionals and have it done. Remember when that construction worker was taking care of some improvements on Mom's house and she asked him to change a lightbulb over the kitchen sink?"

Paul laughed. "Yeah. He was touching the stainless-steel sink and zapped himself while changing the light-bulb. I've never seen a human fly backward that quickly and still land on his feet. I still remember his prematurely gray hair standing on end. His supervisor was laughing, saying that's why his assistant did the dangerous work."

Allan chuckled. "Remember that if the woman who pays for your services asks you to do anything too dangerous. Just call on one of the professionals."

"Works for me."

Allan helped put the groceries away, then paused. "Did you get the impression that the Cooper brothers and their friend might have given our pack members trouble?"

"If they did, they'll regret it," Paul said, serious as hell.

He might not be here all the time, but no outsider would cause trouble for their wolves. It did concern him that the rest of their pack was all female, and two of them were the same age as the men from the Wolfgang pack. The pack had originated in Germany, the name meaning "path of the wolf" or "advancing wolf." It had been fifteen strong, but now only the Cooper brothers and Jerome Huffman were left.

Normally, fewer females existed in a pack. In the Cunningham pack's case, the mix was a little different because of the rabid *lupus garou* and the all-wolf pack that had decimated their numbers, killing off many of their women and children, and all of their men, who had been trying to protect their families. Only two male juveniles, Paul and Allan, had escaped the onslaught.

After unpacking their bags, fixing breakfast, and taking a long wolf hike in the woods, Paul and Allan had lunch with Allan's mother, while everyone else—the Greypaws and Allan's sister—was conspicuously absent.

Paul finished eating Catherine's delightful chicken wings, covered in her special hot-and-spicy rub, and mashed potatoes and pushed his empty plate away. "Are you certain the other wolves haven't caused trouble for any members of our pack?" He couldn't imagine they had left the females alone.

Allan stopped eating his chicken and watched to see his mom's expression.

"Not for me. As far as I know, not for any of the others either."

Catherine sounded evasive, and she glanced at Allan as if worried he might believe she wasn't telling the truth. Paul thought she was getting technical with him. Trying to pin her down, he asked, "So you're saying if someone had difficulty with any of them, she just didn't tell you."

"Well, right."

Paul ground his teeth. "But you suspect one of our women had difficulty with one of them?"

"Maybe or maybe not. The men have gotten into a couple of barroom brawls that I heard about. That's when I learned they were actually living in the area now and working for Somerville. No one in our pack told me that they'd had difficulties with the men. I'm not about to make up something when there's no cause for it. For now, as long as the men are only instigating problems for the humans, we can deal with them."

"As long as they don't get incarcerated. You *asked* the others, and everyone said they haven't had any difficulty with them, right?"

"Yes. Which probably means they didn't."

Paul relaxed a bit. "All right. As usual, the meal was great." He couldn't cook worth a darn, although not for want of trying, which meant he really appreciated anyone who could.

Catherine smiled, but she still looked apprehensive.

"What concerns you?"

"Those three men caused problems for their own pack eons ago, before the rest died. I'm afraid that *eventually* they'll do the same with ours. They were omegas, sure, but when they have no one else to keep them in line, even omegas can behave in alpha or beta ways."

"So you've been keeping an eye on them." He should have known she would. He just hoped that all their wolves would be as wary about the men.

"As much as I can. They stay close to the Somerville ranch for the most part."

"Okay, thanks. I'll…check into it." If Paul had been strictly a wolf, he would have chased the three wolves out of his pack's territory. Or killed them if they persisted in hanging around. But as a *lupus garou*, it wasn't that easy.

If Paul was here all the time, he'd have more of a handle on this. But popping in every once in a while wouldn't deter other wolves if they wanted to cause problems for the Cunningham wolf pack.

When Paul and Allan returned to the cabin, they took a wolf's run through the forest and then did some work around the place, trimming back tree limbs stretching out to the cabin and handling a few other odd jobs before they grilled hamburgers on the back patio for dinner. The time just seemed to fly by. Paul was glad to be back home and was thinking how much he'd like to do this more often. He was a little apprehensive about who would win his services tomorrow night, though, and what he would be expected to do.

He didn't want anyone to feel they didn't get their money's worth out of him, even if it was for a good cause.

At her grandma's home where Lori lived and helped take care of things, they were getting ready to eat dinner. Lori hadn't wanted to worry about the auction, but she knew her grandma was bidding for either Allan or Paul. Lori just hoped that no one would offer too much money and make the bidding go too high, because she didn't want her grandma to be disappointed if she didn't win one of the bids.

The aroma of spicy beef enchiladas smothered in cheese filled the air in the bright yellow kitchen as Lori set the dinner on the table. They settled in their seats, and her grandma smiled at her, her hair in gray curls pinned on top of her head and her eyes alight with excitement. Emma was wearing her favorite green blouse and olive-green-and-brown broomstick skirt, an outfit she fondly called her "earth clothes" because she looked like she could blend into the woods on a summer's day. The green blouse emphasized the green in her amber eyes, and she looked so perky and happy it made Lori smile.

"So," Emma said, cutting into one of her enchiladas, "did you want to tell me about that?"

"About what?" Lori asked, feigning cluelessness. She knew just what her grandma was referring to.

"Paul kissing you."

Lori tried to keep a straight face, but couldn't. She hadn't expected him to kiss her. She only wished he hadn't done so in front of an audience. Rose was still teasing her about it. Lori was glad Rose hadn't taken a picture or video of the deed and posted it on Facebook.

"He was trying to get me to give up my weapon. Or appease me for scaring me to pieces."

"Another man might have gotten angry when you hit him with the broom. I thought that was an...*interesting* way to handle the situation." Emma cut up another slice of enchilada.

Lori sighed. "Totally surprised me. But you know that's part of their training."

"Kissing a woman in distress?"

Lori rolled her eyes. "Using the element of surprise."

"It's about time."

Lori shook her head. "He's not ready to settle down. I'm not sure he ever will be." She took a bite of her enchilada.

"A man like that needs to find an interest that begs for attention more than the mission he goes on. I'd say he might just be looking for something else, even if he's not fully aware of it."

"You mean because he kissed me? It was just a rash, impulsive gesture."

"Don't think I don't know what's going on between the two of you."

"*Nothing's* going on." Which was the problem. But Lori wasn't going to chase after him or beg him to stay with the family. She didn't want to screw up a good thing. Right now she really cared for him and she thought he cared about her, but she didn't want to act like a clinging vine.

"Lori Lee Greypaw, lately, every time he returns home, you conveniently make yourself scarce. He knows why too." Emma speared another piece of her enchilada. "You were there for him when he needed to heal when you both were younger."

"He's a grown man. A SEAL who loves his work more than anything."

"Have you ever stopped to think he comes home to see you?"

Lori frowned at her grandma. "He's too busy doing things with Allan or seeing Allan's family when he comes here."

"And me. He *always* spends some time with me. You think he really wants to see an old lady like me?"

"Of course he wants to see you. You're part of his pack, whether he wants to admit that he's our leader or not."

Emma humphed under her breath. "You know very

well he comes by to see you, and you always skedaddle
out of here for some purpose or another. If you were
around more, he'd do things with you. Not just with
Allan. He knows you are purposefully avoiding seeing
him." She cut into her last enchilada. "You know why
he *really* kissed you?"

Lori let out her breath. She didn't want to hear what
Emma had to say, but she knew she was going to hear it
anyway. "Why?"

"He had to prove to you that he wanted to see you.
And *not* just to say hi. No way was that just a sweet,
little hello kiss."

Lori fought a smile. She had to agree with her
grandma. She couldn't deny that she had been avoiding him. But it *all* had to do with not wanting to feel
more about him than he felt for her. She didn't want him
to feel he had to choose either her and the pack or the
SEAL team and his missions.

"I don't want you to draw any kind of conclusions. I
doubt he's changing his mind about staying around here
for good."

Emma took a sip of her hot cherry tea. "Catherine
warned me. Allan told her that Paul blames himself for
losing a hostage they were trying to rescue on this last
mission. You know how Paul was when his parents
died. He really takes losing someone to heart."

Lori stared at her grandma in surprise. She'd never
imagined that anything could have gone wrong on the
SEAL wolves' last mission. Paul seemed fine to her, and
she felt bad that she hadn't intuitively realized anything
was the matter.

"You know he'll move forward like he's done in the

past. He'll pretend nothing happened and won't work through it."

"What happened?"

"Catherine said Allan wouldn't give any of the details. Just that there were four hostages, and one was killed before they could save her." Emma reached over and patted Lori's hand. "You were the only one he finally opened up to after his parents died."

"He had been taking care of us."

"Yes. Too busy and unwilling to deal with his own grief while the rest of us were in shock over what had happened. He's a natural-born leader like his parents were, and you, young lady, were the only one who could help him to heal back then."

"If he doesn't want to discuss what has happened…"

"Maybe not at first. But make yourself available to him. Let him know you're there for him if he wants to confide in you. You can't keep running away every time he returns."

Lori snorted. "He doesn't even notice that I'm not here."

Emma tilted her chin down. "You can't tell me he would have kissed you the way he did if it didn't mean anything. He notices when you're not here. He always asks about you. I bet you anything, his kissing you was a way to show you just how much he's missed seeing you. Like *you've* taken the easiest way out by avoiding him, *he's* taken a similar path in not chasing you down."

"*That* would be the day."

"Prove me wrong." Emma cut up some more of her enchilada. "*Actually*, Paul already proved me right when you smacked him upside the head with the broom and he kissed you." Her eyes sparkled with mirth. "He probably feels you aren't ready for *him*."

Was that what he thought? No way. He was too hung up on his missions.

Lori let out her breath. "All right. I'll…hang around this time. I already did, didn't I?" Which had everything to do with Catherine entering Paul and Allan in the auction, and Emma getting the notion to bid on them. That meant Lori had to watch out for her grandma. "Not to change the subject, but why don't I do the bidding at the auction for you?"

"Nothing doing. It's my bid, my prize. If you were doing the bidding, he might think you have the hots for him and want him for something other than…*work*."

Lori smiled and shook her head. She loved her grandma. "And what will you have him do? If you win a SEAL's services for the weekend? You just had a bunch of work done on your house…by professional repairmen."

"I'll find plenty for him to do."

Lori leveled her with a warning look. "*No matchmaking*."

"You think I'd spend a whole bunch of money just so you can go on a date? No way. The two of you have to figure that out on your own."

Well, Lori didn't *think* so. Her grandma was level-headed and frugal, and usually did a great job with her expenditures. But still…Emma kept worrying that she'd leave this world, and Lori wouldn't have a mate. And she could be leaving sooner, rather than later. A wolf geneticist had confirmed that the pack's shifter longevity was at stake when he dropped by to take blood samples from pack members to learn if he could do anything to stop the shifter aging from mimicking the human aging process.

"Be sure to wear that teal dress that looks so pretty on you."

Lori raised a brow at her grandma. "I was going to wear jeans like everyone else." She wasn't about to dress up to try to catch Paul's eye.

Emma let out an exasperated breath.

"I'm *wearing* jeans." And Lori wasn't changing her mind about that.

"All right. You young folk don't know how to dress when you go out."

"We're not going out. It's just an auction. And everyone will be wearing jeans. Well, except for you."

"I'll be the best-dressed gal there."

Lori laughed and took the dirty dishes into the kitchen. "You will." She just hoped her grandma wouldn't be disappointed if she didn't win. But also, Lori had to find a way to get Paul to open up to her.

The next day, Lori taught martial-arts classes and scheduled herself to be off from teaching classes for the next week—though she'd have to slip in and do some that her assistant didn't have time for—so she could see Paul and learn what had happened on his last mission.

She had an early dinner with her grandma before they had to go to the auction. When Lori began clearing the table, Emma glanced at the clock on the stove and said, "Oh, oh, we're going to be late." She rushed to help Lori put stuff away.

"We have another hour and fifteen minutes before we need to be there."

"I want to sit right up close to the front. I'll never see over the other people's heads, and what if no one sees my number?"

Emma had never been this interested in any kind of auction. She'd never even bid on anything in the past. Which again concerned Lori. She was going to have to really watch her grandma.

They arrived an hour before the auction started, found several chairs right up front, and saved a couple of seats for Catherine and Rose.

The place filled up fast and Lori was glad she and her grandma had come early, if only to show their support for their pack members. When the men walked single file to the stage, the women all whooped and hollered. What really caught Lori's eye was Paul's Hawaiian-style palm-tree shirt. She'd gotten it for him as a joke three years ago.

She'd never expected him to still have it, figuring he'd gotten rid of it right after she gave it to him. At the time, he'd jerked off his T-shirt right in front of her and his SEAL team members, and put on the Hawaiian shirt. Then he'd gotten a whole lot of teasing from the other men. Now to wear it to the auction?

Emma patted her knee. "He's got your shirt on. I told you he cares for you. It's like he's wearing your favor in a jousting match. He's one brave man."

Lori loved that shirt, but she especially loved it on him. It was all because of a big discussion Hunter's SEAL team members had been having at Allan's family's house. Everyone, except for Paul, agreed that no man in his right mind would wear a flowery pink shirt. Well, she couldn't find a men's shirt that featured just pink flowers, but the Hawaiian shirt had pink palm trees and green flamingos. Even better. She had been surprised when he wore it in front of the other guys to prove to them he would.

Rose and Catherine finally arrived, slipping down the aisle to sit with them. Rose hurried to take a seat next to Lori. Catherine sat on the other side of Emma.

"He's wearing your shirt. I told you he wouldn't give it up, if only to prove a point," Rose said. "Or because he wants to show you how much he cares for you."

Lori folded her arms. "I agree he's proving a point. I didn't think he would wear it here. The cowboys are giving him a worse time than his SEAL team did."

Dusty motioned with his thumb to Paul and shook his head. Dusty was smiling, but it wasn't a friendly smile.

"You're worried about Paul," Rose said.

"Paul? He can fend for himself just fine, alpha that he is. I just don't like seeing anyone being picked on."

"Right. Especially after Paul kissed you yesterday."

Lori knew she'd never hear the end of it.

"You're not going to tell him that the Cooper brothers were up at the lake cottage, are you?" Rose asked, sounding worried.

"I don't plan to. What we do is *our* business. We made a mistake and we handled it. Just like we'd do in any case. Not that Paul or Allan are ever around to help out anyway."

Rose chewed on her bottom lip. "Paul won't think we handled it well, or that we should have allowed the other wolves to see us."

"Then he should hang around and not be running off all the time."

Rose waved at Allan when she caught his eye. "Mom's made a bargain with your grandma. They won't outbid each other for Paul or Allan."

Lori was afraid that others would. "What if someone else gets them?"

"If the price goes too high, Mom will go for one of the cheaper prospects. She doesn't need that much work done around the place. But she wanted to help out the O'Keefes in any way that she could."

Lori settled back in her seat, hoping Dusty wouldn't give them any trouble if her grandma did manage to win Allan or Paul's services.

"So...if Emma wins the bid, what is she going to have him do? She just had a bunch of work done on her house. I didn't think she needed anything else fixed."

"That's what I thought." Lori wondered again what her grandma was up to. She really couldn't imagine Emma paying a lot of money just so that a SEAL wolf could spend more time with her granddaughter. He wouldn't be anyway while he worked on whatever project her grandma came up with.

Yet, Lori reminded herself her grandma's animal spirit guide was the fox, because a little red fox had shown her how to watch and wait, how to blend in, and then how to take advantage of a situation. When she was young, Emma was called Little Fox because she was wily and able to work around tricky dilemmas, encouraging action and moving quickly to overcome obstacles.

She'd been patient for far too long, and Lori wondered if her grandmother had decided to make her move—to make some changes in the pack dynamics. Even though her grandma wasn't the pack leader, Emma was the eldest member of the pack, and as such, she truly was both adaptable and at times the trickster.

Chapter 4

WHEN PAUL AND ALLAN ARRIVED AT TOWN HALL, they found the parking lot full. Paul had expected to be standing on stage well before the auction began, but all the seats in the town hall were already filled, which was surprising, considering the size of the town. The audience ranged from sweet, silver-haired grandmas to wide-eyed teenage girls and women more his age, like Lori and Rose, all smiles, with a smattering of men. All of them cheered the bachelors on as they walked across the stage and took their places.

Paul felt like a celebrity and couldn't help being amused, his cheeks burning a little because he wasn't used to all this attention. Allan was grinning and enjoying all the interest.

Paul glanced at his competition.

The bank loan officer was a little stocky and had glasses propped on the bridge of his nose. He probably could give anyone great financial advice, and he might be a real handyman of sorts. The high school teacher taught carpentry—which meant he would be sought after for that reason alone. The three high school seniors could probably do a variety of tasks. They played on the football team and had been promised extra credit in social sciences if they signed up to do this.

The three wolf ranch hands looked like they could rope some steers, break some horses, and haul some hay.

The redheaded, green-eyed Cooper twins and black-haired, blue-eyed Jerome Huffman were all wearing typical Western attire—cowboy boots, Western shirts, cowboy hats, blue jeans, and fancy belts.

The trio had been outcasts, causing problems for their own pack—not hunting like they should have been, not guarding the pack when they were supposed to—but that proved to be a mixed blessing for them. When their pack killed a rabid elk and consumed it, the three omega wolves hadn't been allowed to eat any part of it. They were lucky to not have contracted rabies and were able to escape their pack's killing spree.

Allan wore a pair of jeans, combat boots, and a blue button-down shirt that made him look as though he was ready to go on a date. Paul had on his palm-tree shirt. He'd worn it on three different missions, sure that it confused the bad guys into thinking he was just a tourist on vacation. Since all three missions had been successful, he considered it his lucky shirt.

But as to what he and Allan could do for weekend projects? They were well trained to hunt down the bad guys and deal with them with finality, protect the good guys, and survive in any wilderness environment. He wasn't sure what he could do here.

He swore Emma was sitting on the edge of her seat in the front row, eager to get the bidding war started. The way she was eyeing him and smiling, he half suspected this was a matchmaking effort between him and her granddaughter, with Emma getting some work out of him at the same time. Every time he'd visited her over the last couple of years, he'd asked how Lori was, wishing he could see her and knowing she was avoiding him.

And every time, Emma shook her head and said she just didn't know what was wrong with her granddaughter. But he was fairly certain Lori didn't make herself scarce because she despised him.

He was damn glad he'd caught up with her at Catherine's house and wondered if the only reason she'd been there was because she hadn't expected him to arrive. That was probably also why she had been bra-less, wearing such hot shorts, and barefoot. Now that she was around, he had no intention of letting her slip away again.

The bidding began then, and the whole affair was not as sedate as Paul had thought it would be. Women were shouting and laughing and cheering the bidding war on. For one hundred and fifty dollars, Widow Baxter bought one of the ranch hand's services.

All the ladies teased her about what she was going to do with Howard Cooper. Paul wanted to give the omega wolves the benefit of the doubt because they might have straightened out. But the business with the woman at the grocery store this morning—combined with Howard's comment about them getting into a bind with their boss and the barroom brawls Catherine had mentioned—fed into what Paul already knew about them. They were trouble and they hadn't changed.

Allan was next up, and the bidding was going strong as he got into the fun of the auction, flexing his muscles and smiling brightly.

"Way to go, SEAL!" Lori and Rose shouted.

"Take off your shirt!" Emma shouted.

Catherine whooped and whistled. Paul had to smile at Emma and Catherine.

Lori's face reddened a bit, probably because her own grandma had shouted out the recommendation.

Allan began unbuttoning his shirt slowly and the crowd went wild.

Paul laughed. He hadn't thought that a honey-do bachelor auction would be anything like this. Then again, Emma was a wolf and they could change the dynamics of a situation in a heartbeat. The ranch hands made a big deal of jerking their shirts out of their waistbands and then starting to unbutton them.

A woman shouted, "Just the shirts, gentlemen."

And that had everyone laughing.

Stripper music began to play, and Paul removed his shirt to the beat like the others did.

Clapping hands, wolf whistles, and shouts indicated the women were just as excited to bid for the SEALs as they were for the cowboys.

Paul tossed his shirt to Lori for safekeeping. When she grabbed the shirt and held it close, he smiled at her.

Allan went for two hundred and fifty dollars to a lady wearing a pink cowboy hat—Martha Madison, the only woman in the area who owned and ran a horse ranch. Paul wondered exactly what Allan was going to be doing at Martha's ranch. Mucking out stalls? Or something a little more glamorous?

Catherine shook her head, disappointed she didn't get to buy her son's time, but she was eyeing Paul when the carpentry teacher went for three hundred dollars.

"New kitchen cabinets!" the woman who bought him shouted, in case anyone thought she was buying the teacher's services for something other than his carpentry skills.

A few of the audience's comments—"Yeah, right!" "Sure thing, Eula Mae!" "You just redid the kitchen cabinets last week!"—brought tons of laughter.

"Auction off the other SEAL!" Mike O'Keefe shouted from his wheelchair.

Paul gave him the Navy greeting "Hooyah!" and a thumbs-up as Allan quickly echoed his response.

Mike shouted the Army's greeting back, "Hooah!"

A female Marine in the audience called out, "Oorah!"

Everyone was clapping and cheering.

Emma was waving her paddle, featuring the silhouette of a man and her number in the center of it, as she continued to bid for Paul. Lori was shaking her head, trying to get her to stop. Paul was smiling at the two of them, hoping that Emma wouldn't pay too much for him because he would drop by her place for free to do whatever tasks she needed.

"Three hundred and fifty dollars going once." The auctioneer paused as everyone became quiet. Emma looked eagerly at him, like she was just about to win the lottery and couldn't wait to claim her winnings. "Going twice." Another pause. The air sizzled with tension. "Sold to Emma Greypaw!" the auctioneer said, slamming the hammer down at the same time.

Emma whistled and Paul winked at her, making her blush. She was so cute and he dearly loved her. From as early as he could remember, he'd always loved her homemade apple pies and tortillas. Emma swore as soon as she pulled an apple pie out of the cast-iron stove, he was standing on her porch, eager to do a chore for her so she'd offer him a piece. And she had always given him an extra couple of slices because he was a growing boy.

Catherine began bidding for one of the high school seniors and missed getting him for seventy-five dollars. That seemed to be the going rate for the boys. The ranch hand, Jerome Huffman, started strutting his stuff and fetched a bid just fifty short of Paul's highest bid.

The bank loan officer came next, but though he was smiling, he wasn't outgoing and waited while low bids came in. Then he finally said, "I do windows," as if that might help raise the money a bit, and it did.

Several women started bidding against each other to win the window-washing service for $150.

The last cowboy, Dusty Cooper, received a winning bid seventy-five dollars lower than Paul's and slanted a glance at him, smiling but not in an altogether friendly way. If Dusty gave any of his pack members grief, Paul was dealing with it in a shifter way.

Michael's *Reflections* was being auctioned off last. Paul hurried to get a paddle to bid for the oil painting that featured the lush, green woods and a beautiful gray wolf sitting and watching the river, just like he'd seen Lori do a million times. Lori was smiling at him. He ended up bidding five hundred dollars, way over the last bid of three hundred. He wanted to help the disabled vet, and he definitely did not want anyone else to have that painting of Lori. It wouldn't mean half as much to them as it did to him.

With the bidding over, Lori and Emma joined him, Lori handing his shirt to him. He quickly pulled it on and began to button it.

"I can't believe you paid so much for that painting," Lori whispered to him. "It's not even my good side."

"All your sides are good," Paul said and grinned, making Lori blush. He loved it.

Sales figures were tallied for all the auctioned
items, and the women met with their honey-do bachelors to discuss the hours they'd be working that weekend. Lori was still shaking her head at her grandma
and Paul.

Emma paid for Paul, then came and took his hand and
smiled up at him. She was like the grandma he'd never
known. "So, Mrs. Greypaw…"

"Emma, please."

"Yes, ma'am. What would you like me to do?"

"You don't have to start the job until tomorrow. Our
lakeside cabin needs quite a bit of work done on it. Lori
offered to show you all that you need to do. I made a list.
She'll be up there helping too."

Pleasantly surprised to hear that, Paul glanced at
Lori. She looked flabbergasted, her mouth gaping as she
stared at her grandma. Paul smiled a little. This was the
perfect way to get to know Lori again in a non-intimate
way. Though he had to say she'd seemed very agreeable
when he had kissed her.

"She's always such a good granddaughter." Emma
patted Lori's arm.

Lori almost appeared a little panicked. Maybe she
was afraid Paul would kiss her again. But he had no
intention of doing anything other than fixing the place
up as much as he could over the weekend. If it took a
little longer, he would be fine with that.

He could work vacation time around it too, if need be.
Maybe he and Allan could even come back to fix some
things later if he and Lori didn't get it done. Emma had
offered to let them stay for a few days at the tail end of
their vacation to go scuba diving anyway.

Lori stretched out her hand to her grandma, who promptly handed her the list.

"I've already paid for supplies at the hardware store. The place needs that one wall around the fireplace painted inside for starters, but you choose the color, Lori. I'm not very good at that."

"Your house is lovely, bright, and cheerful. You are great at color coordinating things," Lori said, contradicting her. Her chin was tilted down and she was eyeing her grandma with suspicion.

"Yes, dear, but so are you. I spent so much time fixing up my house over the past few weeks that I don't want to try to figure out what to do with the cabin. You'll do a lovely job. Let Paul help you decide, if he's got any decorating sense."

He smiled. No one had ever asked him if he had any "decorating sense."

"The hardware store closes in an hour. Let's go get what we need. We can meet over there." Lori waited for Paul to agree.

"Sure thing. I guess I'll be staying at the cabin for a couple of days," he said to Emma.

"No sense in you driving every day from the Rappaports' cabin on the other side of the lake. You can use either of the spare bedrooms. Lori always takes the blue room at the end of the cabin."

Lori sighed dramatically.

"Oh, come on now," her grandma said. "You don't want to have to drive all that way back and forth to the cabin from our house in the country either. And you told me Carmen would take care of your jujitsu classes if you had to manage the bachelor while he did the work I need done. You know she could always use the extra money. I never saw a woman who could buy so many pairs of shoes a year.

"Besides, as long as Paul doesn't wear face paint and scare you to death again, everything should be just fine. Got to run along. You two have fun while you're at it." She hugged the pair of them. Paul hugged her right back, making Emma smile. She took a deep breath and patted him on the shoulder. "If only I were a lot younger." She paused, frowning a bit. "Did Catherine tell you about that doctor who is taking DNA samples of all the wolves he can find to see what's causing the"—she glanced around, and seeing no one nearby, she finished—"change in their longevity?"

"I heard he was making the rounds."

"Well, he's already tested us, but you and Allan were gone when he came. I called him to let him know you and Allan are here for the next couple of weeks."

"Thanks." Paul wasn't worried about it like some of his pack members were. If it was a sign of the times, so be it. As long as they didn't face over-accelerated aging because they had lived so long. That would be the pits.

Then Emma headed for her car. Paul recognized it as the black sedan that had been parked at Catherine's house that morning. So she had gotten a new car too.

"We better get to it," Lori warned. "I'll pick up some groceries after we go to the hardware store, and then I'll meet you at the cabin."

At the hardware store, she picked out a vivid, emerald-green paint that was brighter than what Paul would have selected. He was thinking more of a sage green for quiet, cool, and muted forest colors.

When he mentioned that, she considered the color swatch again. "The cabin has a lot of dark oak wood, so I want to go with something a little brighter."

"We could paint a couple of pink palm trees on the accent wall. The green flamingos probably would disappear in that color of paint."

"I couldn't draw a straight line if I tried. What about you?"

"That and singing, no can do."

He looked over Emma's to-do list while the paint manager was mixing the paint. "Emma wants a new sofa and chairs?"

"Yeah, the old ones were recycled castoffs from forty years ago, so it looks like she really wants to spruce up the place."

"The furniture store is closed by now," he said. He hadn't expected to be picking out furniture too.

"Which is fine. Tomorrow, we can paint, then return to town after lunch and find something that might work nicely for the living room."

"Okay, sounds good."

When they finished picking out the paint supplies, she asked, "Would beef ribs, parmesan noodles, and turnip greens be all right tomorrow for lunch? Chicken wings for dinner?"

"I'd love it."

She eyed the list. "I don't know. It looks like it might take longer to do all this. Well, I can finish up whatever she wants done that we don't complete by tomorrow."

"I'll stay however long it takes."

Lori glanced up at him. "She didn't pay for that much time."

It sounded like he was a bought man. "I'm willing to stay longer and help Emma with whatever she needs done. So we'll need lunch for Sunday. How about salmon steaks? We probably won't need dinner."

Her mouth parted and he was reminded of just how kissable it was. "Um, okay. Breakfast? Forget it. I know what you like. I'll meet you up at the cabin in a little while." She gave him a spare key to the place.

He was going to ask if she needed any help, but he didn't want to make her feel crowded. "Okay, good show. Meet you there. I've got to drop by the Rappaports' place to get my bag." Then he carried the paint out to his SUV and headed to the cabin. He'd decided that this wasn't going to be a bad deal at all. He tended to be a workaholic, totally mission-oriented, so he'd work until everything was done. But what he wouldn't give to have some playtime with Lori—swimming, maybe running as wolves. He'd just have to play it by ear.

When he arrived at the cabin, Allan wasn't there. Paul carried the painting of Lori into his bedroom. When he had a chance, he'd hang it where he could enjoy it most.

He called Allan to let him know his schedule. "Hey, are you doing the job you were auctioned to do tonight?"

"No, I'll be going to Martha's ranch tomorrow. I'm out with one of the ladies who bid on me but didn't win. So I'm buying her dinner. Consolation prize."

Paul laughed. "I'm going to be staying the weekend. Emma has a list as long as Santa Claus's. The jobs will take a couple of days, at the very least." He grabbed his bag, got into his car, and headed over to the lakeside cabin.

"Do you need me to help with anything after I've done my work at Martha's place?"

"Nah. I've got it."

Silence followed, but before Paul could ask if he was still there, Allan said, "Is Lori going to be staying with you for the weekend?"

The tone of Allan's voice said he believed more than work would be going on at the cabin.

"Yeah, to make sure I get everything done right."

"Uh-huh."

Paul chuckled. "What about you? Will you be okay by yourself?"

"With you not around, yeah. I've got another date tomorrow night. I sure like these bachelor auctions."

Paul laughed. "Okay, see you later then."

"Out here."

Paul took the long road around the blue-green lake, noticing that the warm breeze had made the water choppy. The lake was thirty miles long and sixteen miles wide, so getting around it was a bit of a drive. When he reached Lori and Emma's log cabin, he got out of his car and paused to enjoy the hilly woods and the view of the lake and mountains off in the distance. He took in a deep breath and first noticed the smell of pine trees, followed by Lori and Rose's scents, though they had been left awhile ago. None of Emma's, though; she must not have been there for quite some time. He also smelled Dusty and Howard Cooper's scents, which irked him right away. What had *they* been doing here?

Had Catherine suspected something about it? Paul hoped that neither of the ranch hands thought they had a chance with Lori or Rose. He reminded himself that what the women did with their time was up to them, but the thought of the ranch hands still bothered him.

Particularly after he'd seen the way Dusty behaved toward the woman at the grocery store that morning. Paul didn't like the idea that any other wolf had his paws on Lori or that these men had designs on Rose.

He hauled the paint supplies and his bag of clothes up the wooden steps of the deck to the main entrance and set them down. The sun would set over the lake in another hour and a half, and he was going to enjoy it. He hoped Lori would make it to the cabin in time to watch the sunset with him.

He unlocked the door and grabbed the can of paint, the bag of supplies, and his clothes bag. As soon as he stepped inside, he immediately took a deep breath and smelled the scents in the living room. Both of the Cooper brothers had been in the cabin. He growled a little under his breath. Then again, if the men had given the ladies any trouble, they would have said something to him. Wouldn't they have?

Before Lori arrived, Paul dumped his bag in the green bedroom closest to hers. Then he moved the sagging sofa and matching sagging chairs away from the one wall they would paint. The rest of the walls were paneled in dark, reddish wood. Though the color was beautiful, he could see why Lori wanted something brighter on the accent wall that surrounded the white stone fireplace. He began taping the edges of the wood so they wouldn't get paint on it. When Lori drove up, he went outside to help her carry the groceries up the steps.

"The Cooper brothers were here," he said, as if she didn't know it, and as soon as he said it, he realized he sounded accusatory.

He couldn't help it. She and Rose didn't have a pack

to watch out for them. Packs served a purpose—in the wild, as protection for their members, and for *lupus garous*, to keep them safe from humans *and* from other wolves.

Still, the annoyed look Lori gave him made him think that if she'd had that broom in her hand, she would have bashed him with it again.

Chapter 5

"DON'T LOOK AT ME LIKE THAT, PAUL," LORI GROWLED, setting the groceries on the counter. "Like Rose and I committed the crime of the century. The brothers wanted to visit us and go swimming in the lake. And *why* am I explaining myself to you? I don't owe you any explanation!" It was her decision, her mistake, but hers to deal with. And she'd dealt with it. Not fully to her satisfaction, but the best she could have at the moment.

Paul eyed her warily. "You asked *them* to go swimming with you? And you smack *me* in the head with a broom?"

It did sound kind of funny. Lucky for him, he said it with a teasing light in his eyes, or she would have been totally pissed off.

"*They* were invited to the cabin. *You* weren't expected at Catherine's house. What would you do if you were talking to the guys, just having a normal conversation, and I snuck into the house wearing all black clothes and black face paint, carrying a gun, and suddenly appeared out of the dark in a totally alarming way?"

He smiled, albeit a little evilly. "I wouldn't have hesitated to tackle you, take you down to the floor, disarm you, and…well, no telling what else."

Kissed her, she was certain after what happened the last time. She still couldn't believe she'd caught him so off guard and taken him down instead. Then again, he probably hadn't even considered she might do that to him. Now she was thinking of how it would have been if the roles were reversed, and yeah, she could see him doing it too.

"I know martial arts." As if that would have prevented him from getting the upper hand. Though at that point, she'd had no plan to spar with him, instead deciding to just enjoy the sensual moment.

"Yeah, you do a good job at it. So I might have had a bit of a struggle when I tackled you, but in the end…" He shrugged and grinned so roguishly that she fought smiling back.

She was still irritated with his attitude about the Cooper brothers having been there. Rose and she had their reason. She would have told him why, if he hadn't badgered her so about it.

"Did Emma know you allowed the ranch hands to come here?"

Lori's jaw dropped. She couldn't believe Paul's gall. "I can bring anyone here that I like. My grandma hasn't visited the place in over a year. She doesn't care what I do as long as I take care of things."

Paul snorted. "I can guarantee she wouldn't like you and Rose having those wolves up here. And neither would Catherine or Allan."

"Or *you*, apparently." She hastily put the groceries away. "They just came up here to swim and visit for a while."

"Right. The way they were strutting onstage, they would have wanted more than that from two pretty wolves."

She paused, appreciating the compliment, even

though he was annoying her with the conversation. She didn't remember ever hearing him call her or Rose pretty. "Maybe they did, but we didn't have anything else in mind. Besides, if we had wanted to do something else with them, that would have been *our* business. Not *yours*. And if you go sniffing around the place looking for their scents in the bedrooms, you can walk right out the door. I'll paint and do whatever needs to be done on Grandma's list without you."

She was right and he knew it.

Paul leaned against the wall, folded his arms, and watched her put the rest of the food away. "You can't tell me that they didn't want more. And that not getting anything more, they weren't ticked off. I saw the way they acted when Dusty was in the grocery store this morning trying to sweet-talk a woman into going out with him. She said no, and he didn't like it."

"*Noth…thing happened. All right? Give it a rest.*"

At least nothing life-threatening, though the Coopers were lucky Paul and Allan hadn't witnessed it. They would have been in serious trouble with a couple of hotheaded SEAL wolves. It all had to do with their wolf nature. Even a really loose-knit pack would treat this as a pack matter. Just as his parents would have done when he and Allan were young.

Lori closed the fridge door and turned to frown at Paul, letting him know that she wasn't going to put up with anything related to the business with the brothers.

Paul couldn't help feeling wired and aggressive about this. He swore Lori was trying to hide her feelings from him, but he could smell that she was upset.

He was certain the men had given the ladies a hard time about not getting more than just a swimming excursion at the lake.

If nothing had happened, why would she be so ticked off at him?

When she was done putting away the groceries, she changed the subject. "I know it's getting late, but before the sun sets, do you want to pick huckleberries? This is the perfect time to harvest them, and I bought the ingredients we can use to make jam. I'd normally gather the berries earlier in the day, but I want to have the jam ready for breakfast."

"Hell, yeah. Now would be the perfect time. I haven't had fresh huckleberry jam in years. We can make it tonight so we have all day tomorrow to work on the projects." He remembered countless times as a boy when he'd picked the berries for his mother to make into jam, or just ate the berries straight off the bushes when running around in the woods with Allan.

"We only get you for a few hours," she reminded him.

"About that…" He took two of the pails she had retrieved from a closet. "I'm willing to stay here long enough to get everything done that Emma wants taken care of. I'm fine with it." More than fine with it. He realized that this was the first occasion he'd had to spend any real time with Lori without other pack members' involvement. "Allan and I will get together after I put in some work here. He's got dates tonight and tomorrow night anyway, so he might even need the extra time to have the place to himself."

She raised a brow at Paul as they headed outside and began to walk through the woods.

Paul shrugged. "The auction was good for him. He got lots of attention."

"Too bad you didn't luck out with some dates too." She sounded serious and even a tad concerned that he might have that in mind for the rest of the time they were here.

"Hell, why would I want to date anyone when I'm having so much fun here?"

She rolled her eyes at Paul. He laughed. He never dated humans here. He wouldn't when he was *way* more interested in a wolf named Lori.

"I imagine he won't mind helping me finish up when we're here scuba diving at the end of our vacation," Paul said, "if we don't get everything done before that."

"Scuba diving," she said as they sauntered down the path through the woods.

He wondered if Emma hadn't mentioned it to her. "Yeah. It's not going to be a problem, is it? We don't have to stay here if you have other plans." That immediately made him think of Lori and Rose having other guys up there.

"No, no, uh, I was wondering…" She shook her head as she led him into a clearing and pointed to a group of huckleberry bushes with clusters of black berries that looked like blueberries hanging off the branches among the bright green leaves.

He started picking the berries but paused when she didn't say anything further. He glanced at her. "What?"

She shrugged. "I…lost something in the lake. Way out past the dock in the deeper water. Without scuba gear, I couldn't reach it even if I could see where it went."

"What was it?"

"A gold necklace."

He glanced at her bare neck. He hadn't realized she wasn't wearing the gold chain that held a hand-carved turquoise hawk. Except for when she ran as a wolf, she never removed it. "The one with your animal guide?" he asked, verifying it was the same one he was thinking about, since he hadn't seen her in the last two years.

"Yes."

The hawk was her spirit guide. She was the intuitive one, victorious, which he attributed to her having saved her grandma's life when the wolves attacked and decimated their pack. Lori was the messenger, the healer of the group, the guardian. He swore she could remember anything that had happened over the years much better than he could, so the hawk suited her. She was usually the one to convey messages from Emma and Catherine to Allan and Paul when they were off with the SEAL team. He suspected that was why Catherine had wanted Lori to tell him and Allan about the auction.

He continued to pick berries while she also was filling her bucket.

As to Paul's animal guide? Lori swore his was the cougar, which meant Paul was a born leader—loyal, courageous, willing to take responsibility when things went bad, and always had the foresight to get them out of messes before they got into them. The notion that a big cat served as his animal guide, one that normally would love to kill him if they met in the woods, didn't seem quite right. Though he'd had a couple of encounters with cougars that could have killed him and didn't. Paul had to admit he had led the others of his pack out

of several troubling situations over the years, even when
he was still young. He just seemed to have the natural
instinct to perceive danger and steer the remaining pack
members in the right direction.

Though he still thought Lori had said his guide was
the cougar because she wanted him to take charge of
the pack, even when they were small. He thought she'd
used that as a way to try to heal him when he had lost his
parents. But how could he have taken charge of the pack
when he'd been so young? Certainly the grown women
hadn't needed him to provide leadership. And not even
Lori or Rose had needed it for many years.

Lori moved to a bush farther away, picking huckleberries and dropping them into her bucket as he pondered how she could have lost the necklace, as much as
she treasured it.

"So the chain broke?"

"No." She moved even farther away from him
although there were still plenty of berries on that bush.
Wolves were wary creatures. And actions like that got
their notice.

He started to pull off berries from the bush she'd just
left and smelled the anxious scent she'd left behind.
That didn't bode well. "You were swimming when it
happened?" He couldn't fathom how the necklace could
have floated off her head if the chain hadn't broken.

Wolves normally didn't wear jewelry of any kind
because it was problematic if they had to shift outside
rather than at home, where their valuables would remain
more secure. But the necklace was special to her.

She cast him an annoyed look. "Yes. If you can find
it, I'd be grateful. But I'll understand if you can't."

She picked more berries, but he was studying her now, noticing her irritated expression and the way she was no longer pulling the berries off leisurely but yanking them off a little harder than necessary.

"The clasp came undone?"

"No." She acted irritated that he'd asked her so many questions about it, but since she wasn't forthcoming, he suspected something bad had happened.

He wondered just how far the jewelry might be buried underneath the sediment. They hadn't come home since March, and she hadn't said anything to him about it then. Then again, she had conveniently been gone when he came home the last time. But it had to have happened more recently, when the water was warm enough to swim in. "When did you lose it?"

At first, she hesitated to say. Then she finally let out her breath and said, "Last week."

Good. He was glad it hadn't been long ago. He would have a better chance of finding it. If she'd been roughhousing in the water with Rose, that was one thing. Basing his assumption on the strength of their scents, last week would be about when the Cooper brothers were at the cabin. And then swimming in the lake with the women? Had one of them yanked off her necklace? Had she been struggling to get away from him?

Paul ground his teeth and quit picking berries again, eyeing her. He really shouldn't ask, but it bothered him that she was so reluctant to tell him the details. He couldn't see how she could have just…lost it. He suspected that whoever Lori had been with hadn't liked that she put the brakes on with him.

Lori stopped picking berries and gave him the evil

eye. "*Quit* analyzing everything I'm saying. I just need my necklace back, if you can find it. That's all."

He scowled right back at her. "If I learn that Dusty or Howard yanked your necklace off in a fit of rage—"

"What? You're going to kick his ass?"

"Hell, yeah." He meant it too. He wasn't about to let any man think he could treat Lori or Rose in an aggressive manner and get away with it. What might he do when Paul and Allan left again?

She took a deep breath, shook her head, and swung her attention back to the bush.

"So what happened?"

"Nothing that I couldn't handle. Don't keep asking because I'm not saying. It's over and done with."

"Except that your necklace is at the bottom of the lake." That pissed Paul off. Even if the necklace hadn't meant much to her, it would matter. How it got there was what bothered him most. But the necklace *was* important to her.

She again turned away from Paul and continued to look for huckleberries on a new bush farther away.

He let his breath out in exasperation. "It was Dusty, wasn't it?"

She glanced over her shoulder at Paul. He was ready to wring the guy's thick neck. Or take a good bite out of him.

"He immediately regretted what he did. All right? The way he limped out of here, I'm sure he was on some heavy-duty painkiller for a couple of days. We came to an understanding. He's not about to hassle me any further."

Damn it! Paul knew it. But he had forgotten about her

martial-arts training. Even so, he didn't want the guy to think he could get away with what he had done. Or that Lori didn't have someone who'd take him to task for it.

Trying to get a handle on his feelings—wolves protected one of their own—he went back to picking berries.

"Thanks for being so concerned though," Lori finally said.

"You didn't tell Emma, did you?" He couldn't let go of the anger. Damn it.

"No. But she knew something was wrong right away. For one thing, she noticed my necklace was gone. She didn't ask me a million questions like *you* did. I'm sure she realized I took care of the situation to my satisfaction, and that was that."

"Not quite the end of it, since you don't have your necklace. Have you been up here since then?" He didn't believe her scent was fresh enough to indicate she had been.

She shook her head.

He immediately wondered if she'd been afraid to return to the cabin in case either of the brothers showed up. "Are you okay with staying here?"

She rolled her eyes. "Of course I'm okay with it. Even if I wasn't staying with one of the legendary SEALs, who happens to also be a damn scary wolf—with or without face paint—and who is armed to the teeth, I would be fine with it."

"So, you've been afraid to return with Rose or on your own."

"I just said I wasn't. No, I haven't been afraid. I've been working. So has Rose."

But he knew she had been afraid. He could tell by her

stiff posture and annoyed expression, her scent, and the way she turned her back on him again.

He picked more berries and then started worrying about the reason her grandma wanted to fix up the place. What if she was apprehensive about the women coming up here on their own? "Emma isn't planning to sell the cabin, is she?" The land had been the Greypaws' for centuries.

"Of course not." Lori frowned, then shook her head. "At least I don't think so. She never said anything to me about it."

"She would have said something to you." He was fairly certain. Still, if Emma no longer went to the cabin and Lori didn't come out because she was afraid to, it made no sense to pay the high taxes on the lakefront property just to keep it in the family.

They heard movement in the dark woods, and Lori said, "I've got enough berries. What about you? We can always pick more early tomorrow if we don't have enough."

"I've got a bucket full."

Her eyes rounded a bit as if she was surprised to hear it.

"I can talk and pick berries at the same time." He gave her a little smile.

"Start the inquisition rather." She peeked into his bucket just to see how full it was.

He chuckled at her tenacity. "See?"

"You would have had even more if you'd been concentrating on that and not me. However, between mine and yours, that should be enough."

They headed back to the cabin while Lori banged

her tin buckets together, careful not to lose any of her berries.

"You think it's a grizzly?" That would explain why Lori was making such a racket—to chase away anything in the woods.

"It might be. Or anything running around at dusk to find something to eat, just like we would be if we were all wolf. We had a female grizzly recently make the surrounding area her home range, with Flathead Lake in the center of it. She spent close to twelve hours swimming, staying at various islands, including Wild Horse Island for three days. Then she had a day of rest on Bird Island. No one's ever seen a bear that swims as much as she does. So we've been watching out for her in case she comes around here."

"All right. Grizzlies and the Cooper brothers. Gotcha." She gave him an annoyed look.

When they reached the cabin, their wolf instinct was to smell the scents around the place to ensure they hadn't had any unwanted visitors. Paul couldn't help feeling that Dusty or his brother, or both, might come back and retaliate in some manner. He shouldn't have been concerned about it, since nothing had happened in the week that had gone by. But some men couldn't let go of a grudge, and he worried about Lori. And also about Rose.

He noticed then that the sun was beginning to set. He motioned with his head toward the deck. "Come on. Let's watch the sunset over the lake. I can never get enough of it."

"You're a wolf," she said, as if he needed reminding.

They set the buckets of berries in the kitchen, and he walked with her out to the deck.

The dusk and dawn were times for *lupus garous* to enjoy running in their wolf form—and safer if hunters were around illegally hunting them.

They sat on two outdoor, cushioned rocking chairs. Pine trees towered next to the deck on both sides. The dark blue lake stretched out before them, and the distant, misty-looking mountains served as a backdrop for the setting sun. Paul loved seeing the sun set over the lake. The way the top half of the sky was blue and a ribbon of orange and yellow rested on top of the distant mountains, the colorful sunset reflecting off the rippling waters and turning it orange as a motorboat off in the distance clipped the water.

He glanced at Lori, expecting her to be observing the sunset, but she was watching him. She folded her arms and looked crossly at him. So much for simply enjoying the beautiful colors painting the sky, mountains, and water.

"Why did you kiss me? In front of Rose, her mom, and my grandma?" Lori asked.

Paul had thought she was still mad at him for interrogating her about the Cooper brothers. This was a much more interesting topic. "I was making up to you. For scaring you."

"Ha." She continued to study him, watching his reaction and trying to get a feel for what was going on between them.

"I *was*. *And* I was ensuring you didn't hit me with the broom again."

She chuckled and looked back at the sunset.

He smiled, loving the way she was as radiant as the sunset when she smiled or laughed.

"I bet you were surprised." She glanced back at him.

He laughed. "Yeah. I didn't realize I would be attacked by a broom-wielding martial-arts instructor. We thought you needed rescuing."

"Seriously? From the two of *you*, maybe. We thought you had sneaked in Rambo-style because Catherine said you couldn't come over. And you were dying to know what secret activities we were up to at that time of the morning. And you'd have a little fun at our expense."

He was surprised to hear the women had assumed that. "You couldn't have believed that of us."

"You've done it before."

"What, when we were teens? We haven't done anything like that in eons. Besides, we had just come off a dangerous mission. We were still thinking in terms of hostages, hostage takers, and a rescue."

Chapter 6

REMEMBERING HER GRANDMA'S WORDS ABOUT PAUL feeling bad over losing a hostage, Lori wondered how much that was affecting him. None of them had considered that Paul and Allan came into the house like that because they truly thought the women were in danger. She wondered if Catherine had questioned Allan about it privately later, and he'd told her what happened on the job. And then Catherine told Emma. When Lori thought of it like that, it seemed as though the men had brought the mission home when they arrived at the house in full combat mode.

She wondered if Paul and Allan were suffering from post-traumatic stress disorder. She and the pack members worried about that when the men went off on an assignment. What *had* happened on the last job?

As perceptive as she usually was, she should have realized their behavior could have been related to the mission. In fact, Paul's reaction to this business with the Cooper brothers could be too. She felt bad that she hadn't considered it before. Now she was dying to ask Paul about his last mission, though in the past, the SEAL team didn't talk about their missions. Maybe among themselves or maybe to their mates, but not to anyone who wasn't involved in the assignment.

Yet, Allan had to have been sufficiently worried about Paul to mention some of the circumstances of the mission to his mom.

Paul's focus was again on the sunset. "We knew something bad had to be going on at the Rappaports' house. The last time we arrived at the cabin and didn't inform Catherine right away, she wasn't happy about it. She always wants us to come by as soon as we arrive. We planned to drop off our gear and then head over there and pick up groceries afterward. We figured she'd want to fix us breakfast, at the very least. So you have to admit we were rather surprised. Then we heard you and Rose screaming and—"

"I didn't scream."

He turned to study her, his brow furrowed. "In the kitchen you vehemently said you wouldn't do it. I thought some man was trying to force you to do something horrible."

Lori's cheeks warmed a little.

"What was that all about?"

"Catherine wanted *me* to tell the two of you that you were being auctioned off. It wasn't my idea! So I wasn't about to take the blame for it. Or be the messenger either."

"Ah. And Rose's scream? Hell, she screamed when we were on the speakerphone with Catherine, then someone else yelled, and then the phone clicked dead. What would you expect us to think?"

"That someone had a little accident? But really? That was the reason you went all Navy SEAL wolf on us?" She kept herself from probing about his last mission. "Okay, Rose picked up a plate Catherine had been warming on top of her toaster oven. It was hotter than Rose expected, and she burned her hand and dropped the plate. On my foot! Which protected the plate from breaking. I yelled out in surprise when the plate hit my foot. But Catherine must have ended the call with the two of you right after that. She checked Rose's hand to see how badly it was burned, and it wasn't that bad. Rose was startled more than anything.

"Right before the two of you barged into the kitchen, Rose tripped over a box of jams and jellies that she forgot her mother had set on the floor, which made Rose drop the plate she was taking to the dishwasher. This time she didn't have my foot to protect the plate from shattering on the ceramic tile floor. When the plate broke, she said she was giving up on dishes and got another cup of coffee. I got the broom to clean up the broken plate."

"And then used the broom on *me*."

Lori cast a smile at him again. "You have to admit it did stop you."

"Not for long."

"Well, if it had been someone else, I would have continued to fight."

"Not kissed him back."

Now that they had gotten off the subject of Dusty and the necklace, Lori was feeling more relaxed. She hadn't been up here since the incident. Paul had sensed that right away, and she wished she could have said and felt otherwise.

Not that the brothers were inherently bad, she didn't think, or she wouldn't have agreed to them coming up to the lake. She and Rose were trying to learn why the men were now living in the Cunningham pack's territory. She'd thought questioning them was a good idea. The brothers said that they'd had to move from their last jobs and find new homes because the rancher had retired and sold off his ranch. And they'd lived close before so the area felt like home. Now she worried that something more might come of it, considering the way the brothers had given Paul the eye, especially when her grandma outbid everyone for his services.

Paul watched Lori as she looked toward the west, her mouth still curved in a tantalizing smile. "Sunset's gone. Do you want to keep me company while I make the jam for tomorrow?"

He sure did and joined Lori in the kitchen, where she began washing her bucket of berries. He followed her lead and washed his. Then she put them all in a big saucepan and added sugar in the same quantity as the huckleberries. After that, she dissolved pectin and added it to the fruit and sugar mixture.

"Do you want me to break up the berries more? Less?" She paused in stirring them and crushing some to make the mixture more jelly-like.

He peered over her shoulder, breathing in the sweet berry-and-sugar mixture and Lori's sweet she-wolf scent. "Smells great. Looks great." He wasn't just talking about the jam. "Just right." He hadn't eaten homemade jelly in eons, so this was really a special treat. He remembered fondly eating jam on bread before it had even cooled all the way when his mother made it.

Lori looked up at him and smiled a little. He wasn't moving out of her space, just smiling down at her, his mouth close to hers. Hell, he'd never enjoyed watching someone make jam as much as he did Lori. He was ready to kiss her again. She shook her head and turned to finish cooking the jam. He only let her get away with avoiding any further entanglement because he didn't want to make her burn the jam. Otherwise, he would have kissed her.

Lori began to transfer the jam into jars and seal them. She'd let the jars cool down so she and Paul could have some jam tomorrow.

"See? I knew what you'd like for breakfast. Waffles, pancakes, or French toast with fresh huckleberry jam." She licked some of the jam off the spoon she'd used to stir it.

The way her tongue licked the spoon made him think of tangling his tongue with hers again.

"Or honey. Don't forget how much I like honey," he said. He let his gaze switch again from the spoon to her lips and thought about how much he'd enjoyed licking the honey off them.

She chuckled.

Unable to stop himself and hoping Lori was of a like mind, he took the spoon from her and set it in the empty saucepan. Then he pulled her into his arms and kissed her again, tasting the sugary berries on her lips and tongue as she wrapped her arms around his neck and gave in to the kiss.

"I couldn't wait for breakfast." He gave her a firm squeeze. He wanted to tell her she shouldn't have run off every time he came home. That maybe if she'd hung around, *he* might have changed his plans and hung around longer.

This was how he imagined being with her—her soft body pressed up against him, her tongue stroking his, her arms securely wrapped around his neck, telling him just how much she wanted this too.

Then she broke off the kiss and turned away, though

he still had his hands on her hips, not wanting to lose the connection. "Um, okay so I guess it's time to—"

He waited to hear what she wanted to do.

"Retire to bed so we can get up early, eat, then tape up the wall and get it ready to paint." She looked back up at him, her lips slightly swollen from their kiss, her eyes darkened with interest.

Since kissing her further wasn't an option...

"Well, are you ready for bed?"

He raised an eyebrow.

She gave him a get-real look. "I'm not suggesting anything here." Though she couldn't help but be amused.

He laughed. "I wasn't either. What were you thinking of?"

He could sure be cute sometimes. She liked that playfulness when he wasn't being all dark wolf and overly protective. She turned off the living room light and headed for her bedroom at the end of the hall. She wished Paul and Allan would settle down in the area. She wouldn't mind dating Paul, if he was going to stick around. But she had known, even at an early age, that both men loved adventure, the thrill of danger, and excitement—and setting down roots here would be anything but.

"By the way, now that you know why I kissed *you*, I'm curious. Why did you kiss me back?" Paul asked when she reached her bedroom door.

"To prove you weren't the only one who could be so rash." Before she did anything else that was rash, she stepped into her room, said good night, and closed her door.

A big part of his desire to show her how he felt had

to do with the changing of their shifter life spans. At
first it was subtle, as far as they could determine. Once
they reached puberty, the shifters stopped aging—often
showing no real change in their age for many more years.
But as the years went on, they'd seen faster aging in their
older shifters and weren't sure what was causing the
change in their aging process to more closely align with
human ages. Maybe chemicals in the foods they were
eating? Or pollutants in the environment? Or genetic
evolution: now that more shifters existed, maybe they
didn't need such longevity to locate wolf mates. No one
had a clue what it was, but it meant that he didn't have
forever to do something about his infatuation with Lori.

Paul's thoughts were on Lori, and he was certain he
didn't have a lot of time to waste. He thought he had a
good head start, but he could never really know where
Lori was concerned.

He went to bed thinking about Lori—watching the
sunset with her, picking berries, and kissing her for a
second time. For the first time since he and Allan had
come off the last mission, his focus when he retired for
the night was on something other than the woman he'd
failed to rescue.

Despite not discussing anything about the failed
assignment with Lori, he felt better…just being around
her. And despite having some discussion about the
Cooper brothers and being irritated over that, he realized something else about Lori. She got annoyed with
him, and she had every right to be, but she also showed
some sense of understanding. Like when they were little
and he'd lost his parents and he'd kept busy, avoiding
the issue.

He remembered quietly sitting on a riverbank, alone, watching the water flowing over the stones and feeling like the whole world rested on his shoulders. At eleven years of age, he had inherited the pack. His age hadn't mattered. He had always been in charge when he was with the other wolf cubs while his parents were off on a jaunt and other older wolves were busy. He was just a natural leader.

But there he had sat—worried about the pack, about doing the wrong thing and losing the few of them that were left. He'd felt isolated from the others, unable to cope with the grief he felt from losing his parents. There hadn't been any time to devote to processing his feelings. And he hadn't wanted to give in to his grief anyway. It wouldn't have helped the pack to survive.

Then Lori had joined him at the water's edge. He hadn't wanted her to. He'd looked at her with an expression that said he didn't want any company, but she had ignored him and sat down right next to him. He learned right then and there that his alpha-wolf posturing had no effect on her. So he had given up trying and continued to stare morosely at the water.

She began to tell him how she felt about losing her parents and her grandfather, and then he couldn't hold back any longer. The painful memories of seeing his parents attacked as they tried to protect the other wolves of their pack came flooding back to him all at once. The tears had dribbled down his cheeks without his permission, and when he hastily brushed them away so Lori wouldn't see, she had wrapped her arm around his shoulders and told him how much she loved and missed his parents too. Which had made the tears slip down his cheeks even more quickly.

From that day forth, he had seen her differently—the bringer of light, the healer, the only one in the pack who had touched him in that way.

He knew then that, given the right moment, he would give up the ghosts haunting him this time too, and Lori would be the angel who gave him peace of mind again.

Lori tossed and turned in her bed, wishing she had said something to Paul about his last mission. She'd had a lead-in a couple of times, but then the subject had shifted, as if he was afraid she might talk about it. Somehow, she had to let him know she was there for him any time he needed to talk. Instead of discussing anything further about someone like Dusty Cooper!

She couldn't quit thinking about the way Paul had kissed her in the kitchen again, only this time at the cabin. And how much she wished they'd do it again. She was certain he had feelings for her like she had for him. But was it enough to convince him to settle down?

Next time Hunter called, she figured Paul and Allan would be on their way. And it would be several more months before she saw them again. Maybe Emma was right. Maybe Lori did need to just lay claim to him and make him see that he wanted to stay here more than he wanted to run off on missions. But she knew deep down that the reason she hadn't made more effort to chase after him was the fear he would reject her—that the mission would always take priority over her.

She growled and turned over in her bed. She wanted

him, had always wanted him since they were little. Everyone had been so devastated. He'd truly been their knight when the rest of the pack had fallen.

Despite everything that had happened, Paul had set aside his grief to pull them together and ensure they survived.

She closed her eyes. She would not think about this any further. *This* was the reason she didn't like being around him when he came home to visit. She couldn't quit thinking of him and wanting more. Yet when she left town whenever he visited, what happened then?

She still thought about him—wondering how he looked, how he felt about her, if he would ever choose to stay in the area. Not that her grandma had ever let her off the hook when Lori had taken off. Emma had sent texts and phone calls telling Lori about every time Paul dropped by to visit. Not what he said or did or how he looked, because she wanted Lori to come and see for herself.

"Don't you wish you were here to visit with him too?" her grandma would ask Lori.

She growled again.

Chapter 7

THE NEXT MORNING, PAUL GOT UP LONG BEFORE DAWN but found Lori already up, making a pot of coffee.

"I thought we might run in the dark before we have breakfast and start working on the room."

Though Paul had run through the woods with Allan earlier, giving in to their wolf need to explore and race through the forest, they had planned to take another wolf jaunt last evening. Until everything had changed with the auction and Paul being here. Then again, now that Allan was seeing different women on dates, running with him wouldn't have happened anyway.

Paul was glad that Lori was a wolf and wanted to take a run with him.

"You have to ask? Work first? Versus a run as a wolf?" He smiled. "Of course a run as wolves appeals more than anything." Well, almost anything. Kissing her longer, harder…and more—appealed too.

Paul and Allan had needed two months to locate the hostages and then get them to safety during the job in Ecuador. That didn't leave them with time to run even once as wolves. On their South American missions, the team members rarely turned into wolves, though occasionally they did while on guard duty, hoping no one would see them and wonder when gray wolves had been introduced into the jungle. Only a few endangered maned wolves lived there now.

"Good choice." She stalked down the hall to her bedroom.

He wondered how long it had been since she last ran as a wolf. He vowed he would run with her every day he was here if she'd like. Allan and Rose could join them. There was safety in numbers if they ran into some of the wild predators that lived in the forest.

He didn't bother going to the guest room, instead shucking his clothes in the living room. Then he called on the shift that warmed his body as his muscles and bones painlessly stretched to accommodate the change. The change happened so fast that if a human saw it, he would doubt if what he saw had truly occurred.

Standing in his wolf coat, Paul panted, watching for Lori and eager to explore the woods with her. A human who went for a walk in the forest wouldn't notice much more than the changing seasons, unless something major had happened—a storm blustering through the area and taking down trees, or some such thing. But as wolves, *lupus garous* could smell everything around them and see movement that humans couldn't. Because of that, the environment was constantly changing—the animals moving through the area, the insects buzzing among the trees, the flowers hidden beneath the under-brush. So to the wolves, or *lupus garous*, the forest was always interesting.

As soon as Lori ran out of her bedroom as a wolf, he studied her coloration: silver with black tips on her head and back, beige around the face, and a wagging tail indicating how much she wanted to run with him. Feeling just as enthusiastic, he wagged his tail back and gave a little joyful bark. He realized he hadn't had the pleasure of seeing her as a wolf for two long years. Michael's painting of her didn't count.

Paul wouldn't allow her to avoid him again in the future.

He let her go first, then followed her outside through the wolf door. He wanted to raise his head and howl with exuberance, but he curbed the inclination because other wolves, not of the shape-shifting variety, would hear him. He certainly didn't want to attract the attention of another wolf pack.

He ran with Lori through the woods that led into the Flathead National Forest and headed into the higher elevations in the direction of Glacier National Park, where they saw a snow-white, bighorn mountain goat, its shaggy long coat blowing in the breeze. Spying the wolves, the goat quickly left.

Paul and Lori constantly checked for signs that other wolves had claimed the area, smelling the air and the ground, not wanting to cross into any pack territories. Several packs lived in the forest, but they were strictly wolf and most likely would attempt to kill Paul and Lori if they found them encroaching. Not to mention that Glacier had one of the largest grizzly bear populations in the United States, so Paul and Lori were on the lookout for them too.

It still was in the *lupus garous*' nature to run as wolves from time to time—to feel one with their wolf half and explore nature, and to carry the scents home with them—as if they were an all-wolf pack. It was an instinctive behavior they couldn't break, nor would they want to.

After a good jaunt, they headed back through

Flathead National Forest. They had to watch out for both grizzlies and wolf packs there too. On the trip back from his mission, Paul had checked the local news to update himself and learned that some hunter or hunters had been illegally killing endangered gray wolves in the area, so now he and Lori also had to be extra careful because of hunters. Yet this was his pack's home and he wouldn't want to be anywhere else in the world when he needed time to recuperate.

Running with Allan was different. Male camaraderie. A brother wolf. A SEAL wolf. They watched each other's backs. Checked out the sights and sounds, as wolves in a pack did. But with Lori…he truly enjoyed watching her—the way she paused to sniff at a smell, or lift her head and sniff the air, or sit on her butt and watch the stream trickling by. Just like in Michael's rendition of her.

Paul loved seeing her enjoying nature in her wolf coat and just being wild. He'd missed that about her. It was amazing to see how different she was from his SEAL team members.

He'd caught her watching him too, and he wondered what she was thinking. If she was enjoying the run as much as he was.

Other than catching sight of a rare lynx, they arrived back at the cabin without seeing any other animals. And after stretching his wolf legs, Paul felt right with the world. He loved collecting the scents of the wilderness on his fur. Seeing the untouched beauty. Listening to the sound of the winds blowing through the leaves, the water trickling over mossy stones in a streambed, the hooting of an owl. But most of all, he enjoyed running with Lori as a wolf. He hadn't done that in many years.

They paused to watch the sun begin to rise, turning the sky pink and orange before the darkness faded to light, and then they continued the short distance to the cabin.

As soon as they entered through the wolf door, Lori raced for the bedroom, and Paul shifted and began getting dressed in the living room. She was faster than him; he hadn't pulled on his shirt yet when she joined him.

"*That* was fun. I ran with Rose about a month ago, but…" She shrugged. "I think I felt, well, safer with you. But don't read anything into that. You're a male wolf, and you're bigger and scarier looking—to wild beasts of prey, that is. Hunters with guns? None of us stand a chance against them."

"I had fun, Lori. Somehow running with Allan isn't the same." Wolves were social animals, so they did brush up against each other, touch noses in greeting, and lick each other, male to male, female to female, male to female. It was just a way of showing the pack bonds. But with Lori? Hell, rubbing his fur-covered body against hers while they ran or licking her cheek or nuzzling her meant a whole different thing to him.

"You're so used to running with him that you probably know just how he's going to react. Me, I'm an unknown quantity," Lori said.

"Somewhat, but you still have some of the same wolf moves from when we were younger."

"Oh?"

"You used to sit by a stream or river and watch to see if you could catch sight of a fish, and your tail would start wagging vigorously, sweeping the ground."

She laughed. "I'm surprised you remembered."

He couldn't forget how she had behaved as a wolf in their youth. Each of the wolves in the pack had different behaviors, just like humans. But he'd always been fascinated with Lori's antics.

Lori hadn't expected him to kiss her again so soon. Or to…continually get into her space on the run. Not in a protective way, but more like…courting.

She'd like that. If he intended to stay. She made eggs, toast, and bacon for them while he began to tape next to the brick fireplace. After eating, Paul pulled the plastic over the top of the mantel and taped it in place. Lori moved more plastic sheeting over to the base of the wall they were going to paint.

"On the flight home from Ecuador, Allan and I were talking about how you, Emma, Catherine, and Rose need to join a pack. You need to be around more of our kind," Paul said. "I really hadn't thought about it until this Cooper business, and now with a grizzly claiming this as its territory, it's not all that safe to run as wolves by yourselves, or for just you and Rose to run together."

Lori dropped to her knees and began taping around the rest of the fireplace at the base next to the wooden floor. "The two of you were talking about *us*? Deciding what *we* should do?" She snorted. "Figure out what you want to do about *yourselves*." She shouldn't have, but she tacked on, "When you grow up." That earned her a little smile.

Her grandma only shifted on her acreage at night now because of her more advanced age, and Catherine, Rose, and Lori sometimes ran together as wolves because of the safety in numbers. But she didn't need Paul telling her that she and the rest of them needed to join another *lupus garou* pack just so they could run as wolves.

Paul cleared his throat. "We worry—"

She cut him off. "First off, you know it won't happen. Our pack settled this land. We have history here. When that rabid wolf pack killed so many of our kind, we vowed to stay here and to continue on. We promised to be here for each other."

Her face felt tight with annoyance. She hadn't expected him or Allan to stay in the area forever because they'd always been adventurers who loved to right wrongs. Staying here wouldn't have been a viable option for them. But the rest of them were happy where they were.

She shrugged. "This is our home. Besides, do you think my grandma or Allan's mother would leave? They lost their mates here—they'd never consider it. Rose and I certainly wouldn't abandon them. Of course, we've thought about you and the fun you're having in exotic locations…" She paused to glance up at him.

He was smiling a little at her comment.

"Oh, the occasional lone wolf comes through here and thinks he'll settle down, but then he learns that two SEAL wolves visit here on and off through the year, that one is Rose's brother and the other nearly her brother, and off the lone wolf goes."

Paul smiled, then sobered. "If that's the case, he wouldn't be the one for you."

"I'm talking about Rose. *Not me*. With me, they've been afraid of my grandma."

"Emma? How could anyone be afraid of her?" Paul began taping the opposite wall.

"Oh, she starts chanting and pretending she's casting a tribal curse on him, and the next thing I know, the wolf is out of here."

"Emma does that?" He laughed.

"Quit laughing," Lori said, though it *was* funny. She hadn't really been interested in mating the guys. Especially if they were afraid of her grandma. Lori could imagine someone pretending to cast a curse on Paul or Allan. Neither would have tucked tail and run off. "I really liked a couple of the guys." Not enough to mate either of them. If they hadn't been brave enough to stand up to her grandma, how would they react if they ran into a grizzly in the woods? "But Emma's always had her heart set on me marrying one of the two of you. Of course, I told her that neither of you would *ever* settle down, so she should quit scaring off my prospective mates."

Paul quirked his lips a little at that, then frowned again. "So you started dating Dusty?"

"*No*, I didn't start dating Dusty." She stood and gave Paul an aggravated look. She knew he'd keep asking until she gave him the whole story. If she didn't, Allan and Paul would interrogate Rose next, so she might as well give her version.

"He and his brother asked if they could come by and go swimming with Rose and me. We thought that we could learn why they had moved into the area. See if they had planned any trouble for the pack. They brought steaks to cook on the grill, and we made the vegetables. We thought it was important that we check them out. Just like the leaders of a pack would if we had any."

He didn't like that she could have put herself at risk,

but he admired her for stepping up to take charge. And her jab at him for not taking over? He couldn't fault her resolve.

Then he frowned. "But things got out of hand."

"Yeah. We ate, then went for a walk in the woods. It was hot, and when we came back, we went for a swim. Rose and I were wearing bathing suits. The guys didn't mention that they had none and stripped naked. About that time, we were getting a little wary."

"Hell, I'd say so."

"Right, well, we figured they could have worn their briefs at least. As soon as they didn't and we didn't object, they apparently thought we were easy and got way too frisky. Here we are out in the lake in broad daylight. Not that it's that easy to see us because of the size of the lake and how far we are from other houses and the trees surrounding the place, but still, we weren't willing to take the relationships any further.

"Just figured on a nice swim, the walk, lunch, and that was it. We know not to get involved with wolves to any real degree unless we're thinking of a permanent mating. Too risky. They got mad that we didn't want to go any further than just swimming in the lake with them, called us teases. Dusty yanked off my necklace— pulled it over my head, so I don't think he broke it— and just tossed it in the lake. He said that we thought we were too good for them because both our families owned second homes—our cabin on the lake and the Rappaports' place in the mountains. Plus, Rose and I have our own businesses."

"While they're just ranch hands and don't possess anything of their own, I take it."

"Right. Though we thought they were fine before that. It doesn't matter that they're wolves. We weren't interested in anything permanent with them. But it is nice to go out with a male wolf sometimes as opposed to a human. Let our hair down, so to speak. Talk about wolf stuff. When Dusty grabbed my arm, I seized his balls and squeezed hard."

She swore Paul looked a little pained just thinking about that happening to another guy.

"Then he and his brother took off, and we hadn't seen either of them again until last night at the auction. Anyway, Rose and I tried to locate the necklace, but we couldn't find it, despite how clear the water is. It's just too deep."

"I'll look for it, but I need to get my scuba gear. I still think there are possible packs you could enjoy being around. Like Hunter's. They're good people. When Allan and I are gone on missions, you'd have someone in a wolf pack to call on if you needed help."

She let out her breath in exasperation. "I won't tell the two of you that you need to settle down here so we can be a viable wolf pack, and you shouldn't tell me that we should leave and find a pack to live with. Besides, maybe some lone wolf *will* be the right one for me, and he would help us make this more of a cohesive mate-run pack."

Paul shook his head. "Lone wolves don't like to start packs."

"Some do." Not that she knew of any personally, but she was certain there would be cases somewhere. With real wolves there were.

"Emma would surely scare them off anyway." Paul

sounded glad her grandma was watching out for Rose and Lori's welfare.

Lori tried not to be annoyed again that he was suggesting they leave their home here and join another wolf pack.

Chapter 8

PAUL AND LORI SPENT ALL DAY PAINTING, CLEANING, and putting everything back in place. They shared lunch and dinner, watched the sunset again, and took a shorter wolf run into the woods just to stretch their legs. He could really get used to this routine—working with Lori, sharing meals, running with her, and watching the sunset.

When it was time to retire for the night, Lori made a beeline for her bedroom as if she was afraid he'd want something more and she couldn't handle it.

He sighed and went to bed, thinking about how much he'd like to have her in his bed or be sleeping with her. He'd thought about it a lot lately. More so than usual. He guessed she wasn't thinking along the same lines as he was.

No matter how much he tried to sleep, he couldn't help thinking of her in the next bedroom and how much he'd love to be cuddling with her.

The next morning, Paul assumed he was up before Lori because he didn't hear her in the kitchen making coffee. Naked, he left the bedroom, shifted, and noted she wasn't around. Her bedroom door was still closed, and everything was quiet in there. He headed for the wolf door. Not only was it natural for a wolf or *lupus garou* to scent-mark their territory, but it also was essential to ensure that other wolves didn't

encroach—in this case, on Lori and Emma's cabin and
the surrounding area.

If the women had lived in town? Or like Emma and
Catherine, with homes surrounded by a lot of land,
some for grazing and some for cultivating fields, they
wouldn't need to scent-mark. Even though Emma and
Catherine were near the national parks, they still should
have no trouble. But here, out in the woods, he wanted
to keep other wolves at bay.

When he had run with Lori the last two nights, he
hadn't left scent markings that declared the boundaries of her property. So that was his first priority
this morning.

Of course, it was tantamount to saying *he* claimed it,
not that Lori had, but it couldn't be helped. Neither she
nor her grandma had scent-marked the area in a very
long time.

Every hundred yards or so, he scratched or pawed
at the ground or trees, and he urinated in a few places,
leaving an invisible fence that told other wolves to stay
out. Not that a rival pack would honor it. But some
wolves would, while others might actually mark right
over the area to claim it as their own. He smiled a little
as he thought of wolves having their own kind of pissing
contest, literally.

When he was done, other wolves could smell his
new scent marking for nearly two miles. Hopefully it
wouldn't draw them here like some sort of challenge.
He trotted back to the cabin and smelled pancakes and
sausages cooking. His stomach rumbled with appreciation. When he barged through the wolf door, he startled
Lori, who jumped a little. She shook her head at him.

Wearing a peach tank top, black short shorts, no sandals, and lots of bare skin, she looked hot. He looked again at her tank top to see if she was wearing a bra this time. To his disappointment, she was.

"Don't tell me you were claiming my cabin for your own," Lori said.

Hell, yeah. The cabin *and* the she-wolf. He gave her a wickedly toothy grin back, loving that she knew him well enough to realize what he'd been up to, then returned to his guest bedroom. Once he'd shifted and thrown on a pair of shorts, he joined her in the kitchen and poured a cup of coffee. He wasn't much of a chef because he tended to get impatient and either burned his meal or didn't cook it long enough, so he was glad Lori loved to fix meals and was good at it.

"You've got to tell them who's boss around here." He added sugar and milk to his coffee.

"Right. You know what happened the last time I did that? I had three males looking to mate with me. And they were *all* wolf."

He choked on his coffee, half laughing, half trying to clear his throat because the coffee had gone down his windpipe.

"Yeah, you laugh." She waved the spatula at him. "But *you* would have had to fight them all off if you'd been here. As it was, I couldn't leave the cabin for two days."

He started chuckling again.

"Fine. You can chase them off if they decide to venture this way again."

"They *wouldn't* dare."

She gave him a small smile.

"After breakfast, I'm going to pick up my scuba gear from Allan's cabin so I can take a dive this afternoon. Did you want to go with me?"

"Nah, I'll just stay here and clean the gutters on the cabin."

"Why don't you let me help you with that?" When she looked like she was going to object, he said, "Your grandma bid on my services to do this work."

"You *can't* be serious. As long as her list is, you'd need your whole two-week vacation. I don't think she realizes how long it will take to do some of these tasks."

Paul figured Emma wasn't as interested in having him fix up the place as she was in Lori and him having some quality time together to see if they might want something more. Her grandma was good at figuring people out. He knew she only had their best interests at heart.

When he didn't change his mind about wanting to clean the gutters, Lori said, "All right. I'll just see what else is on Grandma's list that doesn't require a highly trained SEAL wolf." She cast him an annoyed look and then served the pancakes.

He smiled at her.

—◆◆◆—

After breakfast, Paul told Lori, "I'll run over to Allan's cabin and won't be gone long."

She waved him off, and he headed back around the lake.

Lori was really hopeful that he would be able to find her necklace. She would have asked him earlier if she'd remembered he was staying at her family's cabin and scuba diving anyway. She'd snorkeled, but couldn't catch sight of the necklace.

She'd even thought of asking one of the guys she'd dated who was with the local police diving force, but she was afraid that he'd think she was interested in dating him again, and she wasn't. That was the hardest part of being a wolf: having no others nearby to date. Other than Paul and Allan, the Cooper brothers and Jerome were the only male wolves in the area that she knew of.

She couldn't go out with a human more than a couple times before she worried that he might see something more to their relationship. She liked the diver and didn't want to hurt his feelings if he really was interested in something more.

That was the problem with dating humans. It was one thing if she and a guy just didn't connect. But if she did really like a human, that was another story. How could she lie and say she didn't feel the same way as the man did? That she'd have to turn him into a wolf before they could go any further in their relationship? Best to go out only a couple of times and leave well enough alone.

She cleaned the dishes but felt the pressure of an impending storm coming on. With her wolf's enhanced abilities, she could sense shifts in temperature, storm fronts, and changes in the weather. She'd thought everyone could do it, but seeing how far off weathermen's predictions could be, she soon realized that her wolf senses helped her to see the changes. Being a weatherman would be a great occupation for a wolf. Everyone would wonder how he predicted the weather so accurately though.

She kept going outside and looking, listening, and smelling the air. Swimmers were hollering and splashing in the water some distance from her place, their laughter carrying across the lake. The sky looked fine. But she knew bad weather was coming, although it could arrive earlier or later, and she wanted to be prepared.

She retrieved a ladder from the storage building, hauled it to the house, and began to clean the gutters.

———⁓⁓⁓———

When Paul reached the mountainside cabin, Allan waved at him from the deck where he'd been stretched out on a chaise longue reading a fantasy, beer at hand. "Did you finish all your chores over there?" Allan asked.

"Nope. I probably need to stay through tomorrow. Maybe even the next day." More, if he could manage.

Allan smiled a little at that.

"Emma had quite a list of projects. Did you finish yours?"

"Yeah, took a couple of hours. Martha didn't have anything much for me to do. Just wanted me to help her move some furniture so she could clean behind it. And take some stuff to the trash and donation site. I'm going to a movie with Rose Tuesday night. She said if I don't take her, she's going out with some guy she's sure I won't like—just because he's human, not for any other reason. So I told her I'd take her. Did you and Lori want to go with us? The seven o'clock showing? It's that new Western that's out."

"You mean the one with the aliens and vampires in it?"

"Yeah, you got it. You know how everything has to

be paranormal these days. I heard there's a new were-wolf movie coming out next year. What will they come up with next?"

Paul shook his head. "And they never get it right. I'll ask Lori if she wants to go."

"Good show. So, if you're not done with your work, what are you doing back here?"

"I need to grab my scuba gear." Paul headed to his room to get it.

"Emma's got you cleaning out the lake around the dock?" Allan asked, sounding really surprised.

With diving gear in hand, Paul returned to the living room and explained about the Cooper brothers, and Allan's sister and Lori having trouble with them.

"Damn it. I bet Rose didn't tell Mom about it," Allan said, red-faced. Then his brow furrowed even more. "Hell, that's the necklace Lori's mother gave her before she died."

"Yeah, so you know how much it means to her. About your sister, she may have told your mom but then Catherine didn't tell you, afraid you'd do something hasty about it. I'm diving for the necklace this afternoon. If I can't find it, maybe you can come over in the morning and help me locate it."

"Sure thing."

"You could have breakfast with us first. We made some huckleberry jam. It's fresh, sweet, and delicious. I know how much you love it."

"You've been picking *berries*? What *else* have you been doing? I thought you said you were working."

Paul chuckled, hauled his gear outside, and loaded it into the SUV.

"Hell, you sure got a real bargain. I bet you even went with her on a wolf run last night."

Smiling, Paul closed the hatch.

Allan folded his arms across his chest, looking highly speculative. "You…didn't want me to come with you this afternoon to look for the necklace? My date isn't until later tonight."

Paul shook his head and climbed into his vehicle. As much as he got along with Allan and loved his company, Paul really wanted to spend as much of the time as he could with Lori. *Alone.*

"Okay. Your loss. Sounds like a deal for tomorrow. Even if you do find the necklace, if you don't mind, I'll just pop on over and get some breakfast."

Paul laughed. "I'll let Lori know and make sure it's all right with her. I'm sure it will be." Paul could just imagine Allan calling his sister next and interrogating her about the situation with the Cooper brothers. "I'll call you about the movie and let you know one way or another, and update you on the necklace search."

"Sure thing."

When Paul arrived back at the Greypaws' cabin, he found Lori standing on a ladder, showing off her tanned legs and cute little ass as it jiggled while she cleaned the gutters.

"I was going to help you with that." He unloaded his scuba gear.

"Storm's coming in late tomorrow or the next day. Don't you think?"

He smelled the air and nodded. "I think you're right."

"At any rate, I figured we'd get done whatever we

could outside today and tomorrow. We can do anything inside later."

"Sounds good to me. I'll start trimming back some of the vegetation around the drive to the parking area."

"Join you in a few minutes."

He took another gander at her shapely legs. "I could just sit here, watch you, and supervise."

She laughed. "I don't think that's what Grandma had in mind when she bid for you."

Paul was fairly certain she did. Maybe not the ogling while supervising part, but having Lori work with him, yes.

He headed for the storage shed and got out a chain saw, then began to trim back branches that were getting ready to scrape the car when they drove in. Otherwise, the Greypaws kept the place in a naturalized setting. No grass yards to maintain. No trying to turn the cabin property into a manicured lot like some did, as if they were still living in town.

He saw movement in his peripheral vision and turned to see Lori wearing garden gloves, a pair of loppers in one hand. She gave him a little nod, then began to clip small branches farther away. He got busy with his work, and with the noise of the chain saw, he didn't realize she'd gone inside after a time until she waved to him from the front deck.

He turned off the chain saw. "We're having lunch and then going to the furniture place, right?" He could smell the food cooking and headed in her direction.

"Yeah, I was just waiting for you to finish up and return home."

The comment about "home" made him pause. He

could almost envision this being home. He liked the idea—wolf runs in the forest, sitting on the deck watching the sunset with Lori, even swimming with her when he wasn't just diving for her necklace. Diving for her lost treasure made him think of something a whole hell of a lot more intimate.

"I invited Allan over to help me look for the necklace in the morning if I can't find it this afternoon. I said he could have breakfast with us, if that's all right with you."

"Uh, yeah, sure. When we go into town to pick out the furniture, we could get a few more groceries."

They both went inside.

Paul washed his hands, then began serving the beef ribs, parmesan noodles, and turnip greens. "This sure smells good."

"Thanks. Hope you like it."

"Everything you cook is great."

"You still can't make coffee?"

"Sure, I can make it. It's god-awful, but I can make it."

She laughed. "I'll have to teach you sometime." They sat down to eat at the rustic pine table. "Did you finish trimming all that you wanted to?"

"There's more to be done."

"I guess we can finish trimming back the tree branches and shrubs lining the drive and the deck tomorrow. Unless you want to cut them back while I go into town to look for the new couch and chairs."

"Nothing doing. Your grandma questioned my decorating sense. I aim to prove I've got what it takes to decorate the place. Besides, it's on the list."

She laughed. "All right. I was just trying to be nice

and let you off the hook. Even if it *is* on the list." She took a sip of her tea. "You seem to be taking this list business seriously."

"I am. I'm going to lose sleep over not cleaning the gutters."

She smiled and he loved that he could amuse her. "Do you make lots of lists?"

He shook his head. "Never. That's why this one is so important."

She laughed again. "I didn't remember you having this much of a sense of humor."

Paul wanted to say she was never around to see it, but he bit his tongue because they were having a good time and he didn't want to ask why she always took off when he came home. Though he had his suspicions.

Lori had just wound a bunch of noodles around her fork when her cell phone jingled. She pulled it out of her pocket. "It's Rose."

Normally, he wouldn't take calls during a meal, unless it was one of their wolves, and then he always did to make sure everything was all right. He understood that Lori would feel the same way.

"Yeah, Rose? What's up?" Lori asked, still twisting the noodles on her fork.

Paul was taking another bite of his rib when Lori's mouth gaped a bit.

Instantly, he assumed Allan had called Rose and given her hell about the Cooper brothers, particularly when Lori's gaze swung around to Paul and she narrowed her eyes. He was in hot water again.

"Sorry, Rose," Lori said over the phone, still giving Paul the evil eye, her voice sympathetic. "I didn't mean to tell Paul, but you know what he and Allan are like. I asked him to find my necklace since he has his scuba gear with him, and he grilled me for an hour to tell him how my necklace found its way to the bottom of the lake. We're having lunch right now." Lori raised her brows at Paul. "*Paul* said we'd go to a movie with the two of you Tuesday evening?"

"I forgot to ask if you wanted to go. It wasn't on the list. It's fine with me either way."

"Okay, sure, we'll go. We'll make the guys pay for haranguing us over the Cooper brothers. We'll meet you at the theater fifteen minutes before the show starts tomorrow night. All right. Bye." Lori set her phone on the table. "You told Allan about us having the brothers up here?"

"What else could I do? Allan wanted to know why I was grabbing my scuba gear. I couldn't tell him it was a secret. Or lie and say I was cleaning the lake because Emma asked me to."

"Humph. You could have said you were going to search for my necklace, and that's it."

"You think I can get anything by Allan?" Paul shook his head. "He knows me too well. And he knows you too well. Besides, he asked. And Rose *is* his sister."

Lori opened her mouth to speak, but then she didn't say anything.

"What?"

"Nothing."

It was killing him to know what she was thinking. He was going to ask again, but he figured she'd tell him when she felt more comfortable about doing so.

After they ate, they cleaned up and headed for the

furniture shop. It was a combination indoor-outdoor furniture place that carried everything from expensive to nice and affordable. Since the furniture was for the cabin, which wasn't often used, Lori said they'd go for something a bit cheaper.

Paul was all for that, but only if the furniture was comfortable enough. He planned to pay the additional expense if Lori thought something a little nicer cost too much. He couldn't remember a time when he actually went shopping for furniture. He didn't have any reason to have a place of his own. He just stayed with Hunter's pack members while he helped plan missions with the rest of his SEAL team, or stayed at hotels or camped in the wilderness while on missions. And Catherine's cabin on the mountain was his and Allan's home when they came back for visits.

Now, looking at couches and chairs with Lori as if they were a newly married couple trying to decide on furniture for their first home together, felt really odd.

"Sally Thurston," Lori said as a woman approached. She looked to be a little older than Paul in human years, brunette, built, and with a lovely smile. "We're just looking for now."

He knew Lori wanted to buy the furniture and get out of there, so they weren't just looking. He suspected she didn't want Sally's help.

"Oh, sure thing." Sally smiled broadly at Paul while Lori turned and checked out more couches, running her hands over the fabric, lifting price tags, and moving on.

"So," Sally said to Paul, stepping into his path when he was about to follow Lori, "what exactly do you do while you're on SEAL business?"

Paul caught Lori rolling her eyes a little farther away.

"The missions are classified." Not that they were with the Navy any longer, and a lot of the jobs weren't confidential, but he didn't want to get in a discussion with the lady about any of them.

"Oh, sure. Did you know I bid for you? But then Lori's grandma raised the stakes way too high."

"She needed a lot of work done."

"I needed a lot of work done." Sally smiled. Then her smile faded. "But now you're furniture shopping with Lori?"

"Part of the job and the fun. Got to check out the couches. Thanks for your help." He stalked off to join Lori. "So what color are you looking for?" Paul didn't care about color schemes as much as how comfortable the seating would be.

"Something to coordinate with the green wall and complement the wood paneling, not get dirty and—"

"Is soft." Paul sat down on one of the softest-looking sofas and found it as hard as a cement bench.

She grinned at him. "Burnt orange?"

"I never noticed. I was going for soft."

"Is it?"

"No. Looks can be deceiving."

She chuckled.

They ended up trying all of the couches they thought might work color-wise and selected a dark blue that looked good with the emerald green. She found accent pillows that matched the wall and two chairs with blue-and-green stripes that would work together nicely.

Lori took a picture of the couch and chairs and sent it to her grandma, but she didn't respond. "She must be busy working with her friends on their new quilting project."

"She'll love it," Paul said. "The brown wood paneling and the flooring are like the trees and the earth, the blue for the sky, and green for the grass and the forest."

"She would feel just that way too. We did a great job." Lori paid for it.

The owner said his son and a helper would deliver everything at four and take the old furniture off their hands.

Sally smiled at them. "Hurry back," she said, more to Paul than Lori.

Lori climbed into Paul's vehicle. "Do all the women act that way around you?"

"Only when Catherine posts a picture of me in my swimsuit on a poster for a honey-do bachelor auction. Before that, no one knew I existed."

"Well, we couldn't very well have posted a picture of you wearing all black clothes and black face paint."

"You are never going to let me live that down, are you?"

"Nope."

He laughed.

"I need to drop by the bank," she said, pointing out the brick Colonial.

"Sure thing."

He thought she was just going to run inside, but she waited for him to come with her.

"I know it's not on the list, but do you want to go with me?" she asked. "It's too hot to sit in the SUV."

He was surprised she'd ask. "Sure." He escorted her inside the cool, air-conditioned building while she went up to the teller and gave the woman a stack of checks, probably from her martial-arts classes.

He glanced around at the people either talking to loan officers or doing regular banking with the tellers. Ten customers total. When Lori was finished, she walked with him toward the exit.

"Sorry. I meant to do that on Friday but totally forgot."

"No problem."

"With Allan coming over for breakfast, we need to drop by the grocery store. I'll pick up more eggs."

"All right." He escorted her outside and saw a couple of motorcyclists drive by. Another pulled into the parking lot. Paul paused to consider the man. He'd seen a description in the news of the man who'd robbed a bank in the next county late last year. The robber had been wearing a black helmet and carrying a camouflage bag. But this guy had a black bag. Still, he was wearing a black helmet, and he was headed inside the bank. Because of his training, Paul couldn't ignore the coincidence.

"What?" Lori asked, waiting with Paul on the sidewalk when he didn't budge.

"I need to run into the bank," he said, eyeing the guy. Instead of removing his helmet, the cyclist was wearing it into the bank, just like the bank robber had done. That was how he had gotten away with stealing the money and no one could identify him.

"What? You don't have an account."

"No, I just want to see something. Why don't you wait for me in the car?"

Lori glanced at the man who disappeared inside the bank. Her gaze swung around to Paul. "You think he's the robber that hit that other bank in Lakeside?"

"I just want to be sure, one way or another."

"And do what? Make a citizen's arrest?"

"Nothing, hopefully. Most likely he's just a bank patron like everyone else. Will you sit in the car?" He really didn't want her going with him. The robber had never shown a gun before, but that didn't mean he wasn't armed. And if Paul took him down, he didn't want Lori in the middle of it. The man had robbed two banks in western Montana and stolen forty-six thousand dollars already. Since the getting was good, the incentive was lucrative enough for the guy to keep "working" at this get-rich-quick business.

"Okay," she said, sounding resigned.

Paul hurried back to the door and pushed it open, then entered the bank. He was certain *he* looked suspicious, returning to the bank when he hadn't had any business there the *first* time he went inside. He watched the man stalk toward the counter, hand the teller a piece of paper, and receive a wad of cash. Everything appeared to be on the up-and-up. The man stuck the bills in his wallet, jammed it into his pocket, and then turned and caught Paul watching him.

He stalked past him and outside.

Paul recognized the man's scent. He was the middle-aged guy who had been checking out the steaks in the grocery store when Paul was. So much for finding the bank robber on a hunch. Paul headed outside and found Lori watching the motorcycle guy as he climbed onto his bike, then took off.

"I thought you were waiting in the SUV for me. He just made a withdrawal. Nothing sinister." But he wished she'd done what he'd asked, because if the guy had been the bad guy… Paul took a deep breath, hating that he worried about her when there probably was no need.

She pointed out two motorcyclists driving by the bank, four motorcycles parked at the Hamburger Stop, and another five sitting in front of Joe's Den of Inequities—a pool hall and diner. "It looks like there's some kind of motorcyclist get-together going on." She handed Paul a slip of paper. "But…here's his license plate number. Just in case."

He frowned at her as they got into his vehicle, skimmed over the note, and then tucked it into his console. "Did he see you writing down his license plate number?"

When she didn't respond, he glanced at her as they drove to the grocery store. She cast him a worried look, and he was afraid that whatever she was reluctant to talk about now had to do with *him*.

Chapter 9

AFTER GRABBING A FEW MORE GROCERIES, LORI AND Paul headed back to the cabin. When they reached the main road to the lake, Lori cleared her throat. "Everything's all right with you, isn't it, Paul?" She couldn't help fretting about him.

"About…?"

Paul had a wolf's wariness, Lori reminded herself. On top of that, he was a highly trained SEAL used to dealing with crises and bad guys. Yet, she couldn't help worrying that his concern about the motorcycle guy, who was just making a perfectly innocent bank withdrawal, had to do with Paul's last mission. That Paul was seeing hostage situations or criminal acts going on where there were none—first at Catherine's house and now at the bank. Was he always like this after a mission? Or was it just because this mission had gone south, and he was having a difficult time coping?

When she didn't say what was bothering her, still analyzing it in her own mind, Paul said, "Something's troubling you. Are you worried about me? I'd rather you get it off your chest, and we'll clear the air. I'm not sorry about being concerned for you and Rose with the Cooper brothers though."

"*Don't* get started on *that* again. I worry about you, okay?" Before he could ask her about what, she continued. "I worry about Grandma. She's getting up in years. Now with this issue of some, if not all, of us aging like humans and not having the extended longevity that we did, I'm more than concerned about her health. And I worry about Rose." She didn't want him thinking she was only concerned about him.

He raised his eyebrows.

"I'm *serious*."

"Okay, so you're a worrywart."

"If you weren't driving, I'd sock you. *No*, I'm not a worrywart. I *don't* worry needlessly about things."

"All right, so what are you worrying about with regard to Rose?" he asked, getting serious.

It was typical of him to ignore her concern for him and focus instead on the other members of the pack. "I don't know." At least nothing for certain. She wished Rose would open up with her.

He smiled.

Lori really *did* want to sock him. "She's canceled a number of dates on me."

"For no good reason?"

"No, she had sound reasons."

He chuckled.

"I'm not kidding around. She doesn't cancel dates with me. Not normally. And not that many in a row."

"Okay, so what do you suspect it's all about?"

"She was seeing some guy, but she didn't want me to know about it. At least that's what I suspect. I don't have any real proof."

"Recently?"

"Some weeks back. And then, well, she wasn't feeling well for a while."

Paul shook his head. "I've lost the logic in this. She canceled on dates for good reasons and hasn't since."

"Right."

"Even with our faster-healing genetics, we can get sick. Have colds or the flu, or eat something that doesn't agree with us."

"Yes, yes."

"But beyond this you...sense something is wrong."

"Right."

"But...not exactly what."

"Right."

He was still smiling indulgently. Cad. "Okay. So what are you fretting about with regard to me? Don't say it's because I wanted to check some guy out at the bank to make sure he was just making a legitimate withdrawal."

"And barging into Catherine's house, thinking we were in a hostage-crisis situation." She let out her breath and said what was really on her mind. "Does this have anything to do with your last mission?"

"*No.*"

He said the word with such finality that she knew she couldn't convince him to talk about it, at least for now.

"Is that it?" he asked, but he didn't sound annoyed with her. Just that he didn't believe she had anything to be concerned about.

"If you don't want to talk about anything, then, yes, that's it." What she didn't expect next was for him to ask a question she was totally unprepared to answer.

"If we're going to get touchy-feely here, without the touching," he said, eyeing her like he wouldn't mind doing the touching too, "do you want to tell me why you make yourself scarce whenever I come for a visit?"

"No." She folded her arms over her chest. If he wouldn't share with her, she had no intention of sharing with him.

—∿∿—

When they returned to the cabin, the weather was perfect for swimming or scuba diving—a nice eighty degrees—and Paul hoped he'd find Lori's necklace without any trouble. He'd tried to ignore her concern about his reaction to the motorcyclist and the circumstances at Catherine's. He believed his reaction to both situations was due to his inborn wolf wariness and his SEAL training. Nothing more. He was not being paranoid, and it didn't have anything to do with the last mission.

"Do you want to show me where Dusty threw your necklace?" he asked as he carried the sack of groceries into the kitchen.

"Sure. Let me put my suit on." Lori quickly put the groceries away. "You have one, don't you?"

He laughed. "Yeah, but I'm only wearing a wet suit for now."

Her eyes grew big. He went into the bedroom and removed his clothes, then put on his wet suit. When he returned to the living room, she joined him, wearing a one-piece bathing suit and with a couple of beach towels featuring hawks slung over her arm. He took a moment to admire her bathing suit. He'd thought she might wear a tiny bikini, but this one was hot too, and perfectly wolfish. A gray wolf's profile was featured against an emerald green backdrop, and the bodice was cut nice and low, which made him want to give a little yank to the zipper smack-dab in the middle. The swimsuit was cut high on the leg, and when she headed for the door, he saw just how low it was in the back.

She was petite, but she had long legs and an adorable ass. He hadn't remembered seeing her in a swimsuit in forever. Although he had planned to scuba dive with Allan, he was already thinking of how much he'd like to teach Lori to dive, which had him thinking about her being naked beneath a wet suit.

He was already embarrassingly hard with the notion as he followed her out the door. Well, it would just show how much he appreciated seeing her in the suit. Wasn't that the ultimate compliment?

They climbed down the steps to the dock stretching out over the water. The lake had warmed up to a nice seventy-four degrees. Not good for the cold-water fish that lived there—they had to swim closer to the bottom of the lake where it was in the high sixties—but the temperature worked well for swimmers.

Lori dropped the towels at the end of the dock and dove into the water with grace and precision. Beautiful. He waited to see where she ended up before he entered the water. When she paddled in place, he slipped into the water and joined her.

"Out there somewhere." She motioned in the general vicinity.

He was still angry that Dusty Cooper had yanked her necklace off and tossed it into the lake when the jewelry meant so much to her. If Dusty had broken the chain, the turquoise hawk would have fallen off, and Paul would probably never locate it.

He swam underneath the water, lower, until he was close to the bottom, searching with the beam of the

waterproof diving flashlight, looking for any sign of
something gold sparkling in the illumination. But the
necklace could be buried in the sediment and he'd never
find it.

Because of their scuba-diving training, he and Allan
had taken a few jobs salvaging items from sunken
ships off the islands, or locating valuable artifacts or
those with sentimental value for folks who had lost
them in various lakes. He always wanted to find the
valued treasure, but this time it was even more of an
imperative because he personally knew how much the
necklace meant to Lori—first, because her mother had
given it to her and it was one of the few mementos
she had left of her, and second, because of the spiritual
meaning it held.

He had never been scuba diving in this part of the
lake, so he didn't know what he might find. At Lake
McDonald in Glacier National Park, divers could find
rakes, pitchforks, and axes once used to take out the
trash. The lake was frozen over during winter when the
locals put their trash on it, but when the spring thaw
came, the trash would sink to the bottom of the lake.
Sad, but true. Still, divers discovered the implements
and placed them upright in the soft soil at the bottom of
the lake, creating an underwater forest of shovels and
pitchforks. Now divers came to see them and take pictures of the artifacts of an earlier century.

What would he find in this lake? Nothing that seemed
out of place or unusual, he suspected.

After about twenty minutes, he saw a glitter of gold
in the beam of his flashlight. Excited that it could be
Lori's necklace, he swam closer, reaching for it. His

fingers brushed something metallic covered in green
moss—in the shape of a gun. An old gun. A flintlock
pistol with a wooden body, a rusted ten-inch steel barrel,
and a curved pistol handle. It looked to be from the nine-
teenth century.

He suspected from the moss growing on it and the
rustiness of the barrel that the pistol had been there a
long time. He lifted the necklace off the trigger guard,
examined the carved turquoise hawk, and was relieved
that it was Lori's. Best of all, the chain wasn't broken
and the turquoise hawk was intact. He slipped the necklace over his wrist and left the gun there for now. He
would use it to help find the location when he returned
to see if anything nearby could tell him why the gun was
there. But he wanted to let Lori know first that he had
found her necklace.

He rose toward the surface, making his safety stops
on the way up. When he broke the surface of the water,
he saw Lori had returned to the dock.

Standing so she could see into the water at a higher
vantage point, Lori was waiting with her brows furrowed, her whole posture stiff and anxious. He held the
necklace up for her to see, and her face broke into a
sunny smile. "You found it!"

Her enthusiastic response was reward enough. She
looked at him as though he were her hero, and for the
moment, he felt like it. He was more than thrilled that he
could make her that happy.

He considered where he was in relation to the dock
so he could retrieve the pistol next. He would explore
a bit, though he planned to swim to her and hand over
the necklace first, afraid he might lose it while he was

retrieving the gun. He removed his regulator mouth-piece. "I found a flintlock pistol there too."

Her cheerful expression quickly turned dark. "Grandpa Greypaw's gun?"

Hell. Why hadn't Paul thought of that? He hadn't considered that it might belong to her family, but they had lived on this lake for over two hundred years, right here where the newer cabin of fifty years had replaced the old one. "Your grandfather's gun?"

"Yeah. We never found his body either."

She sounded anxious, and now he worried what else he might find.

They had looked forever for all the families in the pack that had been killed by the rabid wolves. Her grandfather's remains were the only ones they had never recovered; the others had been buried in the old cemetery plot set aside for their families on the Greypaws' land.

He began to swim toward Lori. "Let me give this to you, and I'll return to get the gun."

"Wait, let me swim to you and get my necklace so you don't lose the place where you found the pistol." She dove into the water and swam to him.

He lifted his mask, and when she reached her hand out to him, he didn't give the necklace to her. Instead, he placed the long, gold chain over her head.

Then he held the turquoise between his fingers. "This is where it belongs. With you. Always."

With tears in her eyes, she wrapped her arms around his neck and kissed him. It wasn't just a thank-you for finding her treasured memento, but something deeper, more heartfelt, and he realized this wasn't a thank-you at all.

He felt the same wolfish need, the same lustful attraction and, he was fairly certain, the same desire to take this further. He was torn between ending the kiss and wanting to prolong it, while she wrapped one leg around his, anchoring herself to him, her body moving against his in the gentle ripples of the lake, up and down. Despite the wet suit and her bathing suit between them, he felt his erection rising to the occasion again. Of course, all he really needed was to see her in that bathing suit, her nipples standing out against the stretchy suit, to make his cock stir.

With her body moving against his in such an erotic way, he was suffering. Their tongues were doing a slow slide together, back and around, as he kept one hand against her naked back and the other cupping her head for maximum kissing pleasure. The sun shone off the water, the heat of their bodies keeping them warm. He sure loved kissing her like this and felt like one hot SEAL wolf wrapped around a wolfish mermaid. He wanted to be sliding between the sheets with her inside the cabin.

But he knew he had to be careful how he handled this. She was special to him and to the pack. He sure as hell didn't want to screw things up between them.

He'd certainly thought about them being tangled beneath the sheets when he'd visited before, or even on a mission. Not seeing her the last couple of times had only made the yearning stronger. Yet he hadn't wanted to chase her down. Maybe she hadn't really wanted to see him. Then again, maybe her avoidance had to do with the knowledge he'd have to leave again, and she didn't like having to always say good-bye.

He kissed her intimately, lovingly, knowing he was going to have to make real changes in his life—for the better. When she finally pulled her mouth away from his, tears streaked her cheeks.

Hell, he hadn't meant to upset her. He hugged her close. She nestled her head against his chest, and he rested his chin on the top of her head.

"Are you okay?" he asked softly, hating that she was feeling bad and that he could have been the cause of it.

"Yeah. You don't know how much this means to me." She slipped her hand around her turquoise hawk. "But..."

Suddenly it dawned on him. Her grandfather. She felt bad about having never found him, and now they'd probably located his gun which brought the memories back to her. They all had been devastated by losing their families, but at least they were able to bury them, keep them in their memories, and get on with their lives. With her grandfather, they knew he couldn't be alive, but not knowing what had happened to him had been the hardest part.

Paul kissed the top of her head, relieved she wasn't upset that he had been kissing her. This was only the beginning, and he knew she had to be feeling the same way that he was about their relationship. "Okay. I'm returning to get the pistol and see if we can at least identify it as his. As long as you're okay."

"I am. Go ahead. I'll just stay here."

He brushed away the tears on her cheeks, and she smiled up at him, but her smile was only for show. She was trying to indicate she was all right when he knew she wasn't.

"Be back in a moment." He went for another dive and reached the area where the pistol had been, or so he thought, but with the way the water was moving, he and Lori had drifted a bit. He swam back to the location and saw the shape of the pistol. When he grasped it, the barrel hung up on what he thought was a stick, until he realized it was a rib snapped in two. Hell. In that instant, his stomach tightened with concern. This was definitely a mixed blessing.

Gently using his fingers to brush away the sediments collecting around the ribs and other bones, he found a human skull. A chill crawled up his spine. It had to be her grandfather's. Their wolf pack had been attacked near the lake by a mix of *lupus garous* and the all-wolf pack that the Wolfgang pack had also infected. Those in the Cunningham pack who hadn't been killed had hurried to leave the area as quickly as they could.

Eventually, the rabid wolf packs died from the rabies, or Paul and the rest of the pack finally hunted them down. They couldn't have allowed any settlers—humans in the area—to kill off the *lupus garous* because the wolves would have turned into humans upon death. The wolves that were all wolf was a different story, but it was difficult to tell the two apart when they were in wolf form. So Paul and those left in his pack had to take care of them.

Paul brought the gun with him, planning to come back for the bones later when he had his diving bag in hand and could retrieve them.

He hated to mention what he'd found. Lori and Emma would want to know. After spending the required amount of time to return safely to the surface, he resurfaced and said, "I...found bones."

More tears pooled in Lori's eyes and he hated that he'd upset her further.

"What do you want to do? We can let anthropologists know. They'll take them and analyze them to determine age, sex, and origin or we can…"

"Give my grandfather a proper burial. Grandma has always wanted that."

Paul knew that would be Lori's choice and Emma's. It would have been his own, if her grandfather had been his flesh and blood.

He gave her the gun and she wiped away some of the moss. "It's his. He carved an eagle on the handle."

Paul recognized it too. His own grandfather had given Emma's husband the pistol and taught him how to shoot it. The pack had been a mix of Native Americans and settlers, but they were all *lupus garous* and had worked together as a pack.

"What if the bones aren't his?" Paul asked, though he couldn't imagine they wouldn't be, not when the pistol had been with them.

"The gun was with him, wasn't it?"

"Yeah."

"It was him then. He never let that gun out of his sight when he was in the woods or near the lake because of the all-wolf packs, grizzlies, and cougars in the area. He was the only one of our pack members still unaccounted for. So we bury him in the family plot. I don't want scientists cutting up his bones. Grandma wouldn't want that either."

He hated to tell her he couldn't get them right away. "I've…got to get some equipment and come back for him later."

She looked disappointed that he couldn't do it this minute.

"I can only dive one more time, but not for as long as it will take me, and then not again for another twelve hours or so."

She nodded. "We've got to make sure the Flathead County sheriff's office doesn't get word of this and send out their search-and-recovery dive team. If they do, we're going to lose Grandpa's bones. How would we be able to explain we knew they were his?"

"Agreed. We should be fine. No one should ever suspect what we're up to. People get caught at stuff like this because they show it off on Facebook, or tell friends or family who share it with the world. Then they're in trouble." The two of them swam back to the dock.

When they climbed out, Paul was curious about the local dive team, since that always interested him. "Is the search-and-recovery dive team a good team, do you know?"

"Yeah. Rated one of the best in the state of Montana. They have twenty-four divers with all kinds of dive agency ratings—dive masters, master divers, rescue divers. But they also have training in underwater criminal investigation with specialties in underwater body-and-evidence recovery. So we really don't want to get them involved, or we'll have to make up some story about how my grandfather died so long ago. We'd have to say he was an older descendent because no one could know about how long we actually live."

"Right." But Paul's thoughts were already headed in another direction. "How do you know so much about

the recovery team?" He suspected that unless she had
read a bunch of stories of missions they'd gone on, she
wouldn't know that much about them. He hadn't realized how much it bothered him that he hadn't been here
in her life all this time. He assumed if she hadn't dodged
seeing him for the past couple of years, things would
have been different between them.

"I dated one of the guys."

Surprised, Paul raised a brow.

She shrugged. "He's human and I only went out with
him twice. He was nice, but I had to let him know pretty
quickly that I couldn't do anything long-term with him.
If I'd still been seeing him, I would have asked him to
locate my necklace."

"He would have found your grandfather's pistol and
bones." Paul couldn't help frowning, not only because
the guy would have uncovered them and then the situation would have been out of the family's hands, but
also because she'd dated him. Paul couldn't help being
a little jealous when he had no right to be.

She sighed. "Yeah. That would have been a disaster."

Paul would like to meet some of the team members
and swap stories, maybe even let the guy she dated know
she was off-limits. It truly was a wolf condition—at
least that's what he told himself. She was part of Paul's
wolf pack, and wolves looked after each other. With just
a few of them in this area, they needed that *lupus garou*
support system.

When he didn't say anything, she teased, "If you
had been around and wearing your wet suit, I probably
wouldn't have dated him."

He smiled a little at her comment. He knew for

certain she wouldn't have dated the guy, wet suit or no, if he had been around.

He'd tried damned hard to see her only as part of their decimated wolf pack and not a potential mate, because that meant giving up what he loved doing. But didn't Bjornolf, Hunter, and Finn end up doing that in the best way possible? Got the girl and still went on missions? Though while the babies were on their way, the guys were sticking closer to home—as good wolf mates would do. Which was why Allan and Paul had been taking a lot of jobs as a two-man team lately.

She let out her breath in exasperation. "I'm only kidding."

He recognized the frustration in her words, but they didn't ring true. He reached out to touch her arm and… well, he wasn't certain what he could say, but then they heard a truck's engine rumbling as it drove up the dirt road to her cabin.

Lori turned to look in that direction. "It's got to be the furniture truck. I'll go see to it." She sounded like she was relieved to have a chance to leave.

"All right. I'm going to make another sweep over the area." He was off the hook for the time being, but he knew these…feelings between them were bound to come into play until they dealt with them.

He'd considered that Lori and the other women needed to locate a wolf pack and even find a mate among them, since he and Allan weren't home long enough to make a difference. Yet, every time he thought about it, he hadn't liked the idea.

This was their home and had been forever. Like territory marked by a wolf, this was theirs. He didn't like the idea that another alpha male would show up and take control of their pack. They were a pack of a sort. Semi-autonomous, though he'd kept in touch with Catherine and Emma to ensure everything was all right back home. They'd gotten along fine for years like that.

In his heart, he knew that if an alpha male tried to take over, Catherine or Emma would apprize him of the situation immediately, and he and Allan would chase the interloper off. Which meant it was past time that they did something about the situation with the pack and how it was currently being run.

Chapter 10

THE FURNITURE MOVERS WERE EARLY! LORI'S HEART pounded as she worried she'd be caught holding her grandfather's flintlock pistol. She quickly hid it underneath the dock—she couldn't let the men see it. She hurried to the end of the dock and grabbed one of the beach towels. Wrapping it around her, she ran up the steps to the front door. Emotions warred within her as she went inside and threw on a long T-shirt before she had the men haul out the old couch and chairs and carry in the new ones.

Between being overjoyed that Paul had found her necklace, saddened to learn of her grandfather's final resting place, and confused about Paul's interest in her, she felt her feelings ping-ponging all over the place when she never thought of herself as that…well, emotional.

She couldn't believe that her grandfather had been so close by all these years and they'd never discovered his body. She wanted to call her grandma, but the furniture movers had to leave first. She hated that she and Paul had to wait to bring her grandfather out of the lake now that they knew he was there. Yet she reminded herself that after all the time that he'd been down there, no one would be the wiser. Still, knowing he was there, she kept feeling like someone else would discover him.

She glanced out the window, looking for Paul, but he must have gone diving again. In a way, she wished the furniture guys hadn't come when they did. What had Paul planned to say to her when they were at the water's edge?

She let out her breath. When it came to him, she was always overthinking things.

But how could she not, when he'd kissed her so passionately in the lake? Like he'd wanted her, every bit of her, just as much as she did him. And then? He'd leave her again.

———

Still feeling hot and, well, aroused, and unable to get his mind off Lori and the kisses they had shared, Paul continued his descent to see if he could locate anything else in the vicinity of the pistol. He ended up back at the bones. He couldn't help but be drawn to them, remembering the terror when he and the others had fled, every wolf for himself, trying to get away from the rabid wolves that senselessly attacked everyone they could reach: young, old, and every age in between.

Then he saw more bones about ten feet away—wolf bones, three ribs broken, and a war hatchet lying next to them. It was definitely her grandfather's weapon; though the iron blade was rusted, the wooden handle still was intact. Lee Greypaw had shown all the youngsters how to throw it, and Paul and Allan had gotten quite good at that.

Lee seemed to have thrown the hatchet at the wolf, hitting him in the side and possibly breaking the three ribs, but the wolf had still managed to attack him. Then both had died. Since the bones were of a wolf, even in death, it had been a full wolf, not a *lupus garou*. What if her grandfather had used the gun to defend himself but it jammed—and then he and the rabid wolf ended up in the water, and her grandfather didn't make it?

Saddened that her grandfather had died, Paul was glad to know that the wolf that caused Lee's death had perished at his hand. Paul knew the elder would have felt some satisfaction that he'd been a warrior in his last fight. Paul took hold of the hatchet and made his graduated return to the surface. That was enough diving for the day. He'd gather up the bones tomorrow.

When he left the water, he removed his tank and flippers, then slipped the hatchet under the dock where Lori had placed the pistol. He could imagine her walking up to the cabin with a weapon in hand while the men were moving the new furniture into the house. Grabbing the towel that Lori had left for him, he stalked up to the house.

When he reached the living room door, he noted Lori had thrown a long T-shirt over her wet bathing suit, though it was clinging to all her curves. That had him thinking about kissing her in the water again.

He greeted the three men and headed for the bedroom to strip out of the wet suit and throw on some clothes.

By the time he left the bedroom, the men had packed up the old furniture in the truck and driven off.

Pleased at how well the furniture looked, Paul sat down on the couch, sank into the soft cushions, and ran his hand over the velvety material. He loved this couch. He could just stay here forever.

Lori disappeared into the bedroom and returned wearing a pair of shorts and a tank top. She sat next to him and patted his bare leg. "They look great, don't they?"

Yeah, with her sitting on the couch, her leg pressed up against his, the whole setup looked even better. "Yeah, your grandma is going to love it."

"I'll bring her up to see it when you leave to stay with Allan at the Rappaports' cabin." She sounded a little sad.

"We haven't even gotten to half the work we need to do. Did you want to call her about your grandfather?"

"I hate to, but yeah, I'll do it now that the furniture guys are gone."

"I'll give Allan a call and see if he wants to help me retrieve the bones in the morning. It would be quicker and better if the two of us could do it. One other thing…" Paul explained about the hatchet and the wolf, and what he suspected had happened.

Lori let out her breath on a heavy sigh. "Good. I'm glad to hear he had a fighting chance. He would have been pleased to kill his attacker but saddened at the same time. He was a fighter to the last, but they were brother wolves. We know they weren't responsible for their actions, not when the rabies had infected their brains. They couldn't help what they did."

Paul put his arm around her and pulled her close, feeling it was a natural thing to do. She snuggled back, as if she felt the same way. He stroked her arm soothingly. He just wanted the closeness, the comforting, the knowledge they had been through so much in the past. Now they were coming full circle on the event that had turned their pack lives upside down.

"I know. As upset as all of us had been, we never blamed them. We knew if we had been infected instead, we would have reacted in the same way," Paul said.

"I wholeheartedly agree." She raised her head off his chest and looked up at him. "Did you get it? The hatchet?"

"It's down by the dock next to the pistol. I didn't want to carry it up to the house and have anyone see it."

"I don't blame you. No telling what the furniture movers would have thought. Do you want to go get the weapons while I fix a light dinner? I was thinking we could trim the branches next to the deck after that. If we have any more time before it gets dark, we could trim back some of the trees beside the private drive."

He wished Emma had asked him to help out before. He realized then just how much work they'd needed to get done. He certainly didn't mind doing any of this kind of work when he came home on vacation. That was what being part of a pack was all about.

"Sure thing." He didn't make a move to leave the couch or release Lori.

She chuckled. "It sure is comfortable. No springs stabbing us in the butt, no rough wool scratching our bare legs."

"No musty smell, feels like velvet, and is cushiony soft." Having Lori tucked under his arm was what he loved most. He sighed, really liking the feel of Lori nestled against him and thinking how he'd like to do this again. "If you'll fix dinner, I'll get the weapons."

She left him on the couch and then went to prepare the chicken wings. He finally dragged himself off the couch and left the house. He ran down the steps to the dock to the beach and called Allan. "Are you busy?"

"From the dark tone of your voice, it sounds like a SEAL mission. What's up?"

"I found Lori's necklace, but I also found her grandfather's remains."

Allan was silent for a moment, then he said, "In the lake?"

"Yeah, all along. After all the rabid wolves had been killed, we searched for him everywhere, but no one thought he would be in the lake. Do you want to help me bring the bones up in the morning?"

"Hell, yeah."

Paul explained what he assumed had happened as he walked to the end of the dock, then stared out at the dark blue water. He wondered if he and Allan would have found Lee Greypaw while diving together here near the end of their vacation.

"Emma will be glad to know the truth after so many years of not knowing," Allan said. "How's Lori holding up?"

"She's saddened, of course. But glad he had a fighting chance and died a warrior's death." Paul left the dock, picked up the pistol and the hatchet, and headed back to the house.

Allan sighed. "Wish we had gone scuba diving there some years back."

"Yeah, me too. Who would have thought we'd find anything important there? We've always gone to the sites where other divers have reported special finds."

"I agree. We're going to have to be sneaky about retrieving the bones."

"Yeah, figured we'd go at first light. Most folks aren't out on the lake that early. No one should really know what we're up to anyway—the lake's big and the property is secluded."

"Sounds good to me. Are…you about done with the other chores?" Allan asked.

"About that…I'm going to be up here for a while longer. We need to put sealant on the deck, trim back some tree branches overhanging the deck, clear some of the wood and underbrush along the dirt road to the cabin, and some other things."

"What have you been doing all this time?" Allan asked, sounding a little surprised Paul had so much work left to do.

"Painting, buying new furniture…diving for Lori's necklace."

"You've been doing *what* with the furniture?"

He knew Allan would wonder about that. "Emma wanted a new couch and chairs for the living room at the cabin."

Processing it, Allan didn't say anything for a moment. "Sooo, why the new furniture?"

"It was old. It needed to be replaced. Why else would she need it?"

"No one hardly ever goes up there."

"So?"

"Well, sounds like someone's setting up house."

"Maybe she's thinking of renting it out for visitors to the area," Paul said, having given that some thought. "She could make a good income." Though she'd never done so in the past.

Allan laughed. "Hell, it's…okay. See you in the morning."

"It's…what?" Paul asked.

"Emma's pairing the two of you up. She's giving you the fixings for your new nest and it won't—"

"We're wolves, not birds."

"Den, then. See you later."

Paul had considered that scenario, but he couldn't believe Emma would really think something like that would work. Getting Lori and him together so they could get to know each other better, sure. But actually setting up a household for them? Nah.

He called Catherine then and let her know about Lee Greypaw, afterward calling Emma. He wanted to talk to her after Lori did and make sure she was all right.

"Thank you," Emma said, her voice strained. "I can't thank you enough, Paul."

They talked for several more minutes, and then she said she needed to talk with Catherine about arrangements. "See you tomorrow then."

They ended the call and he ran up the steps to the deck. When he opened the door to the cabin, he smelled chicken wings frying. He took in a deep breath of the lemon-and-pepper seasoning. He definitely could see the benefits of sticking closer to home: enjoying home-cooked meals and sleeping in a comfortable bed. Plus he didn't have to run through the jungle to save a life and ensure he and his teammates weren't injured during a mission.

As if on cue, Hunter called him. Paul shut the door to the house and sat down on the new sofa, certain this had to be about another mission, despite the fact that they were on vacation. "Yeah, what's up, Hunter?"

"Got a mission for you and Allan, if you want it. I know it hasn't been that long since the last one and that you're on vacation, but you know the rest of us aren't available right now."

As if Lori knew what the call was about, she walked into the living room, drying her hands on a kitchen towel, and said, "You can go, if you need to. I can take care of everything on Emma's list. You just need to do what you need to do."

She looked so stoic standing there, still drying her hands that had to be well dried already. He knew she didn't want him to go and he wasn't about to.

He cleared his throat and said to Hunter, "I've got a really hot mission here I've got to take care of."

Lori frowned at him. He smiled at her.

"Hell, it's about time," Hunter said. "Let me know if you need the SEAL team for anything. We'll be packing and heading that way."

Paul chuckled. "Will do. Talk to you later." He ended the call with Hunter. "Chicken wings smell great."

"You don't have to feel obligated to stick around here if someone needs rescuing." Lori stalked back into the kitchen, sounding annoyed that he wouldn't leave.

Was this a reversal of Lori's avoidance? He realized that this was all about his job. He left her behind all the time. Now that he was here and had no intention of leaving—well, not until after Allan's and his vacation were done—was this a new way for her to try getting out of…

He pondered the conclusion he'd been reaching before he joined her in the kitchen.

…a relationship with a very interested wolf?

Lori didn't want Paul to feel obligated to stay because of Emma's to-do list. He'd already done plenty for them.

After he'd discovered her grandfather's bones and her necklace, nothing else mattered. It would be easier if he just left, before she started feeling like this was meant to be—together at the cabin, enjoying meals and sunsets, running in the woods as wolves, working on projects together, picking huckleberries like they used to do as kids, and…kissing.

She served the meal while he set the table. "What was the mission?" she asked, curious why he would have turned it down, thinking it couldn't be that serious if he didn't agree to go.

He took his seat. "I didn't ask."

In total surprise, she stared at him a little too long.

He shrugged. "I'm on vacation."

Without approval, her mouth curved up a little. "You are a hot SEAL wolf."

"Thank you."

She noted he was trying hard to keep a straight face. "I mean," she said, tilting her chin down to let him know she was being perfectly serious, "I can't see you turning down a mission when someone could need rescuing. How could you not ask what it was all about?"

"It's like I told Hunter. I have a hot mission here that needs to be taken care of."

She frowned at him. "You're not being serious."

"Like hell I'm not. There's always a situation going down. And there are others who contract out to do what we do. We're not the only ones available for this sort of thing, whatever it was. But if we don't get some downtime, we'll be worthless. Besides, I've already signed up for this job and here I'm staying."

He sounded serious, but she couldn't believe it.

"You didn't exactly sign up for it," she said, still feeling guilty that she hadn't sent word that Catherine and Emma planned to put him up for auction.

But some part of her knew he'd do it even without having been asked, and another part of her said she wanted to visit with him this time, to see if maybe she could change his mind about what was important to him. Not that she had any intention of chasing after him. If he wanted to stay because it was his idea, then she'd be happy about it. She knew it could never work out well between the two of them any other way.

"You're right," he said. "If Catherine had asked, we would have done so anyway. You know I would have helped Emma out with this stuff no matter what. All she had to do was ask."

Lori knew he would have too. "You come home to have a vacation. There was no way she'd normally ask you to do a bunch of work for her."

"Working on stuff like this is fun." He cast her a sexy smile that hinted at liking something more than just the work, then shrugged. "I don't mind it at all. It gives me more focus. Besides the pack obligation," he continued, slanting a look her way that was roguishly sensual, "I wouldn't want to be anywhere else in the world but here right now."

Right now. Not as in forever. Well, maybe not with her either, but just here, in this place.

"Damn, you're a good cook."

"You do a great job painting," she said, glancing back at the wall.

"Thanks. Can't say I've done much painting before. But it's kind of relaxing."

Again, she thought of him and his last mission. She sighed. He needed this, she supposed. He probably preferred staying busy to sitting on the deck and staring out at the lake, which would have given him more time to brood over what had gone wrong on the mission. He was a doer, not a couch potato.

Then again, that was part of his trouble: keeping busy instead of dealing with his issues.

They finished eating, and he looked like he had thoroughly enjoyed the meal. She loved to cook, so she was glad he wasn't picky about what she fixed.

"I'll clean up the dishes, if you want to get the trimming tools out of the storage building." She grabbed up their plates.

"Sure. And then later, we could watch the sunset."

She stared at him. She didn't believe he'd want to watch the sunset with her on a regular basis. If she kept sitting with him and watching sunsets, and swimming with him, and kissing him while he was turned on in that hot wet suit, she was going to lay claim to him and declare that he couldn't leave. Forget letting him decide what he wanted to do with his life.

Now how would that be for alpha posturing?

She smiled to herself over the notion. Wouldn't he be surprised?

"Yeah, sure." She collected the rest of the dishes and cleaned up while he headed outside.

She had just finished putting away everything when gunshots sounded in the distance in the national forest. Her heart gave a little skip. Wolves, even if they were *lupus garous*, always were wary of the sound of gunfire.

She expected to hear Paul on the deck with the

clippers and garden gloves. She should have known he would be back to his SEAL self.

He stalked inside. "I'm going to take a look and see what's going on."

"Do you think someone is in trouble?" Lori asked.

"Maybe. There shouldn't be any hunting right now." Paul headed for the bedroom and changed into jeans, hiking boots, and his bright palm-tree shirt, then headed out of his room. "I don't have anything else that is bright enough to wear to ensure I'm visible to the shooter."

"I'm going with you."

He nodded, and she was a little surprised he'd agreed. But if someone was fighting off a bear, he might need her help.

"Have you got something bright to wear?" Paul asked.

"A neon-pink T-shirt."

"Why don't you wear that so the hunter doesn't think you're prey? If it *is* a hunter and not just someone in trouble."

"That was just what I was thinking." After she changed into jeans, boots, and her colorful shirt, Paul armed himself with a gun and knife—which made her think of the invasion of Catherine's house—and they quickly headed out of the cabin and made their way through the forest.

After a fast twenty-minute run, they heard a man moving about in the underbrush ahead of them, hidden by the foliage.

"Hot damn," the hunter said to himself, but with their wolves' hearing, both Lori and Paul heard him before they could even see him.

What instantly irked Lori was that the man didn't sound like he was in danger. That was about to quickly change.

Alerting Paul, she pointed out fresh bear scat—larger than a black bear's, which meant it was a grizzly's. Paul nodded.

Armed with a rifle, the hunter was dressed in camouflaged clothes, his hat shoved on his short-cropped, rusty-colored hair. He was headed for trouble as he stalked toward the large, dead bull elk.

"The bear could be anywhere," Lori whispered to Paul as they hid in the woods, watching the hunter. Even without seeing the bear, she was certain it had to be in the vicinity and would claim the fresh kill for its own as soon as it smelled the blood. Like wolves, bears had great hearing and scent capabilities.

The hunter wasn't wearing anything bright, she assumed because he wasn't worried that others were out illegally hunting and might shoot him by accident. But what if others were being asses, just like he was?

"The hunter is putting himself in real danger," Paul said.

"We can't call out to him or the bear will be alerted that we're here, if he doesn't already know."

Paul agreed. "I can run faster as a wolf. I'll shift."

Lori started stripping. "But the hunter is liable to shoot us."

"He'll be too concerned with protecting himself from the bear, which will show up when I distract the hunter."

"You mean we're going to be the *bait*." She ignored the part about how he intended to do this alone.

Paul jerked off his shirt. "I don't want the bear to see you. If he makes his appearance, you return to the cabin."

"We work as a team—as a pack," Lori said with finality as she finished removing her clothes and shifted.

Chapter 11

"HELL, LORI." PAUL YANKED OFF THE REMAINDER OF his clothes as he spied the bear headed through the woods toward the fresh kill and the unaware hunter.

In her wolf form, Lori was watching the situation with the bear and the hunter, her tail still, her whole posture in eager readiness as she waited for Paul to give the signal to rescue the man.

"*Watch out for the bear!*" Paul shouted. "At one o'clock."

The man spun around to see the bear standing tall on its hind legs. The hunter tried to get off a shot, but his rifle jammed.

"Whatever you do, stay calm," Paul called out, still hidden in the trees and the brush. Lori remained near him, ready to take the heat off Paul if the bear charged him instead of the hunter. Paul couldn't move toward the man or cause the bear to see *that* as an aggressive action. "He's curious about you, checking you out. Don't run. Wave your arms and speak in a loud voice. Stand your ground. But if you can't, back away slowly, diagonally. Don't look him directly in the eye. That shows your aggression."

He hoped the hunter would just stand his ground. The bear huffed and popped its jaws. Then it suddenly dropped down on all four paws and slapped the ground.

"Steady, man," Paul said. The hunter looked like he was about to have a heart attack.

Suddenly, the bear charged the hunter.

"Don't run! It could be just a bluff!" Though bears were unpredictable, if they were predatory, they often gave no warning of an attack and just…charged. But protecting its food, no matter whose kill it was to begin with, could make the bear behave in a much more aggressive manner. Still, running from the bear was *not* a good idea.

The bear veered off at the last minute, at the same time that Paul shouted, "He's bluffing. I'm sending my pet wolves to distract him. So don't shoot the wolves, or you're on your own. Get the hell out of there as soon as the wolves go after the bear."

Hoping the poacher didn't un-jam his rifle and shoot them, Paul shifted. Lori and he raced toward the kill, startling the hunter, though he had to realize they were Paul's "pet" wolves, as they came from the same vicinity that he had hollered from. Paul hated that Lori was with him though. As big as the grizzly was, either of the wolves could easily be killed in an instant.

He was used to SEAL-type missions where, alongside his teammates, he fought the bad guys in human form. He'd fought wolves, well, *lupus garous*, when protecting Hunter's pack. But Lori had little experience with this sort of thing. Not that he'd done it more than once either.

They snarled at the bear, distracting him from the man, hoping the hunter was backing away and getting out of there. Paul and Lori had to remain focused on the bear and hope that they wouldn't be injured in the process.

The bear charged Lori and she made a hasty retreat

through the woods. Grizzlies and wolves could run at
the same average speed of thirty-five miles per hour, so
no advantage for the wolves there, though they could
turn quickly. And she was doing a terrific job of it—
dodging between trees, using hairpin turns.

The bear's strength could be the deciding factor if he
caught her.

His adrenaline pumping through every vein, Paul
chased after him, growling, snapping, and snarling,
getting way too close to the bear for safety's sake,
trying to draw the bear's attention away from Lori.
The grizzly suddenly swung its massive body around to
fight Paul. His heart doing a double take, Paul twisted
around and headed in a different direction, running full
out. He swore he'd never run from anything so fast in
his life.

He just hoped Lori didn't chase after the bear again
to get him off Paul's back. He figured she wouldn't have
any run left in her. Not enough to stay ahead of the bear
for another round of the chase. Even Paul was quickly
wearing out. But like Lori, he was running away from
the kill. The farther he distanced himself from it, the
more likely the bear would stop following him.

The bear was huffing and snorting as he ran after
Paul, but finally ended the chase when they were far
enough away from the kill. Because Paul didn't hear
Lori growling at the bear, he figured she was off somewhere safe now. He was glad for it.

The bear must have gone back to his dinner. He
would protect it and bury it, while he fed from it for several days, so Paul hoped the hunter realized he'd lost his
prize. Hell, he wasn't even supposed to be hunting elk at

this time of year. Paul had every intention of reporting the poacher as soon as he was able.

Paul had planned to leave their clothes where they were and return to the cabin, waiting to retrieve their things until the bear had settled down a bit. As long as the wind was still blowing in Paul's favor, he'd be all set. Then he realized he had his cell phone in his pants pocket, and Lori might have had hers with her too. One of his guns and a knife were also with his clothes. Not that he expected anyone to come across their things and grab them when the bear was so close by.

Beyond that, Lori had her necklace with her things, and after finding it in the lake, he didn't want her to lose it again. As much as he didn't want to return to the area where the highly agitated bear would be protecting its prey, Paul needed to.

Keeping low like a wolf on the prowl, Paul finally reached their clothes. Through the cover of the trees and underbrush, he saw the bear behind the elk remains, snorting, clacking his teeth, and then swaying his head. The hunter was gone, not foolhardy enough to believe he could carve up his kill and haul it out of there while Paul and Lori were distracting the bear.

As a wolf, Lori suddenly materialized out of the underbrush and joined Paul. He shifted and remained crouched, then proceeded to put on his clothes as quietly as he could to avoid alerting the bear. Lori stayed in her wolf form to protect him if necessary. He sure as hell would be at a disadvantage if the bear caught sight of him now, half-dressed. Even if Paul could scramble up a tree, some grizzlies could climb them also, and even if this one couldn't, it could reach up to a height of ten feet.

At least Paul and Lori were downwind of the bear.
The problem was that bears' senses of smell and hearing
were exceptional. Eyesight not as much. So as long as
the bear didn't smell or hear them, Lori and Paul should
make it all right.

Once Paul was dressed and he had Lori's clothes in
hand, he walked at a crouch until they were deeper in the
woods. Then he sprinted for the cabin. Lori stuck close
to him like a wolf guardian. She would make a damn
good SEAL teammate in wolf form, he thought.

He planned to track down the hunter next, but as soon
as Lori entered the cabin, she shifted, took her clothes
from him, and began to dress. "I picked up his scent
trail. I followed him for a while, but I wanted to make
sure you were okay."

Distracted at seeing her naked, Paul barely heard
what she was saying. As soon as she slipped into her
black, silky panties, his focus turned to her beautiful
breasts, with rosy nipples, rigid and mouthwatering.
She grabbed her black lace push-up bra and secured her
breasts, but when she folded her arms across her naked
belly, he finally glanced up from feasting on her beautiful body and saw her raised brows. "Did you hear what
I said?"

"I'm still getting over being chased by a bear." The
bear was nothing compared to seeing Lori naked.

"Right." Then she pulled on her jeans.

He hadn't wanted her anywhere near the bear, but
then again, he wouldn't have wanted her anywhere near
the hunter either, just in case he decided to shoot a wolf
too. A poacher couldn't be trusted.

"I remembered we'd left our cell phones with our

clothes and couldn't even call the sheriff about the poacher," Lori said.

"And you left your necklace behind."

She pulled her shirt over her head. "And your shirt."

He did love that shirt. But mostly because she had bought it for him and grinned so broadly when he'd shown the rest of his SEAL team that he had no qualms about wearing it. "I'm going to throw on something a little less noticeable." He got an olive-green T-shirt from his room. "If we're going to chase after the hunter, maybe we should wear clothes that will blend in more."

"Agreed."

"Do you want to go hunting with me?"

She smiled and he realized just how much asking pleased her.

She hurried to her bedroom and replaced the hot-pink shirt with an olive-green one that matched his, only hers dipped low enough to show off the swell of her breasts. "If we're wearing clothes that disguise us, won't he be liable to shoot us and say it was an accident?"

"Only one of us," Paul said. "A second shooting would be too risky."

She chuckled.

He pulled her in for a hug. "I don't know, but I think we're going to do some heavy-duty talking once we return."

She looked up at him with a serious expression. "You mean cutting back the trees and shrubs comes later?"

He didn't answer her right away, thinking about the weather and wanting to finish the tasks on Emma's list.

Lori's eyes sparkled with mirth. "The list comes first."

"We can talk while we work."

"Yeah, somehow I knew that list would take priority."

"Not a priority, but we can do both at the same time."

Smiling, she shook her head. Then they headed out, Lori with a couple of cans of bear spray repellent, and Paul with his 9 mm semiautomatic Glock pistol and a knife.

For two miles, they tracked the man. He was a typical human, and though he was wearing some hunter spray, both Paul and Lori smelled his sweat and fear and...

Paul wrinkled his nose.

Urine. The bear charging him probably had something to do with it. In any event, they had no trouble tracking the hunter's scent. They heard a truck engine's heavy-duty rumbling. It sounded like it had a performance exhaust upgrade, so Paul would recognize it anywhere if they heard it again. By the time they raced to where the hunter had parked the pickup truck, the vehicle had driven off. He was probably worried that the man who sent the wolves to distract the bear would call the police about him poaching.

Wishing he could have at least gotten a license plate, Paul said, "I guess that's it for now. Ready to do some more of our chores?"

Lori let out her breath on a heavy sigh, looking totally peeved. "Too bad we missed him."

"Agreed. I'd love to see him get a hefty fine and maybe some jail time to deter him from doing it again."

"*Lengthy* jail time," Lori said.

When they reached Lori's place, they still had a couple more hours of light, but Paul wanted to stick close to the cabin. Tomorrow, they could trim more of the tree limbs next to the drive. He called the sheriff, told him where the man had headed, what he looked like, what he was wearing, what he'd killed, and where the elk was, not to mention the bear that was now feasting off it.

Lori removed her boots and socks, and went barefoot onto the deck, where she began clipping back twigs and small branches next to the deck's railing. When he'd ended the call, Paul put on a pair of work gloves and started pruning the branches on the opposite side of the deck so he wouldn't be in Lori's way.

"So what did you want to ask me in the SUV earlier?"

Looking a little surprised, she glanced at him and hesitated to say.

"I want us to talk. I want you to tell me what's bothering you."

"Okay." She still hesitated, as if she was either gathering the courage or wanted to be careful about what she said.

She should know she didn't have to tiptoe around him. If he didn't like the question, he just wouldn't bare his soul.

"I wanted to ask about your last mission. About how you feel once you've been on one. Do you keep thinking about it? Do you wish you'd done anything differently? Is it hard to let it go?"

That was it? Hell, the number of questions was almost as long as Emma's honey-do list. "Anything else?"

"Well, for starters, that's it."

Although he didn't want to discuss this with anyone but Allan, since he'd been there and lived through it with him, Paul knew he couldn't avoid telling Lori the truth. Not when he'd told her they'd talk. He was just as happy to push it out of his mind completely, not wanting Lori to hear how he'd failed to protect the woman he was meant to rescue. In truth, he'd let it go while he'd been busy working or spending time with Lori. Dredging it all up would make him remember what he'd prefer to forget.

"All right," he said with reluctance. "Do you know anything about this last mission?"

"No."

He suspected she knew something or she wouldn't be asking.

"Four third-year botany students from a college back east went trekking into the Amazon jungle without anyone to watch their backs. Many of the researchers who venture into the jungle take armed muscle with them for protection. It's just one of those things. Some get by without any trouble, but others don't. It's always better to be safe than risk being taken hostage." Paul continued to chop away at the overgrown limbs. He felt better talking about it if he could remain physically active.

"The students were all young, between twenty and twenty-two. Three guys and a girl. It took us forever to locate them because their captors had moved the students around a lot. We finally found them tied to trees, starved and dehydrated. Which wasn't good. They were weak and we were going to have problems getting them out of there quickly and safely to a point where we could rally for help." He paused to exchange a tree-limb lopper for a saw. The trimming had been sorely neglected over the years, and he vowed to help out more around Emma's places when he could.

"What about the guards?"

"We were fortunate that nobody was watching the students. We guessed they figured the students weren't going anywhere, and as isolated as they were from civilization, no one was likely to come across them. If it wasn't for our keen wolf sense of smell, we might not have found them either."

"You couldn't call for a helicopter to come pick them up right there at the campsite?" she asked.

"We had to assume that their captors were still in the area. We needed to get the students as far away from there as possible and to a better extraction point where a helicopter could reach us. We freed the students, gave them water and nutrition bars, and then hiked for nearly three hours, barely resting, despite their condition. Not one of the students complained about it, knowing all our lives depended on it. The woman was having the worst time of it. Both Allan and I had taken turns carrying her."

Paul put the saw down, grabbed a smaller clipper, and cut away at the twigs, but he realized Lori wasn't working any longer. Either she was done, or she was too engrossed in what he had to say. He didn't want to look at her, didn't want to see how she would view his failure. He realized then how hard that was for him to deal with—Lori seeing him as less of a hero and less of a man.

"We had safely crossed several streams, but after the last one, we heard men shouting in the distance. Their shouts were coming from every direction. Except for up above the cliffs. We had one choice. After climbing the cliffs, one of us would lead the students out, while the other pinned down the kidnappers with a barrage of gunfire.

"At that point, neither Allan nor I could carry the woman up the cliff. The male students could barely make it on their own. We had a rope harness attached to her, and I was guiding her up. Allan had climbed the rest of the way to the top with the others. I left her, hurried to the top, and between Allan and me, we were pulling her up. I grabbed one of her hands and then the other while Allan continued to tug her the rest of the way up using the harness."

Paul took a ragged breath. "The bastards began shooting from across the stream. Allan had to stop pulling her up by the rope harness to return fire. I continued to draw her the rest of the way as quickly as I could. But I was too late."

Lori touched his arm, and he realized she'd crossed the deck without him even being aware of it. She took his clippers and set them aside, and then pulled him into her arms.

He swallowed hard. "She didn't make it," he said, barely able to get the words out. "I couldn't let her go, Lori. I had to get her home to her family."

"I know you, Paul. You would have done all that was humanly possible. Just think of the men you saved who might have perished along with her! You've always been there for us when things were so bad. We were broken. The whole pack. Yet you organized us and made sure we had shelter and could fend off the rabid wolf pack until you, Allan, and Catherine killed them. And then when we were starting over, you were the one who took charge and got us back on our feet. You've always taken care of us. But sometimes we need to take care of you."

He looked down at her and saw she was dead serious.

She tilted her chin up stubbornly. "You're always concerned about everyone else, Paul. You've always felt you should carry everyone else's burden. And…well, you should."

He hadn't expected her to say that. Somehow, she always knew the right thing to say to make him feel better. "Oh, I should, should I?"

"Yes. You should. Your pack needs you. More than ever before."

"What if Allan took over and—"

"Not only does he not want the job, but you're the one who always took charge. Everyone expects you to take it over and be here for us." Lori let her breath out on a heavy sigh. "I know you don't want to give up what you do. When you do, we'll be waiting for you."

"What about you? Will you be waiting for me the next time I come home? Not disappearing to avoid me?"

"Who says—"

"I do. You can deny it all you want, but it's the truth. I can live with it for now, as long as you're not avoiding me because you hate me or something."

"Yeah, right. I wouldn't want you to lead our pack if I hated you."

"Then it's because you get upset that I'm leaving again."

"Like I don't have anything better to do than think about you every minute you're gone?"

"Every minute?" He smiled a little.

Lori was glad she'd made him feel better. He'd make

her feel better if he stuck around. She noticed the sun was beginning to set, so she led him over to the outdoor chairs. She was beginning to think she'd made an awful mistake in leaving every time he'd come home before. But she knew he hadn't been ready to settle down, and every time he'd left, she'd felt bad.

He didn't let go of her hand when he sat down. She wasn't sure what he was up to until he pulled her into his lap and wrapped his arms around her waist. They sat there like that, watching the sun set in silence.

He still hadn't once said he wanted to stay here for them. Not yet. And she didn't want to push him on it. Which was why she hadn't said anything more about her concern for Rose.

Chapter 12

LORI SAT IN PAUL'S LAP, LEANING BACK AGAINST HIM. She felt his arousal take on a life of its own, his hand gently caressing her arm while they were supposed to be watching the sunset. She decided he was sleeping with her tonight. Wolves mated for life, so she couldn't have sex with him, but she wanted him in her bed and wanted to share the closeness. She did not want to mate him though, not if he was so determined to stay away from the pack for months on end.

She had no qualms about being his mate and sharing in the responsibilities of leading the pack that, unbeknownst to him, would be growing by leaps and bounds once he declared he was their leader. There was time enough later to share that news. But she wouldn't be his mate if he was going to leave all the time, possibly getting himself killed in the Amazon jungle and leaving her to run the pack alone.

She took a deep breath and let it out, loving this side of him, the sexy tenderness that was Paul. She was so sorry for what he'd been through—for the woman they'd lost and for the woman's family. Yet Lori sensed he was somewhat relieved to have shared the story with her.

Something clicked with her at that moment, and she wondered if he needed someone to convince him to stay. She'd always thought he should make the decision on his own. But she was coming to the conclusion that he didn't believe they truly needed him. That maybe he thought he'd step on toes because they had managed for themselves ever since he joined Hunter's SEAL team.

It was late and she normally would have felt tired, but the way he was stroking her arm, the way she felt his arousal pressed against her back, she couldn't help but think of him in bed, and any tiredness that might have claimed her slipped away.

The sun had long ago disappeared behind the distant mountains, and yet they still sat there together, neither of them calling it a night. Was he thinking of asking her to come to his bed? Or was he hoping she'd ask him?

She couldn't believe how nervous she felt about it. What if he said no? That he didn't want to compromise her? What if he really didn't want to go to bed with her?

"Do you want to go to bed?" he asked, breaking through her muddled thoughts.

Maybe she *was* a worrywart.

"Yeah, the sun has already set." As if he didn't realize it had. She didn't make a move to disengage herself from him, loving the closeness they shared. It was the first time when he'd been home that they'd been really close like this.

The night air grew cooler while the warmth of his body heated hers. He continued to run his hand over her arm in a soothing manner. Well, more than soothing. She was already getting turned on.

And he could smell it. Just like she could smell his arousal and his piney scent from the run through the woods.

He leaned down and nuzzled her cheek with his face. She smiled at the scratchiness of the hint of stubble on his cheek. "You're scratchy."

His lips swept over her cheek and they were soft and masculine. She turned to look at him, to see his expression. His eyes were dark with interest. He leaned down and kissed her mouth, and she wrapped her arms around his neck, wanting to press her breasts against his chest, wanting to crush her body against his.

She barely registered that he'd lifted her in his arms and carried her into the house, slamming the door behind them. He stalked toward her bedroom, not pausing at his room, but she still wasn't certain what he was going to do. Leave her in her room alone so she could sleep? Join her in the bed?

He laid her on her bed and looked down at her with such longing that she was certain he wanted to stay with her as much as she wanted him to.

"Tell me I'm out of line and I'll leave without a whimper," he said.

"I could never see you whimpering."

"A growl, then." He gave her the most devilishly sexy look.

"Stay with me," she said, reaching for her zipper.

"Gladly." His voice was filled with lustful need as he yanked his T-shirt over his head.

This was what she'd wanted as soon as he'd kissed her in Catherine's kitchen, black face paint and all.

Not a mating, she thought. But she wasn't wearing jeans and a shirt to bed. Naked probably wasn't a good idea either.

She unfastened her zipper, yanked down her jeans

and tossed them aside, then climbed under the covers. She meant to pull off her shirt, but she hesitated.

He removed his boots, socks, and jeans. Wearing only his briefs, he climbed into bed with her.

She was going to take off her shirt, but he moved in next to her, ran his hand underneath the fabric, and cupped a lace-covered breast, making her feel sexy.

Especially when he pulled the lace down and exposed her breast, his hand rubbing against it and making her nipple grow erect. He suddenly stopped, and she nearly growled at him, but he lifted her shirt over her head and tossed it. And then he quickly unhooked her bra and pitched it over the side of the bed.

His mouth latched on to her nipple, and she was rethinking the mating scenario, whether he left her behind while he went on missions or not. Just his mouth closing around her nipple was enough to make her come off the bed, but then he used his wicked tongue on the sensitive flesh, and she groaned out loud.

"You shouldn't have run off," he said, moving his seductive mouth to hers.

Before he could press his lips against hers, she said, "Ditto."

He smiled against her mouth, and then he began kissing her possessively, yet waiting to ensure she wanted this as much as he did. She did. She cupped his head and held on for dear life, kissing him like this was the end of the world and they were meant to be together.

She wasn't sure what he had in mind to do, how far he wanted to take this, but she knew what she wanted. She slid her fingers underneath the waistband of his briefs and began stroking his ass.

His lips paused against hers with that wickedly hot grin, and then he was on his knees, pulling off her panties and tossing them aside.

She thought to say something about waiting to mate, or that she loved him, but she was afraid she was jumping the gun. Instead she soaked in the hot and sexy way he was making her feel as he licked at her nipple again, then lower, down her belly. His tongue curled into her navel, and she was about to come unglued. Until he took a deep breath of her aroused scent mingling with his and began to stroke her already swollen nub.

She was so keyed up with him touching her, so caught up in the feelings swamping her. She wanted all of him, not just a teasing simulation of where this could lead. The mating, the commitment for life, all of it, now.

Slow down, she told herself, but she was already yanking off his briefs so she could see the arousal that she had encouraged, loving the beautiful sight of him— all wolf in human form, strong, muscular, SEAL and wolf man combined. And what a devilishly hot combination that was.

He was hers, she decided. He'd never mate any other wolf. She wasn't letting him go.

"Lori," he said, his voice husky, making her name sound as if it was the most beautiful word he could manage to get out. Then he was leaning down to kiss her mouth again and stroking her to completion. This time she let herself go, quit analyzing everything between them, and gave in to that happy conclusion that had her writhing at his practiced touch and crying out with release.

She wanted him to join her, to mate her in the worst

way, her body thrumming with the most delicious
climax. Yet, again she was torn, not wanting him to
reject or put her off.

She sighed, wrapped her hand around his cock, and
began to stroke him. He kissed her mouth, which was all
he needed to do to let her know he wasn't willing to go
any further. At least not yet.

Lori wasn't ready for a mating, Paul knew. Even
if she smelled like she was, and her eyes and lips said
she was.

Was he? He wasn't certain. For now, this was
damned good. Even to get this close. This was near
to heaven.

She appeared to enjoy stroking him and watching
his expression as she worked him hard, pulling on his
every sense, pushing him to the end, to completion, and
making him spill his seed all over her.

She smiled at him. "Mmm."

He smiled back and carried her into the bathroom to
shower. Together.

Paul and Lori had cuddled the rest of the night in her
bed after showering. He decided that if they didn't mate
soon, he wasn't going to last. How would it sound for an
alpha SEAL wolf to beg?

For now, he just loved being with her as her breath
lightly caressed his chest. Then he began to wonder what
they were supposed to do today. He didn't remember
what was next on the agenda until he heard Allan drive
up in the old Pinto—the one he left at the cabin until he
returned from missions—and parked.

Both Lori and Paul groaned as he realized he had to leave the she-wolf behind and hurry while he grabbed his clothes and dressed. By the time he reached the front door to let Allan in, his SEAL buddy was grinning. "Looks like you had kind of a rough night."

Paul should have run a comb through his hair. He heard Lori in the kitchen and was damn glad she was quick.

But then Allan's smirk turned to concern. "Not having nightmares still, are you?"

Hell no. Not with spooning Lori the rest of the night. He'd only had thoughts of her when he'd awakened. Hot, sexy, wanting-to-do-it-all-over-again thoughts.

"I'm fine," he said, not wanting to discuss *why* he was fine.

Allan was studying him. They hadn't moved from the deck and Paul closed the door. "So how did your dates go?"

Allan smiled again. "Probably not half as great as being with Lori has been. I mean, working with her. You know."

Yeah, Allan had guessed there was more going on than he was saying. Paul leaned over the deck and looked out across the water. He loved it here. He could see staying here with Lori. He could see... Well, he could see being mated to her. He realized he'd never thought there would be anyone else in her life, just like he'd never imagined anyone else in his.

"Are you sure you're okay?"

"Yeah, I am." Paul didn't want to tell him that talking to Lori had made all the difference in the world to him, again.

"Okay. How about Lori? Emma? About Lee Greypaw?"

"They're fine. I talked to Emma and she's sad but relieved he's finally going to be put to rest with the others in the pack. We need to call her when we're ready to drive over there. She still has the pine casket she had made so long ago for him, stored in the storage shed. We'll go over after we get dressed, bury him, and say our good-byes to him."

Lori poked her head out of the door and greeted Allan, though she still looked rather tumbled herself. So much for her being quick at getting ready in a hurry. Allan considered her thoughtfully, then smiled a little. "Morning. Heard you made some tasty, homemade huckleberry jam."

They enjoyed breakfast and the company as Lori good-naturedly grilled Allan about his dates with the women the last two nights. Allan told about the fun he'd had, glancing at Paul from time to time. Paul knew he wanted to ask about how Lori and Paul were getting on. But he knew enough not to broach the subject as Paul eyed him with a warning look.

Allan smiled even more. "Food was delicious," he said and finished the last bite of his egg.

"Thank you. We'll feed you again sometime, I promise." She took their plates to the kitchen. "I'll clean up while you dive."

Paul hoped she wouldn't be too upset when they brought her grandfather's bones up. It was one thing to rationalize it, another to see the evidence of his demise.

Everyone had been close to Lee Greypaw, had listened to him recalling the adventurous tales of his youth, including one of finding a wolf cub in a flooded den that the parents couldn't reach, rescuing it as a young boy, and then raising the cub. The rest of his tribe wouldn't permit the wolf to come into camp, so he had lived outside the camp. From then on, his kin had called Lee "Runs with Wolves."

Every time Lee went on raiding parties against another Native American tribe to steal their horses, the wolf warned him when danger was near, saving his life twice when he was young. But wolves had to follow their natural inclinations, so the cub grew into a mature wolf and left Lee and found a mate. He still returned to visit Lee, but the female wouldn't approach. And then they had cubs of their own and left the area.

Lee had taught the children in the *lupus garou* pack that they were brothers to the wolves and to treat them with respect. He'd been a storyteller at heart and Paul had loved to hear his tales. He missed Lee's stories and how he'd taught the children of the pack to fight and move stealthily through the woods as humans. He had been a wonderful mentor, patient and understanding.

Allan also was quiet when they walked down to the water, following Paul's lead, both of them carrying soft brushes, mesh diver bags, and their flashlights. They heard the roar of a motorboat headed in their direction, and Paul glowered at the driver who sped past, too close to shore for the rate of speed he was going. Paul couldn't make out who was in the boat, just three men with base-ball caps on their heads, the two in the back looking away from the dock. The driver was focused on the front as the boat kicked up water and waves, and sent them crashing into the dock.

"If we weren't diving for bones, I'd call the sheriff's office and report them," Allan said.

"You and me both."

They got into the water and then made their descent. After swimming a short distance, Paul motioned to where the wolf's bones were. Allan nodded and swam over to their location, then began removing them from the sediment.

Paul swam over to where Lee's skeletal remains were and carefully, reverently began to collect his bones, knowing Lori's grandfather's spirit had long ago left them. Yet, Paul treated them with respect. When he had gathered all that he could find, he swam over to see if Allan was done. He motioned to the surface, indicating he'd also found all he could. Using up the maximum time they could safely spend on the dive, they headed for the surface, pausing every twenty feet for a couple of minutes to decompress properly. They were still ten feet from the surface when they heard the roar of a boat headed their way.

Surely it couldn't be the same reckless idiot who had passed them more than an hour ago.

Then the engine slowed down and they saw the boat idling by the dock. Hell. Now what? Each of them had a skeleton in his bag.

When they surfaced, they realized the driver of the boat was Dusty Cooper, along with his brother, Howard, and the other ranch hand, Jerome, who had been at the auction.

Lori was talking to them, arms folded across her waist. She'd seen Paul and Allan surface, her gaze shifting that way for a second, but then she quickly ignored them as if they hadn't been there, giving them cover in case the cowboys decided to get really reckless and try to run them over.

"I heard you were still up here at the cabin." Dusty got out of the boat and stepped onto the dock.

Paul was itching to climb out of the water and knock the bastard into it.

"I'm still working on fixing the place up," Lori said coolly.

"Do you want me to come over and help you?"

A red hawk soared overhead screaming *kee-eeee-arr* for two to three seconds as if warning her that the men were danger.

"No. Thanks."

Dusty couldn't be serious after what he'd done to her necklace.

"Paul is still helping me. Allan came by to lend a hand too. So we're doing fine and I don't need your help."

She sounded as pissed off as Paul felt.

"So where are they? Up at the cabin working? We saw them on the dock getting ready to scuba dive, so it doesn't look like they're doing much work for you."

Paul motioned to Allan, and they disappeared beneath the water.

Lori knew that Paul would be just as pissed at Dusty as she was, but since Paul wasn't able to help her if she riled up Dusty, she continued to play it cool. Not that she wasn't ready to use a jujitsu move to take him down if he tried anything. But she was certain the other two would get involved, and she couldn't handle all three of them at once.

Dusty glanced down at the necklace that she was

proudly wearing around her neck. The notion that he had ripped it from her and tossed it into the lake aggravated her all over again.

"Paul retrieved it from the lake for me. Wasn't that nice of him? After you threw it into the water, and I was afraid I'd lost it for good. I've got work to do. See you around." Lori didn't trust Dusty. He knew Paul and Allan were in the water, yet he'd barreled toward the dock without regard to speed regulations or the divers' safety. She hoped Allan and Paul stayed way below the surface of the water so that if Dusty barreled out of here, they would be safe. She was afraid to look out at the lake to see where they were now and give their location away. Instead, she turned and headed back to the house.

She prayed Paul and Allan were able to dive deep enough to stay out of harm's way.

"Maybe we can see a movie or something sometime," Dusty called out to her.

She ignored him and listened to him climb back into the boat. It seemed strange that the three cowboys were riding a boat across the lake, instead of galloping across a range on their ponies. She wondered where they'd gotten the boat. They yelled, "*Yee-haw!*" and then tore off across the lake toward where Paul and Allan had been swimming.

She turned then and watched the boat speed away. Her heart racing, she dashed back down the steps and ran down the dock. When she reached the end, she saw a hand grasp the edge.

"Paul? Allan?"

"It's me," Paul said and set his bag on the dock.

Allan followed behind him and also deposited his bag.

"Where were you when that idiot peeled out of here?" she asked.

"Underneath the dock. When he was talking to you, we swam underwater to reach the dock. The other two men must have been watching you and Dusty. Has he been hassling you since the day you were here together?" Paul asked, getting out of the water. "I thought you hadn't seen him again."

"I haven't. I think this all had to do with you being up here. Maybe he was trying to learn if you were still staying here to help out." She stared at the bags, feeling a mixture of relief and sorrow. In their hearts, they'd known her grandfather had died with the rest of their pack members, but still, there'd always been a little bit of hope that he'd lost his way, and they'd find him some day. "Were you able to get all of them?"

"As many as we could find. We need to get these up to the house and secure them." Paul took Lori's hand in a way that meant courtship and led her back toward the steps to the cabin.

She liked that. And she was past ready for it. She noted Allan's smile when he saw them hand in hand. She really hadn't expected Paul to show that much affection in front of Allan or anyone else in their pack yet, but she appreciated it more than he could know.

Allan agreed with Paul. "I wouldn't put it past Dusty and his buddies to return to further harass you."

"They'd been drinking. I saw a couple of six packs of empty beer cans lying on the floor of the boat. I'll call Grandma and tell her we got Grandpa's remains."

They all headed up to the house while Lori made the call to Emma. "We've got Grandpa and the wolf. As soon as Paul and Allan get dressed, we'll come out to your place and bury him."

Once they had changed, Lori said, "My grandma had a couple of wolf farmers from the next county drive there and dig a hole for the coffin."

"Is she okay?" Paul asked as he drove them to Emma's home. Though she had acted fine the night before, she might be feeling bluer today. He glanced at the speed limit sign and slowed down a little, mindful of all traffic laws. They couldn't afford to be caught with Lee's bones. The sheriff's department probably wouldn't care about the wolf's bones.

"Yeah, she's saddened but relieved that he'll be with the family."

"Good."

Emma lived out in the country and had thirty acres. Since the Greypaws had lived there forever, they had set up a cemetery for the wolf pack centuries ago. Rose, Catherine, and Emma were already there, waiting for them, when they arrived.

A wrought iron fence enclosed the graveyard, which was surrounded by woods to give their wolf pack members a feeling of being at home in their natural environment. Several of the families had been grouped together—a father with his six-year-old son, a mother with her three-year-old twin daughters—as a way to keep the families together even in death. Thankfully, Catherine and Emma had been able to hire farmers and men from a nearby town back then to dig the graves and make the pine boxes and granite headstones.

Now, those left of the original pack gathered around as Paul and Allan laid out Lee's bones—on a hand-woven blanket Emma had made long ago—inside the colonial pine box made in the same style as the ones for the rest of their lost kin. She placed his ceremonial deerskin breechclout, leggings, shirt, and moccasins on top of him.

Allan laid the wolf skeleton at his feet, as if it were his companion, like the wolf cub Lee had raised. Paul and Allan added Lee's pistol and his hatchet to rest beside him. The ladies placed wildflowers of yellow columbine, red paintbrush, and white bear grass on top of him. Then last, the blanket was wrapped around the two wolf brothers.

After closing the lid, Paul and Allan lowered the pine box into the hole, and Emma said a prayer. They covered the coffin with earth and gave their silent blessings.

Lori wrapped her arm around her grandma. Emma had been more than relieved to learn of her husband's final resting place in the lake but was glad to move him to where the rest of the pack was buried. But she had been sad too, fighting tears since she learned he'd been found.

Now, appearing a little lost and unable to hold back any longer, she cried, which caused Lori to sniffle.

Even though it might not be legal for them to take Lori's grandfather's bones from the lake, since the lake was state property, it was right for them to bury him with the rest of the family in Mother Earth so he could continue his spiritual journey.

Lori had considered that moving him from his resting place would disturb his spirit too much, but the notion that someone else—a perfect stranger with no connection to her grandfather or their wolf pack—might come across her grandpa and take him to a forensics lab to be studied had made the decision for her. She could just imagine the difficult time she and her grandma would have had in getting his bones back. That would not have been a good alternative. Even in death, he needed to be with the rest of the pack.

While the women prepared the meal, they talked about all that Lee had meant to them. He had taught the younger members of the pack—Allan, Paul, Rose, and Lori—how to find food in the forest to keep them alive and how to move like the wolf even when they were in their human forms. Emma shared how gruff he could be, and how loving and gentle. And Catherine told how he had helped her husband build their first cabin on the mountain, along with others. When the rest quit for the day, Lee and her husband would still be at it, talking about the pack and what it meant to them. It was a sad time, and yet the pack members were glad to be able to share in this and say their good-byes.

Afterward, they ate a meal of ribs, corn on the cob, and watermelon that the ladies had prepared.

Following the meal and conversation, to Lori's surprise, Paul took her aside and said, "I was looking over Emma's to-do list and we need to seal the deck."

"Hey, let me help with it," Allan said. "I want to feel like I'm doing something worthwhile."

Lori eyed Allan for a moment, then suspected the guys wanted to talk. Since she needed to be there for her grandma anyway, she agreed. "I'll go with you to the home supply store, and we can pick out the deck sealant."

"All right," Paul said.

They told the ladies good-bye and headed out in Paul's vehicle.

As soon as they arrived at the store, she heard the rumble of a truck engine that she recognized, courtesy of her wolf hearing. As if confirming her suspicions, Paul glanced that way. The truck was parked at Joe's Den of Inequities, but a hedge between the parking lot and the road blocked their view of the truck's occupant.

"It's the hunter's truck, isn't it?" she asked.

Allan looked clueless. Lori realized she and Paul hadn't told anyone in the pack about their run-in with the hunter, the dead elk, and the grizzly—just the police.

"Sure sounded like it. He caused some trouble for us yesterday. Poached an elk, and then invited a grizzly for dinner," Paul explained to Allan. "I'm going to check it out. Why don't you pick out the sealant we need for the deck, Lori, and we'll join you in a few minutes."

"Wait. What exactly are you planning on doing?" she asked.

Allan smirked. "Looks like we're going on a hunt."

"I should go with the two of you," Lori said, not liking that they might find trouble in there. "I can just envision the hunter giving you a hard time in the pool hall. He might have more buddies there who have been drinking and would jump on the chance to back him up."

"We're not going to do anything but make sure that the guy who owned that truck is the same one who was poaching in the forest."

"I'm going with you." Lori didn't trust that the two

SEAL wolves wouldn't get into a brawl and end up in jail.

"See, Paul, if you were our pack leader," Allan said, "she'd have to listen to what you told her to do."

"He's not," Lori said, not that she'd agree with him anyway. She realized then that having Paul lead the pack would take some getting used to. Like Allan said, they had to listen to the pack leader, or why have one?

Paul put his arm around her shoulders. "You want to get a beer before we go shopping for sealant?"

"Yeah, I'd go for that."

Allan shook his head and walked beside them. "You know what's bound to happen if you start taking her on missions."

They both looked at Allan, waiting for him to continue, but he only shook his head again.

As soon as they walked around the hedge, Lori saw the Cooper brothers' pickup truck. "Maybe we don't want to do this."

Paul and Allan glanced in the direction of the truck. "Don't tell me. It's Dusty or his brother's truck. We're not after them, even though they were driving that boat recklessly."

"Not to mention they could have hit us while we were diving," Allan said.

Not to mention that Allan and Paul were removing bones from the lake without reporting it to anyone in authority.

"Or that he got violent with you in the lake." Paul gave Lori a look that said he wasn't giving up being aggravated about that.

"Okay, good to know you don't hold any grudges

and no one's going to have any difficulties. If you get into trouble and I go to your rescue, *well*, Emma and Catherine might be annoyed with the lot of us and just leave us in jail if we end up there," Lori said.

"Do you know how to use a pool cue?" Paul asked her.

"To play pool or to fight?" she asked as Paul pulled the door open and Allan went in first. "Balls are my specialty."

Chapter 13

PAUL, LORI, AND ALLAN ENTERED THE DEN OF Inequities, which smelled of beer and whiskey, of predominantly male testosterone, aftershave, and sweat. Paul reminded himself that Lori was a wolf and a martial-arts instructor with her own dojo. She would be all right even if there was a confrontation. He wasn't sure what Lori meant by her "balls" comment, whether it was in reference to her handling Dusty Cooper the last time in the lake, playing a game of pool, or using a pool ball as a weapon.

And here he thought he knew her so well.

As soon as they walked into the place, he and Lori looked around for the hunter and smelled the air for his scent.

"Over there." Lori nodded with her head to the man who was still wearing hunter clothes, cue stick in hand. He was playing pool with Howard Cooper and the guy Paul had seen at the grocery store and the bank—the motorcycle guy. Dusty Cooper was talking to a woman at the bar. Jerome, the other cowboy, had a drink in his hand while he watched the others playing pool and was the first to see Paul, Lori, and Allan.

He lifted his head in recognition, eyes widening a bit. It was like a wolf standoff with Paul and Jerome eyeing each other and waiting to see what the other would do.

"A drink?" Lori reminded Paul, slipping her arm around his waist.

He maintained eye contact, the natural tendency for an alpha to show he was in charge, waiting for the other man to shift his attention elsewhere. Jerome finally did, glancing back at the bar to see if Dusty knew who had just arrived.

A three-man country and western band was strumming guitars and singing while other men were playing pool at three more tables covered in blue felt. On the perimeter, patrons were gathered around small tables, eating and drinking and sharing noisy conversation. Paul and his group took a seat at one of the empty tables.

They ordered beers while Paul watched Jerome tell Dusty they were here. Lori patted Paul's thigh, dragging his attention away from them.

"You know, if I were a beta, you sure would have me shaking in my boots," Lori said.

He glanced down at her sandals.

Her lips quirked up. "Or sandals. We're only here to make sure that was the hunter we saw so we can report him to the police, right?"

"You got it." Paul would have liked to do more than that—like taking Dusty to task for the incident with the necklace. He wanted the men out of the area permanently.

"If you're still mad about the necklace—" Lori said.

"And that they tried to run us over in the water." Paul cast her an annoyed look.

"Well, yeah, there was that."

Paul got his phone out and called the police to tell

them he had identified the poacher, and where he was now.

When the waitress served their beers, Allan paid for them.

"You know, they're going to have it in for you for calling the police and ruining their pool game," Lori said.

"Too bad. The problem with men like that is they are stupid enough to poach—and if they get away with it, they'll do it again. Even if they get in trouble for it, they may continue to do illegal crap if the punishment isn't severe enough. The only way to stop them is to deal with it and not let them get by with it."

Lori took a sip of her beer. "I agree. Totally on your side, Paul."

Howard took his turn at the game while Dusty watched Paul. Paul gave him a slight smile. Not friendly in the least.

Lori shook her head.

"Hey, we're the good guys here," Paul said, "and we believe in doing what's right."

Lori let out her breath. "Yeah, I know, but you're doing your alpha-wolf display of aggression."

He gave her a predatory grin and was leaning down to kiss her when Allan cleared his throat. "We've got company. Police just arrived."

"I'll see to them." Paul left Lori and Allan at the table and headed toward the front door where two police officers had just walked inside.

Several of the patrons glanced in the officers' direction.

Paul showed the officers his ID, motioned to Lori,

and said, "Lori Greypaw was with me when we caught the hunter just after he had killed the elk and caused trouble with a grizzly." Paul pointed out the man wearing hunter clothes, pool cue in hand, who was watching the officers and Paul. "As soon as Lori and I heard the gunfire, we figured he was in trouble. Since I'm a SEAL, I thought I could assist him."

"And Lori Greypaw?" Officer Killington asked.

"She was worried he might be injured and need help. I couldn't convince her to stay behind. Anyway, we distracted the bear, the hunter got away, and we outmaneuvered the bear. Then we tried to learn where the hunter was headed, a campsite or a vehicle, but we missed seeing his truck before he left the scene of the crime. We saw him in here, both of us recognizing him, and I called you." That was the good thing about a wolf's sense of scent. While a human's recollections of a person's appearance could be faulty, a *lupus garou*'s combined visual and scent identification of the man made it a sure thing.

"All right," the taller of the two policemen, Haversly, said.

The officers walked over to the table where Lori and Allan were sitting, and she gave her version of the story, minus the part about Paul "releasing his wolves" to distract the bear.

The one cop was smiling a little too much at Lori. Paul frowned. Had she dated him too?

"Anytime you need us to demonstrate for your class again, just call on us," Killington said. "We got two recruits from your class, and they're top-notch academy graduates."

"I'm so glad it worked out for you and for them. They're good guys," Lori said.

Well, that worked to their advantage, because the officers believed Paul and Lori were reliable witnesses. Both of the men told Paul they were former Army military police officers, and with Paul's SEAL background and Lori's work with them, the officers were more apt to trust their judgment.

The officers glanced back at the hunter, who was no longer playing pool, but standing with his buddies. Then the hunter headed for a back door and the officers took off after him.

Paul said, "Let's go watch his truck in case the police officers don't grab him in time."

Heading outside, Paul, Allan, and Lori were in place when the hunter came running around the hedge, the sound of footfalls in pursuit. Paul did what he would have done in any case where he was trying to prevent a lawbreaker from escaping—one who happened to be right in his path. He tackled the man and took him down to the asphalt.

"Thanks," Killington said, and then he and the other officer handcuffed the man. They found a rifle in his pickup with the serial number scraped off, which they seized and would send to the federal Bureau of Alcohol, Tobacco, Firearms, and Explosives for further investigation.

The one officer read the hunter his rights, and after he finished, Killington said, "Looking to serve some jail time over this, big fine, the works. Assaulting an officer…"

Paul noticed then that Haversly looked like he'd been

punched in the eye, the area turning red and swelling a little.

"Resisting arrest, hunting for elk without a license, hunting elk out of season…"

The police officers hauled him toward the cruiser.

"Who knows what else?" Killington said.

"Six months in jail, you think?" Haversly asked.

"At least. And a big fine too."

If Paul and Lori had had any doubts that the man should be arrested, they didn't now. Not that Paul had been having any doubts.

He glanced at one of the dark windows of the pub, saw the three cowboys watching them, and slid his arm around Lori's shoulders. "Let's pick out that deck sealant before it gets too much later."

—~~~—

Lori arrived back at Emma's house, where the ladies had already cleaned up after the meal and were sitting around talking about Paul and her.

They all smiled when she walked in.

"You *know* I heard you talking."

Emma motioned for her to take a seat.

Lori poured herself some of the pink lemonade in the big glass pitcher on the coffee table and then joined them.

"Well? How's it going for the two of you?" Emma's eyes were alight with eagerness at hoping to hear the good news.

"Well, Paul and Allan have probably already made enemies of the three wolf cowboys on the Somervilles' ranch. And Paul apprehended the poacher we discovered who had killed an elk and turned him over to the police. So he's probably not really a fan of Paul's either."

Emma tilted her chin down and gave Lori *the* look. "That's par for the course when it comes to *that*. What we wanted to know was if you'd convinced Paul that he needed to settle down and take a mate."

"You know I'm not going to do anything to convince him to stay if he doesn't want to." She shrugged.

Rose groaned. "If he liked me the way he likes you, I would be all over him to stay."

Lori chuckled. "I think he's…thinking about it. You know him. We have to keep suggesting something to him and then he keeps mulling it over and then he makes a decision, imagining that he came up with the idea himself."

The ladies all laughed.

But Lori was thinking that until he made up his mind, he needed to sleep far away from her.

"Yeah, you've got that right," Catherine said, then sipped her drink.

"But still, I'm not making any kind of commitment to him if he's not going to make a commitment to the pack." Lori took a sip of the sweet lemonade. "Oh, this is sooo good. We haven't had pink lemonade all summer."

"Well?" Rose said. "How *is* it going between the two of you?"

No matter what, Lori couldn't keep from blushing.

<center>~~~</center>

Paul and Allan were each having a beer as they swept the leaves, twigs, and dirt off the lakeside cabin deck.

Using putty knives, they cleaned between the boards. Then they washed the deck with a mixture of bleach and warm water. Paul was thinking that he hadn't done too badly as a handyman. He liked working while being out in nature but not getting shot at, just enjoying the view and the company.

"I've been thinking it over. Are you sure you don't want to take over the pack?" Paul asked, waiting for a reaction as they began to apply the waterproofing deck sealer.

"Just because my mother and sister are my family members, you think I have more invested in this. I don't buy it. You're part of the family just as much as they are. Between the two of us? You've always been the bossy one."

Paul hadn't really seen himself in that way.

"You're *always* in charge. Which is fine with me. I can just imagine *me* taking over the pack, which I could very well manage, but then *you* would be telling me what to do."

Paul laughed out loud. He supposed Allan was right.

Allan continued to brush the sealant over his side of the deck. "What we really need is a mated pair. I'm not finding a mate and returning here to create the pack."

"What about Lori?" Paul stopped to take a swig of his beer.

"Hell, yeah. Just what I was thinking."

Paul wondered why he hadn't realized Allan also had an interest in Lori until Allan said, "She's perfect for you, man. Her hawk spirit guide means she's the visionary. Your cougar guide proves you are the leader of this woeful pack. Me? Mine is the wolf. I outwit our enemies, take advantage of change, love family values, and will always have your back."

Paul snorted. "You don't even believe in animal spirit guides."

"Hey, when it comes to the two of you, I do. How many wolves can say that a cougar saved his butt when he was a kid? Cougars fight over the same territory as wolves. A lone wolf cub would have been dead meat at the claws of an angry cougar. Instead, she protected and took care of you until you found your way back to our pack. Not to mention that years later, after you were a full-grown wolf, you came across a cougar, and he watched you but didn't make any attempt to attack you. Didn't chase you off. Didn't run away. Face it, the cougars have your back."

Paul shook his head.

"Well, it's all true, isn't it? You smelled like a cougar when you found your way back to us. So we knew you weren't just telling tall tales. As to Lori's spirit guide, she's always been the most intuitive of all of us. I used to tease her that she was Lady Hawk because when she was around, red-tailed hawks were too. Besides, she'd sort of outgrown her original name of Little Hawk."

"The hawk led her to her grandma when the rabid wolf pack struck. And Lori saved her grandma," Paul said. That had made him believe there was something to it where Lori was concerned.

"Right. That was the first time we knew something was going on with it. It was like that day when we were in such a panic, fleeing for our lives, and each of us— you, me, Lori, and Rose—found our animal spirit guide to lead us out of danger."

"That would have meant a wolf helped you." Paul knew Allan had been on his own during the killings. Allan would never admit to believing in a spirit guide.

"It did. It was *me*. I used my nose to find my mother and Emma, and I outwitted the two rabid wolves that tried to kill me."

"True enough."

"And Rose's is the dragonfly. She loves the water. She was disappointed that the family cabin wasn't closer to the lake because she's always in the water whenever she has a chance to be. She's better at seeing things from a different angle than the rest of us. If she hadn't been down by the lake chasing after dragonflies, the rabid wolves would have found her. She pursued a dragonfly that flew low enough to keep her attention for three miles until she reached Lori's grandma and forgot all about the dragonfly."

"Emma said that Rose's spirit guide led her to safety." Allan shrugged. "What do I know? Except I do know you're interested in Lori, more than you try to let on. You're afraid that running the pack will end your life of adventure. But maybe it's time to settle down. We've lost two of our SEAL team to matings and also our shadow SEAL. Maybe that's our cue to make a home here for ourselves for good."

"So who do you have in mind to mate and settle down with?" Paul asked.

Allan didn't say.

Paul thought of one of their salvaging assignments and the wolf Allan had gotten interested in. "Wait, you're not thinking of that cute diver we met off Grand Cayman Island, are you?"

"We had something in common. And she's a wolf."

"And has a wolf father who's damned protective. And he wouldn't want her to leave the area."

Allan laughed. "There is that. I don't know. Every time I come home and see our sad pack with no leadership, I realize…you need to do something about it."

Smiling, Paul shook his head. "If I did…"

"Hot damn!"

"No, wait. I'm just considering this, but if I did, would you be my second-in-command?"

"Hell, yeah. You know I would."

"No chasing after a wolf in the islands?"

"I'm not sure she even took notice of me." Allan shrugged. "But yeah. My home is here with the rest of the pack. So, will you do it?"

When Paul didn't answer fast enough, Allan added, "Okay, look at it this way. If any male wolf came here and tried to mate with either my sister or Lori and wanted to take over the pack, we wouldn't like it, would we?"

"Hell, no."

"Even if he was a good mate for one of them, right?"

"Yeah." Paul had to agree to that.

"So that means either Rose and Lori can't have mates in this area, or one of us mates one of the ladies. You have been raised alongside my sister and she's too much like a sister to you. That leaves only Lori and—"

"And she'd have our balls for lunch if she knew we were talking about one of us mating her and taking over the pack as if she was just part of the deal."

Allan laughed. "Yeah. Speaking of balls, what did she mean before we went into the Den of Inequity?"

"Your guess is as good as mine."

"Okay, so you've got to be persuasive and convince her that this is the right thing to do. Did you kiss her again?"

Paul smiled. He couldn't help it. Allan would know anyway, one way or another. "She kissed me. For rescuing her necklace from the lake."

"Ah," Allan said, sounding like he didn't believe that was all there was to it.

Which there wasn't. But Paul was trying not to let on.

"Hey, I was thinking about diving around Lake McDonald. About the time the wolves killed our pack, the water level was low enough that a forest grew near Sprague Creek. Do you remember it?"

"Vaguely. We got chased by a momma grizzly through those woods, if it's the same place I'm thinking of."

"It is. Six years ago, divers found a forest in the lake. And it's that same forest. I was thinking we might go diving and see it for ourselves."

"That would be weird. Everyone else who goes there is a present-day visitor to the area and would see it as a waterlogged forest a couple of centuries old. For us? We ran through those woods as wolves."

"Yeah. Now, at about fifty feet deep in the greenish-blue water, the trees would still tower way above us, stretching toward the sun. And instead of birds flitting about the trees, schools of kokanee salmon swim through the branches. We could sit atop a branch high above when we sorely wished we could have climbed when that grizzly was chasing us."

At the time, he and Allan had been scared witless.

"We had a bad drought back then. I remember my dad saying that he'd thought of trying farming, but he stuck to hunting and created just a small garden for Mom."

"Yeah. So what do you really think about setting down roots? Viable option?"

Paul stared at him for a moment, surprised that Allan would *really* be serious about this. They'd been like brothers growing up, and Allan hadn't once said he wanted to settle down. "Is this because of the rest of the SEAL team is mating?"

"That and I worry about our family." Allan always talked of his mother and sister as though they were truly Paul's mother and sister, and Paul appreciated it. "And Lori and her grandma. Hell, while we were gone, Lori and Rose could have gotten into some real trouble with the Cooper brothers. I don't like that those troublesome wolves are in the area now. Do you?"

"Agreed. So that's what this is all about."

"Some of it. Plus this business with us no longer aging like shifters, and from what we've been hearing from Hunter and other wolf packs, it's permanent unless that scientist can figure out how to change it back to the way we were. That means you don't have forever to figure this out. Besides, don't you want to have a house that's a home? A lovely wolf to come home to? Something more permanent?"

"How long have you been thinking of this?"

Allan sighed. "I have to admit that when Hunter got mated, I was a little bit envious. I knew Finn had a thing for Hunter's sister, but I never thought he'd mate her."

He had always wondered what took Finn so long. Paul finished sealing his half of the deck.

"Then Bjornolf mated our own female operative in the group. And he was a real ghost on operations. No way did I think *he'd* ever settle down. Nor did I think Anna would. So it got me to thinking of what was really important."

"Family."

"Right."

"Why didn't you say so before?" Paul had thought of it, but he wouldn't have let Allan go on a dangerous mission without watching his back, and vice versa.

"So you'll do it?"

"If I did, it would have to be something that everyone wants."

"That's a given. Hey, are you about done?"

"Yeah, finished here. It's about time for me to pick up Lori and bring her home."

Allan smiled a little.

Paul shook his head. Yeah, he knew how that sounded. Like he and Lori were together in a permanent way. But he knew it would be a quiet night, a time of reflection after the funeral.

They finished the job and returned to Emma's place.

When Paul picked Lori up to take her home, she *was* quiet.

"Are you okay?"

"Yeah. But the lady who takes over when I can't be at the dojo has to take off tomorrow. I need to be there for the day. And truly, it will feel good to teach some classes."

"That's fine. I'll take care of whatever is next on the list. And then we go to the movie in the evening with Allan and his sister."

"Yeah, you can come by and pick me up."

When they arrived home, they watched the sunset and he kissed her, but he could feel the tension between them and said good night, hoping tomorrow would be better for her.

———

When Paul heard Lori leave in the morning, he got up to start his workday, not believing he'd missed seeing her off. He was glad she'd made the coffee for him before she left, but he wished he'd had breakfast with her. He wondered if she felt she needed to pull back from him a bit. He understood, though he had every intention of proving he wanted more with her and that she needed the same with him.

He worked all day, grabbed a tuna-fish sandwich, and picked up Lori at the dojo. She was all smiles and gave him a big hug and kiss.

"Hmm, this is better. I missed you early this morning," Paul said, not letting her go.

"I had to get to an early-morning class for those who work during the day. Did you get a lot of work done?"

"Yeah. But I missed the distraction."

"Me?"

He chuckled. "Ready for the movie?"

As soon as they arrived and got out of their vehicle, Allan and Rose met up with them, and Allan said to Paul in a rush, "We're switching dates."

"What?" Paul asked, not getting what Allan was up to.

"You're with Rose and I'm with Lori."

"We're not exactly on a date," Paul reminded him.

Lori was smiling.

Rose whispered just for their ears only, "Allan just spied Widow Baxter's daughter, Tara, headed this way. If Allan's with his sister, she's bound to try to sit with him in the movie theater. But if he's dating Lori, and you're here with me, problem solved."

Lori laughed. "You're a SEAL, for heaven's sake, Allan."

"I *am*, and when it comes to taking out the bad guys, no problem." Allan moved around and took Lori's hand.

Allan had the appearance of being a really sweet guy, with his round face and jovial features. And he was a really good guy. But put him in a firefight, and he was just as lethal as any of the SEAL team members. Paul hadn't expected him to be a marshmallow when it came to a woman.

"Yeah, but you're like a sister to me," Paul said to Rose as she grabbed his hand and pulled him to the concession stand inside.

"Tara has only lived here five months. She doesn't know anything about our family dynamics because you're rarely around." Rose switched her focus to the concession stand. "Okay, for getting me in trouble over the Cooper-brother fiasco, I want a large popcorn, bottled water, and a package of red licorice."

"What would you like, Lori?" Allan asked as Paul paid for his "date's" order.

"I'm good. We just ate."

Allan looked amused. "I got the cheap date."

"On second thought, get me everything Rose wanted, but instead of licorice, make it something chocolate. Call *me* a cheap date." Lori cast Allan a look.

Paul smiled at Allan. "The chocolate will cost you

more than the licorice cost me." He was glad that Allan had suggested the movies for tonight. Paul hadn't been to them in ages. Though he'd rather be on a date with Lori than pretending to be on one with Rose.

Still, when they sat in their seats way up above, he made sure he was seated between Rose and Lori. Allan missed the opportunity and Tara came to join them but was polite enough to ask, "Is this seat already saved for someone?"

She was a quiet, blue-eyed blond and always seemed serious.

"No. You're welcome to it." Allan was his typical nice-guy self, and Paul was glad that he wasn't gruff with Tara, even though he didn't want to date her.

Allan was more into women who were vivacious and not pushovers in the least. Paul could understand Tara's desire to mingle with them though, since she was a wolf too. Yet, he was surprised she'd joined with them, since she tended to be more of a rabbit and kept a low profile. No one knew exactly why the mother and daughter had settled in this area. They were rather secretive, Paul thought. He wondered if they'd had trouble at their last residence. Something to do with their wolf halves? Or something else?

If he took over the pack and invited them to join, he would have to learn what their story was.

"So what are you and Paul doing while you're here?" Tara asked.

"Vacationing." Allan was watching the advertisements on the movie screen.

"Did you finish your work already for Martha?"

"Uh, yeah," Allan said. "And now we're vacationing."

Paul stifled a laugh.

"So when are you leaving again on one of your SEAL assignments?" Tara asked.

Lori was smiling. So was Rose. Poor Allan.

The movie credits began and Allan relaxed in his seat as Tara turned to watch the movie.

The place was packed that night. Paul settled down in his seat and shared popcorn with Rose. Though she suddenly didn't seem to want to eat anything.

At one point, Rose leaned over to whisper, "Emma was grateful you found Lee and helped to bury him yesterday."

"It took us too long to locate him, but I'm glad we finally did and now he's with the family." It might be weird to consider it, but Paul thought Lori's grandfather would also be more content to be with the rest of their fallen pack members.

He thought it was odd that Rose would bring that up now when she was normally really quiet and just as engrossed as Allan during a movie. Lori and Paul tended to privately share comments during movies.

He realized Rose was still leaning toward him, but not because she had any intention of pretending she was his girlfriend, he didn't think. He suspected she wanted to tell him something privately. She was tense, not eating or drinking anything. She looked down at her lap and wasn't watching the movie either. He knew her well enough to know something was the matter. She must have felt this was the first time she had him to herself where she could talk to him. The shooting and shouting in the movie—which for wolves was a little too much—continued to hide their voices, and the theater was nice, cozy, and dark like a wolves' den.

He slipped his arm around her shoulders and pulled her closer and whispered to her, "What's wrong, Rose?"

She didn't say anything, just leaned her head against his shoulder. That really worried him.

Lori glanced at them and he wondered if she knew what the matter was. Allan was too busy getting into the alien cowboy movie to notice.

"You'll tell Mom and you'll tell Allan. And Lori." Rose looked up at him with tears in her eyes.

His stomach tightened with concern. He couldn't fathom what kind of trouble she might be in that she didn't want the rest of the family to know about.

"You have to be our pack leader."

He frowned at her. "What brought all this on?"

This was certainly not the time to talk about that. But her concern over the others finding out her secret made his heart pick up the pace a bit.

She looked to the side and brushed away the tears suddenly trailing down her cheeks.

"Rose..." He caressed her shoulder. What was she so concerned about that she wanted him here, watching the pack? Instantly, he thought of Howard Cooper and the trouble she could have gotten into with him at the Greypaws' place. Had he bothered her further and she was afraid to tell anyone about it? Hell, if the bastard had hurt her...

Then she let out her breath and whispered, "I'm pregnant."

Chapter 14

WITH THE ALIEN MOVIE MAKING SO MUCH NOISE, LORI couldn't hear what was being said between Rose and Paul, but she highly suspected it had to do with what she'd been worried about—that Rose was concerned about something and needed help dealing with it, despite Rose's denial that anything was wrong.

Lori was glad Rose was finally telling Paul, and she knew he would help her to see that the pack would back her up, no matter what the problem was. When she heard Rose sniffling, Lori wanted to give her a hug and wished Rose had felt comfortable enough to talk with her about it before this.

But Rose, like the others, saw Paul as the leader and was inclined to talk to him about issues that would affect the pack. Lori suspected it was something really important. Not just some frivolous concern.

She knew she'd learn soon enough, though she had her suspicions. She tried to watch the movie and let Rose and Paul have their privacy, but she couldn't help straining to catch any words that would confirm that what she was worried about had happened.

His mouth gaping, Paul stared at Rose in disbelief as the cowboys in the movie fired their six-shooters at the aliens.

Wolves rarely got pregnant if they had sex with a human. Paul had only heard of a couple of cases. He supposed that had to do with ensuring their *lupus garou* kind survived. When they did have offspring with a human, the baby or babies normally didn't have the wolf parent's ability to shift.

In any event, Paul was ready to kill whoever the man was who had gotten Rose pregnant. Not that she was completely innocent in this. Unless…hell, it better not have been one of the wolves at the ranch who forced himself on her. "Howard Cooper?"

She quickly shook her head, her eyes wide, and he realized he'd spoken the ranch hand's name out loud.

Attempting to get his temper under control, Paul tried to look at this in a more reasonable way. "Are you certain you're pregnant?" he asked, when he wanted to turn wolf and take on the father.

"Yeah, I'm sure. Pregnancy tests work the same on us. I've taken three over the last three weeks, and it comes back positive every time."

He needed to talk to her alone, not with the noisy movie playing in the background, and without disturbing others in the theater. He turned to Lori and Allan. "We'll be right back." He handed their popcorn to Lori. Both Lori and Allan raised their brows in question.

He motioned for Rose to exit the row in the opposite direction, where they were closer to the aisle. "Let's talk in the car."

So much for going to the movies. Now *this* conversation would be what he'd always remember whenever he went to see another movie.

"You need to mate with Lori," Rose said as they left

the theater while she shoved her unopened bottle of water into her purse. He assumed that's where the licorice was too. "You need to be our mated pack leaders. If you don't settle down here, Lori's liable to get herself in the same bind."

He didn't think Lori would get herself into a mess like this. Though he did wonder what would have happened if Dusty had taken the business with her further…

Paul glanced down at Rose's stomach but couldn't see a difference.

"Who is he?" he asked, trying to keep his cool when he felt anything but, and to keep the focus on Rose where it belonged.

"You don't know him. He was just passing through. We hit it off, dated for about two weeks, got too drunk on the last day, and went a little too far. He left the following day."

"Two weeks?" They never dated humans more than a couple of times. "Wait. He was a wolf?" Paul couldn't have been more surprised. Though he was glad the man hadn't been human—if that had been the case and the man wanted to share custody of the baby, someone would have had to turn him. What a mess that could be if he had family or was already married. The ramifications could go on and on.

"Yes. Yes. You didn't think I got pregnant by a human, did you? That's so rare. I wouldn't have even considered it."

"It had crossed my mind. You have to tell your mother and Allan. Everyone will know before long anyway."

He and Rose climbed into his vehicle.

"I want this baby," she said, running her hand over her belly.

"You know we wouldn't have it any other way." Paul was surprised she was even worrying about that. Unless a *lupus garou* child lost his pack and ended up being taken in by humans, children born to their kind were not adopted or sent to foster homes. They remained with what was left of the pack.

Paul smiled a little at her, trying to break through the tension in the car. "The family will be happy for you. But you have to know how I feel about it. And how Allan will too, when he learns of it."

"That's why I want you to talk to Allan. You can talk him out of searching for the father and killing him."

Paul took in a deep breath. "He wouldn't. Hell, he might like the guy." Paul was sure he wouldn't. Not at first. Just like Paul wanted to do some bodily harm to the wolf. It wasn't that Rose and the man might not be right for each other, but he'd left Rose to take care of a baby on her own. "No one suspects that you're pregnant?"

"No."

"Who is the wolf?"

"Everett Johnston. He was a lot of fun. He said he had some issues he had to deal with, and he'd be back. He was in town for the two weeks and we went swimming every day, saw movies, and took wolf runs. He loves the water as much as I do. We just really hit it off great. I've never felt that connection with another wolf before. Like what you and Lori have. What we shared, well, it was really special."

"But he took off," Paul reminded her, growling a little.

"Yeah, like you and Allan aren't here most of the time. And you have feelings for Lori."

Paul hadn't seen that coming. Rose was right, though he hadn't gotten Lori pregnant.

"I told you he had issues. He couldn't stay. I kept hoping he'd call or write or text or return, but it's been eight weeks and, well, I'm pregnant."

"Have you tried to contact him about the baby?"

"Of course not. He hadn't planned to mate me. It was just a mistake."

"We mate for life, Rose."

"As if I don't know that!" She looked out the window. "He was fun, but I think he's like you. Not ready to settle down."

"He needs to know what his recklessness resulted in."

"I never got an address for him. I don't know where he lives or anything. And his phone has been disconnected."

So she had tried to get hold of him.

She started to cry. "Allan and Mom are going to kill me."

Hating to see Rose upset, Paul pulled her into a warm hug. "They love you and they'll love the baby. We all will." Though because of their wolf genetics, many *lupus garous* had multiple births and she might be looking at twins or more. Now, he wished Allan and he had been in the area at the time. This never would have happened. Or at least they would have known the wolf before everything had gone this far. "As to the father, that's a different story."

"It's not just Mom and Allan. It's this small town business. Everyone will be whispering behind my back about how I'm having a baby out of wedlock."

Many wolves didn't feel the necessity to have a regular wedding because they mated for life, so there was no reason for them to make up a binding document that said they were husband and wife. Even so, they let on to the rest of the world that they were married, so Paul could understand her concern.

"I've thought of moving," Rose said, in a small voice, sniffling and soaking the front of his shirt with her tears.

He knew she didn't mean it. The pack meant everything to her.

"You can't. No way would any of us let you run off on your own. You need to be with us. Your mother would be beside herself if her daughter and grandbaby were gone. You'll need help raising one of our kind. We need a pack to raise the cubs, to show them our ways."

"Then you and Lori will be our pack leaders."

"Everyone keeps saying that. Lori and I have never even talked about mating one another."

"She's often talked to me about it."

Hell, why hadn't she said anything about it to him? "Oh?"

"You're like the knight in tarnished armor to her."

He chuckled. He couldn't help himself. "Really." He could see Lori thinking of him in terms of a wolf coat, but tarnished armor?

"Yeah. You pulled our pack together when we were lost in grief. You did that as a leader. But you also did it to avoid working through your own grief for your parents' loss. She recognized that. She's always wanted to be your mate, but she's never wanted to push it because she knows how much it means for you to work on these dangerous assignments you go on. She will wait for you forever. Why do you think she rarely dates lone wolves who pass through here? She won't even consider them in terms of a mating because she's waiting for you. You're going to be old and gray before you ever get a clue."

He couldn't believe it. He knew Lori cared for him, just as he did for her, but he'd never realized she'd sacrificed the chance to fall in love with another wolf because she had been waiting for him to settle down.

"Your team members are all setting down roots. Your family needs you. I need you. And a few months from now, a new member of the pack will need you."

Suddenly, Paul felt like he was going to be a father, not of a wolf cub, but of a whole wolf pack, as small as it was. He guessed that in the back of his mind, he always knew it would come to this, but still…

He went back to the real issue at hand. "The father needs to know. We won't push him into anything with you. I only want your happiness and the baby's. But the father needs to know." One way or another through their SEAL team sources, Paul was going to locate Everett Johnston and learn the truth. "You have to tell your mother."

"If you tell her, she won't get as mad. She never does, because…because she sees you as our pack leader, even if you don't."

"This is not the same as breaking her favorite lamp because you were playing chase with Lori and caught your foot on the rug. And she never was angry with you over that. Or any of the other things you got in trouble for in our youth."

"I can't do it."

Paul sighed. "All right. We'll have to tell her now because if you're that far along, we need to find a wolf doctor to check you out."

"And learn how many babies there are."

He hadn't wanted to mention it.

"I know I could be carrying multiple babies. Our kind often does." She took hold of Paul's hand and placed it on her hard belly. Because of the baggy T-shirt she was wearing, he hadn't noticed. She wasn't very big yet and if she hadn't told him, he wouldn't have guessed it this early on, especially when he hadn't known she'd been with a wolf.

"How were you able to go swimming with the Cooper brothers at the lake a week ago without anyone knowing the truth?"

"I was wearing a long T-shirt and said I didn't want to get sunburned. I didn't actually plan to get into the water. Besides, I'm barely showing." She shrugged. "I wasn't out there long anyway because Dusty forced a kiss on Lori, and she grabbed his balls. He quickly let go of her and they took off."

Lori *hadn't* told Paul about the forced kiss. What was to stop Dusty from trying again? Further, what bothered Paul was that neither Lori nor Rose had said what Howard had done during the fiasco. Paul hoped that meant nothing, but he wasn't about to assume such a thing. "What did Howard do this whole time?"

Rose didn't say anything.

Paul let out his breath. "Rose," he said in the pack leader voice that he hadn't used in a long time.

"You have to promise me you won't kill him."

"I wouldn't kill the bastard unless it's warranted." Beyond that, Paul wasn't promising anything.

"From the end of the dock, he…he threw me in the lake. I told him I didn't want to swim. He wouldn't take no for an answer. I was afraid my T-shirt would cling to my belly, and Lori would be able to tell I was pregnant."

Paul ground his teeth. "Did he hurt you?"

"No. I shrieked because I wasn't expecting it. I cursed him, then swam toward the beach. But he jumped in and tried to stop me. I might not know martial arts like Lori, but I rolled over on my back and kicked him in the face. After that, I made it to shore, saw Dusty pull Lori's necklace off, and you know the rest."

Paul wanted to take a bite out of the bastard. "He didn't follow you out? Hassle you any further?"

"Not when Dusty started cursing up a storm. The two of them left then."

He knew Lori hadn't told him everything. "Are you sure you're not farther along, Rose? Wolves usually don't show this early unless—"

"They're having twins or triplets."

Just what he suspected. "Catherine isn't going to like that I'm calling her about this," Paul said, really feeling it was Rose's place to tell her mom the truth. He pulled out his cell phone.

"I'd rather you do it," Rose said.

"All right." Paul placed the call. "Catherine, I've got to talk to you. We're still at the movie theater. I'll let Allan know I'm bringing Rose home, but we need to talk."

"Okay. See you in a little bit."

He suspected Rose's mother already knew. Catherine's voice was tense, but she didn't push for any

further word than that. Since she was so close to her
daughter, he thought she must know.

"Let's go back inside the theater, and I'll tell Allan
and Lori we'll see them later."

"I could wait in the car."

"No, you come with me." Paul wasn't sure why he
wanted her to, but he really didn't want to leave her
alone. Maybe because she was so upset. He thought
someone should be with her until she talked to her
mother and brother—well, Lori and Emma even. That
was their pack. Everyone should know. And everyone
would be behind her on this.

"Paul," Rose said, taking hold of his hand as they
returned to the theater. "We should ask Tara and her
mother to join us. They're in our territory. They should
be in our pack."

He hadn't officially taken the job. He wasn't ready
to add any more wolves to the equation until he let the
original pack have some say in things. Then he thought
of how Rose was so upset over this and had to have been
for a couple of weeks. Had she waited all this time to
speak with him and not said anything to anyone about
it? "*Did* you tell Lori?"

Rose shook her head.

"You should have."

When he reached the bottom of the stairs to the theater, he said, "Why don't you wait here while I tell Allan
and Lori where we're—"

"Allan's coming."

Paul glanced up to see Allan headed down the stairs.
The two of them were so close that Paul swore Allan
already knew what it was about.

"You're leaving?" Allan asked, sliding a glance to his sister.

"Yeah. I'm going to take her home. Tell Lori, if you would, that I'll see her back up at the cabin after a bit."

"You don't want us to come with you?"

"No," Rose said.

Allan cast her a big brother's look that promised he would know what was going on before long. It was just the way of the wolf. Paul knew he'd definitely want to find the guy who had made his sister pregnant. "All right. See you in a bit."

Allan turned and strode back up the stairs. Lori was watching them from her seat. Paul gave her a little wave, she nodded, and then he and Rose headed back outside.

He smelled Rose's nervous scent and saw her wringing her hands. He glanced at her, checking to see if she was crying again, and she stuck her hands in her pockets. "She's going to want to kill me."

It was just an expression the family used and they didn't mean it literally.

"Your mother might be upset, but everything will be okay."

"You won't put a hit out on him, will you?"

Paul smiled at her and wrapped his arm around her shoulders. "No. That's not what we do. Unless the guy has taken some of our kind hostage or something. Then, if we have only one way of safely freeing the hostages, he could be a dead wolf. But in a case like this, we just want to talk to him and learn more about him. Discover what his 'issues' are."

When they arrived at Catherine's house, Rose looked

like she was going to be sick, as pale as she was. "Are you all right?"

"No."

He hurried to get her passenger door for her, and then took her arm and led her to the house. To his relief, Catherine quickly opened the door and took her daughter from Paul, moving her to the kitchen. The scent of spices filled the air, and he saw jars in a row where she'd been working on filling them with her spice rubs to sell at Rose's shop.

"You're pregnant, aren't you?" her mother asked softly, her eyes a little misty.

Paul wasn't surprised her mother knew, and she'd be calm about it. Not happy, but not really angry either. Maybe a little mad at the man who'd gone too far with her daughter and left her in such a way. Well, maybe a little angry with Rose too, for getting herself in this predicament and not telling anyone.

Paul followed them into the kitchen in case they needed assistance.

Catherine sat her daughter down at the kitchen table, then got a wet cloth and ran it over Rose's face. "Can you get her a little water?"

"Sure thing." Paul filled a cup of water for Rose.

"I got dehydrated when I was pregnant with you kids. I wasn't drinking enough water. I nearly passed out because of it. So you need to keep hydrated." Then Catherine glanced at Paul and raised her brows a little.

He really didn't feel it was his place to tell Rose's mother what had happened, but since Rose looked like she might expire on the spot and her mother was waiting for an explanation, he just said what he felt she needed to know. "She can't get hold of him. He's a wolf but a drifter, or he would have been in the area, and he hasn't had any contact with her since…since they met."

Then he talked about what was really important for now, considering she might be carrying multiple babies. "We need to get her to a wolf doctor. I don't know of any in the area. That's the priority for now: finding a wolf doctor she can see and ensuring the babies are going to be healthy. Beyond that, we have connections and we'll find the wolf father."

Rose started to cry, and Catherine looked just as distraught as she leaned down to hug her daughter.

"Not to force them to mate," Paul said, not wanting to upset her further. "This is strictly to learn what we can about him and go from there. If we determine he's one badass wolf, well, since she's my sister too…"

Rose looked up at Paul through her tears and managed a small smile.

"Well, if he is real trouble, I don't want him near her or the baby. Rose can make more of an informed decision when the time comes."

"We should find a wolf doctor close to home," Catherine said. "I don't want her to have to fly or drive a long ways from here. And the further along she is, the worse it will be."

Paul agreed. He didn't like that there wasn't a doctor in the area if members of his pack were going to start having babies. It wasn't something he had even considered before now.

"Our SEAL team can check with our sources on that. 'Wolf' doctors aren't listed in any registers or phone books as such. They're usually with wolf packs and take care of their own, though an occasional lone wolf is known to doctor strictly human patients. But we have enough friends who are with other wolf packs that we can see if anyone knows of a doctor that's closer than the others. We'll get right on it." They talked for about an hour while Paul took notes about Everett Johnston: what he looked like, how he dressed, anything Rose recalled about him. Then Paul texted Hunter with the information.

Hunter texted back that they'd look into it.

Paul's phone rang and he looked at the caller ID. "Yeah, Allan?"

"Hey, buddy, the movie's over. My engine was making an awful knocking sound, and then it just died. I'm going to wait with the car and I've called a mechanic to help me out. Can you take Lori back to her cabin if things are all right with you and Rose?"

"Okay, I'll pick Lori up. Thanks. Be there in half an hour." He ended the call, then told Rose and her mother, "I've got to pick up Lori at the theater and take her home. Are you going to be all right, Rose?"

She nodded.

"We've got to tell the others—Allan, Lori, and Emma. You need to let everyone know."

Rose still looked ill at ease, and he suspected she was worried her mother would take her to task after he left. "If you would, could you tell them?"

"All right. I'll call you all later." He gave Rose and Catherine a hug, and he thought Catherine looked somewhat relieved to know this business was now out in the open. She was smiling a little, and he knew that meant she was thrilled to be having her first grandkids.

And then he headed out the door. Before he even got into his car, he called Allan back.

"Okay, I'm on my way over there. I need to talk to you about some stuff."

"She's pregnant, isn't she?" Allan growled. "Who's the guy?"

Chapter 15

LORI HAD SUSPECTED ROSE MIGHT BE PREGNANT. SHE hadn't wanted to swim when she absolutely loved swimming, and she'd been sick for a couple of weeks. She'd tried to hide the fact she had been ill by working longer hours at her shop, but Lori knew something was wrong. Even her grandma and Catherine had questioned Lori. Rose hadn't said anything to them, and they thought she might have told Lori something. And she was certain it all had to do with the time a few weeks ago when Rose didn't have a minute to spare to see her.

Lori wasn't sure how to feel about Rose's pregnancy. She worried that Rose didn't want to be with the father, worried that he wasn't a wolf and they'd have to change him. Would Paul now see they needed a pack leader? Maybe they had needed something like this to turn the pack upside down again and make him realize they needed him.

No matter what, Lori would love Rose's baby, or babies, as the case might be. She just hoped that Rose was ready for this too. Though she didn't have much choice now.

Lori was dying to know who the father was though. And how Paul planned to handle this. Well, and Allan too, as he paced back and forth across the movie theater's parking lot, his brow furrowed and his voice growly as he spoke to Paul over the phone.

Shaking his head, Paul drove to the theater while Allan was still on the phone with him. Paul couldn't believe he was the only one who had been clueless about Rose's pregnancy. "Does Lori know?"

"She guessed it. So did Lori's grandma. Mom would have too. It's not something Rose could have hidden that well from them. Not when they see her all the time. From you and me? Yes. They've just been waiting for her to tell them the truth, hoping she'd talk to you about it since she hadn't told anyone else. She really looks up to you. When I grilled Lori about what she thought was going on, she told me what she suspected."

Why hadn't she told Paul? "Good. I'm glad we're already all on the same page then. We need to locate a wolf doctor." He was fighting to keep the SUV on the road, the winds already picking up from the storm they'd sensed was headed their way.

"And find the bastard who got her pregnant."

"Does Lori have any idea where he might be?" Paul asked.

"Lori said she was really busy with her dojo and other projects. When she had a moment, she asked Rose if she wanted to go out to dinner, but she said she had other plans. She didn't elaborate, and Lori didn't ask. But for about two weeks, Rose was unavailable to see her. Same excuses. Was busy, couldn't break free to get together with her. Lori figured she was seeing some guy—human though."

So that's what Lori had been talking about when she told Paul she'd been worried about Rose for no good reason. "At least he is a wolf. She said she was eight weeks along."

"Lori said that was the right timing—eight weeks."

Paul shook his head. "Okay, one other thing—are you really sure you want to be my second-in-command?"

"Hot damn! You finally agreed to be our pack leader. And, yes, I do."

"I have to make sure that Lori and Emma are all right with it."

"Lori's grinning, thumbs-up. And she said Emma's going to be so happy."

Paul still hadn't been sure that everyone would feel that way because they'd been doing their own thing for so long. "Okay, well, if after a while all of you decide that you don't like it, that's tough. You're stuck with me."

Allan laughed.

Paul turned into the theater parking area and found Allan and Lori standing next to Allan's car, all smiles. Paul got out, and before he could say anything to either of them, Lori rushed to join him, threw her arms around his waist, and gave him a big, warm hug. And then kissed him full on the mouth.

When he came up for air and looked into her smiling face, he smiled right back. "Well, hell, if you had let me know that this was the way I'd be treated as the pack leader, I would have done it a long time ago."

"Right," she said.

"Seriously." He sure as hell got the impression she was willing for him to be much more to her than just their pack leader. He loved this initiation into being the one in charge. He kissed her again for good measure, letting her know this thing between them meant a whole hell of a lot more to him too.

When he finally and reluctantly broke free of the kiss, she immediately said, "Thank you. Now we have to ask Tara and her mother to join the pack."

"We can do that a little later. We've got some other concerns." One of the next major issues to consider was if Lori would be his mate, but he intended to talk to her in private about that.

"Do you need a lift to your cabin?" Paul asked Allan.

"No, the tow truck is on its way. They'll be here in a minute. They'll take me out to the cabin, and they'll drop my car off there after they've fixed it."

"Have you been having trouble with it?" Paul asked, sniffing the air, glancing around the area, and checking just in case someone had tampered with Allan's car.

"The car's old, but it's been running pretty good lately. Let you know what the mechanic finds out."

"All right. I'm going to start making calls then."

"To my grandma first," Lori said, climbing into Paul's SUV. "You have to tell her that you're going to be our pack leader."

"What do you want me to do?" Allan asked.

"Call Leidolf and see if he knows of a doctor who lives near here. Rose needs to see a doctor as soon as possible to ensure she's getting the proper care. I asked Hunter to check into this Everett Johnston."

"I'm on it. Thanks again for taking over the pack."

"Hell, you're going to work harder than me."

Allan just smiled, then he waved at someone. Paul turned and saw the tow truck.

"Okay, we're out of here," Paul said, and as soon as he got into his SUV, he immediately called Emma with the news about the pack leadership. "I know it's long overdue, but—"

"You're mating Lori. I knew the two of you would come to your senses before long. Oh...I'm so happy for both of you. And it means you're taking over the pack. This is the best news ever. I've got to go. Bread's in the oven and I don't want it to burn."

Emma hung up before he could clarify that he was just taking over the pack for now. He'd have to work a little harder on the rest of it. He wasn't sure about Lori.

He set the phone in the console. Either Emma just assumed he'd mated her granddaughter, or she hoped her saying so would make it a sure thing. He was reminded of Emma's animal guide, the fox.

He cleared his throat, his face feeling a little warm with embarrassment. Lori might not like that he hadn't set Emma straight. Not that Emma had given him any time to do so.

"You didn't tell her you were going to take charge of the pack. You didn't even say good-bye to her," Lori said, frowning. "She would be ecstatic. What happened?"

"She assumed it. And had to go quickly before she burned her bread."

"Oh."

By the time they got on the main road, the wind had really begun to pick up. Paul opened his mouth to speak, but Lori beat him to it. "The winds finally got here."

Paul wasn't interested in talking about the weather. Was Lori nervous about what they needed to really discuss? "You know how the weather is. The changes can come earlier or much later, or not at all. But what I really want to discuss is *us*."

She patted his leg, which made him think of the way she'd kissed him when they had been in bed the night before last. He knew he couldn't continue sleeping with her and not mating her. He'd never last.

"Now that you've agreed to be our pack leader for certain, you need to find a mate. Like the king of the beasts."

He chuckled. "That's lions."

She laughed. "You need a pack mate. But you'll have to prove you're a good pack leader first."

Not believing her in the least, he glanced at her. "Does that mean if I asked you if you would mate with me, you'd say you had to decide later?"

"Absolutely." She folded her arms and watched him. "I'm not mating with a wolf who might decide he has to go on another important mission when here I am trying to raise triplets on my own."

"Triplets, eh?" He knew she was going to give him a hard time. But he was digging in and winning her over, one way or another. "You'd have the pack to help you out." He glanced at her flat tummy, unable to imagine her belly swelling with babies, but he liked the idea she would be his. He would never have been able to accept the notion she'd have babies by any other wolf.

"Yeah, right. Allan would be running off on the mission with you. And here Rose and I would be, saddled with all these babies and no pack to help us out. Just Catherine and Emma, but she tires easily."

"Is she okay?" Paul asked, concerned, realizing that Lori had brought this up a couple of times now and wondering if there was something more going on with Emma's health.

"Sure. It's just her age, but now that our life spans match humans more closely, you know how it is."

He understood her concern. "I can't believe you've turned me down. You don't know how hard it was to even ask. I will be scarred for life."

"You *didn't* ask."

"But you just said—"

"You have to prove you're a good pack leader first. Everyone, including me, knows you can do it. But you have to truly want to lead the pack with all your heart."

"And you think I still have reservations."

"I think if Rose hadn't asked you to step in and be our pack leader, you wouldn't have decided to do this."

"Catherine asked me."

"Same difference. I have to admit, I admire you for stepping up to do so because of the circumstances."

"Do you know why I turned down the mission that Hunter called me about?"

"Why?"

"I wanted to visit with you. To be with you. I didn't want to be saving the world when I felt I needed to be here. It had nothing to do with Rose. Well, a little because I worried about this situation escalating with the Cooper brothers. You didn't tell me that Howard got physical with Rose. Or that Dusty forced a kiss on you."

"I handled it, all right? As for Rose, it was her place to tell you, not mine."

He still wasn't satisfied. "At the same time, I wasn't sure you needed me. You've all been doing fine for so many years."

"What would you do if while you and Allan were gone, some alpha male wolf tried to take over our pack? I'd fight him off, but what if that wasn't good enough?"

"I'm not like some pack leaders who decide every-thing for their packs. I have every intention of being as democratic as I can."

"Everyone loves you for always taking everyone's feelings into consideration. But the others will expect you to lead."

"And I will. But I'll also listen to what everyone else wants to do." He took a deep breath. "I asked Allan to be my second-in-command. But everyone has a role to play. We need to set up a good time for all of us to have a pack meeting." Since Lori hadn't agreed to be his mate, he wasn't going to push it. *Yet.* "You think Rose is going to have more than one baby, don't you?"

"Yeah. I think it's inevitable. Her father and mother had triplet brothers and sisters. Allan and Rose are twins. I think the likelihood she'll at least have twins is a good bet."

"Allan said you suspected she was pregnant."

"Yeah, though she's been careful to wear clothes that aren't revealing, I've noticed she's showing, just a little, when the wind blows her loose-fitting clothes against her belly. And then her frequent bouts of sickness. The first couple of times, we figured it was food poisoning. Maybe a touch of the flu."

"Why didn't you let me know?" Paul asked.

"You've been in the Amazon for the last two months! And I wanted to tell you, but I didn't want to say she was and then learn she wasn't."

"Okay, you're right." He realized then why Lori was

so worried about him tearing off on another assignment. Often, the missions could last for weeks. And during the last mission, Rose had gotten pregnant. What if he was mated to Lori? What if she found out she was pregnant and she couldn't even tell him for weeks?

"What about us?" He couldn't help it. He wasn't letting go of them. Maybe if he kept talking like they were a mated pair, she'd see he was serious about this and agree.

Her eyes lit up. "There *is* no us."

"Right. But if you and I did mate…?"

"Sextuplets, no doubt."

He groaned a little, though he was amused she would say so.

She chuckled.

Humans didn't usually have that many children, but being wolves, it was possible, and without fertility drugs. He was thinking a couple, for starters.

The winds were really picking up by the time they reached the dirt road that led to the cabin. Tree branches were swaying, the wind was howling, and the car was being pushed across the road. Paul gripped the steering wheel, struggling against the gusts.

"So what you're saying is that you don't want me to take any missions in the next ten months or so," he said, though he figured since he was taking over the pack, he was hanging around for the duration. Besides, he had to build on something more with Lori.

"You'll probably have to do some of it so you can support your mate," Lori said, glancing out the window.

He smiled. "You don't think I could be a handyman?"

"I think you need some adventure in your life."

"The truth is that Hunter's not going on any missions right now because of Tessa and the twins. Finn's staying home and dealing with pack matters with Meara. Anna's had her triplets so she and Bjornolf are sticking close to their pack and family. So the SEAL team is really not doing much of anything these days."

"You and Allan are still working."

"Our own contract work. Maybe I can find some around here."

Lori snapped her fingers. "That police unit that does dive work."

"Yeah. Like that. I've got lots of credentials. Plus my specialized SEAL training. If they have an opening, though it might be volunteer, I could do that until I find something else."

"You could help me teach the kids at my martial-arts center."

He didn't answer.

"You'd be good with kids."

"I could do it. I might have to let you handle the older kids."

She chuckled. "They usually have better control over their actions."

"They can punch harder, and they might try with me, while with you, they're being careful."

She just smiled.

"I may still have to go on a mission from time to time if something vital comes up and the team needs me, but for now, I'll stay put for a good year. How's that sound?"

"It could... Stop!" Lori said, bracing her hands against the dashboard.

Paul slammed on his brakes as they heard the ponderosa pine tree snap and fall across the gravel road right in front of the car. For a moment, they stared at the downed tree. Paul cut the engine and reached for his door handle. "We'll have to hike up the road. We're about two miles from the cabin. I can return with the chain saw, cut up the tree, and move the car after that."

"That's going to take some work."

They got out of the car, locked the doors, and walked up to the tree. The way the wind was gusting and the ponderosa pines were bowing over, Paul was afraid more would topple in the storm before long. He climbed to the top of the four-foot-high diameter of the trunk, reached down to pull Lori up, and then they jumped down on the other side.

"That will take you a while to get back down here and saw that up," she said. "It's already got to be close to ten thirty. Maybe you should wait until morning. It's so dark now that even with a lantern and our wolf night vision, you'd have a time cutting the tree safely." She sniffed the air. "Besides, it's getting ready to rain."

"You're right. The car should be all right down there for the night."

She took his hand, and he smiled down at her. "No mating yet?"

"It depends on how…persuasive you could be."

"Hot damn, woman. I can be persuasive." He knew she wouldn't want to wait. Not if she'd told Rose he was her knight in tarnished armor.

Three more trees had fallen across the road. The ponderosa pines were up to a hundred feet tall. In the dark,

Paul couldn't tell if they had been uprooted or broken in half.

He and Lori jogged against the thirty-mile-per-hour winds—the gusts probably close to sixty miles an hour—barely making any headway, hoping her cabin was okay. When they finally reached it, he thought it looked fine, no trees on top of the roof, and the deck was like he'd left it after sealing it.

They both hurried inside, and she reached for the light switch and flipped it up. Nothing happened. "A tree must have hit a power line somewhere in the area."

Just then the rain broke free from the clouds and pounded on the roof and the deck with a thunderous torrent as Paul quickly shut the door.

"You stay here," he said and started to check the rest of the rooms. Then he heard her in the kitchen getting a couple of glasses out.

He hoped she wasn't irritated with him, but he couldn't help himself. In the business he was in, he was used to being cautious and not assuming anything. He checked the breaker boxes. Nothing had been flipped and he didn't smell anyone else's recent scent in the cabin. When he rejoined her, she'd lit a cinnamon-scented candle, and had a bottle of wine and glasses ready. With her feet bare and her dark hair tussled by the wind and falling in disarray all about her shoulders, she looked wolfishly delicious, like she'd just risen from his bed, and he sure as hell loved the idea.

It was time to seduce the she-wolf.

"By the way, thanks for sealing the deck. Especially before the rains came."

"My pleasure."

"Do you remember the time I got stuck up in that tree when I was nine?"

Paul opened the bottle of Chablis, poured the wine into two glasses, and then moved from the kitchen to the new sofa. "Yeah, when you weren't really stuck. You just wanted me to come rescue you."

He sat down on the sofa and she joined him, brushing up next to him. She smelled wild—of the piney woods, the stormy wind, and she-wolf, sweet and spicy. He breathed in her scent and luxuriated in it, like a wolf would enjoy his mate.

"You knew?" she asked, sounding surprised before she sipped her wine.

"Sure I knew." He was amused that she thought she'd pulled one over on him.

"You never let on. You acted as though you truly did have to rescue me. It was all an act?"

"I had to impress all the other kids."

She chuckled. "I figured if it was too difficult for you to make it all that way to reach me, I'd suddenly get the courage to meet you halfway. But even then you were good at rescuing people."

"I thought you might be considering that. It wouldn't have been half the challenge for me—as far as the other kids would have thought. So I was glad you stayed put. But what if I hadn't come for you? Because I knew you were just trying to get my attention and—"

"You had to impress the other kids."

He laughed.

"Besides, you wanted to impress me even more than you wanted to impress the others." She raised a brow in challenge.

"You're right, you know." He took her hand in his and squeezed, looking into her warm brown eyes, flecked with green. "I *wasn't* going to let you avoid me this time. After Allan and I got settled, I was going to see you. Although I hadn't envisioned you smacking me in the head with the broom."

She laughed.

He drank the rest of his glass of wine and put it on the coffee table, then pulled her into his arms.

She finished off her wine and set the glass beside his. "I wasn't planning to leave this time," she said, cuddling against him.

She felt right in his arms. "You shouldn't have left the other times."

"You wouldn't have been ready for—"

"This?" He kissed her mouth, one of his hands cupping the back of her head, the other combing through her silky hair as he soaked up the scent and feel of her.

She cradled his face with her hands and kissed him right back with such feeling that he knew, despite loving his work with the SEAL team, that he regretted not having gone after Lori. Yet he understood why she had left the way she did. She hadn't wanted him to have to choose between her and his jobs. But he'd already made the decision that if she was agreeable, they'd be mated wolves before long.

Which was why he hadn't taken the job Hunter had called him about. It was time to change the rules at home.

Chapter 16

PAUL KISSED LORI'S FOREHEAD AND HUGGED HER TIGHT as the wind continued to blow around the cabin, the rain still pouring down. "You know, when the lights go out, there's nothing better to do than—"

"Go to bed?" Lori asked.

"I thought you'd never ask." He'd scooped her up into his arms before she realized what he was going to do, and she gave a little cry of surprise. He walked over to the kitchen counter, blew out the candles, and carried her back to her bedroom.

She smiled up at him, thinking he was finally going to take charge and get the job done. That's what she loved about him. She was the same way, except when it came to this.

"Someone wise told me I was going to be old and gray before I ever figured out what I was missing in my life," he said very seriously.

"Oh?"

"Yeah. She was right. I've had a crush on you ever since we were young, you know." He set Lori on the bed. "You were the only wolf that chased my tail around, trying to grab hold. No other cub would dare."

She chuckled, remembering how he'd whirl around and tackle her. But he never hurt her.

"Yeah. You couldn't keep looking at me with those big, dark brown eyes and with such a wolfish grin, your tail wagging with enthusiasm every time you saw me, and hide the attraction," she teased as he began to slide his shirt up his abs.

Tan, sexy, hot, sculpted SEAL abs. She tried hard not to drool.

"I was trying to be subtle about it. Was I *that* obvious?" he asked.

"Your tail gave you away. Well, and all those beautiful wolfish teeth. You always were the top wolf, setting the others in their place among the juveniles, but when it came to me…"

"You had my respect because you were my alpha match. I never could think of you in any other way."

He yanked off his shirt and then shucked his boots, socks, and jeans. She waited for him to join her in bed. He pulled off his briefs, baring his glorious naked self, and she sighed.

He joined her in bed and then began caressing her breasts lightly through her cotton blouse and bra. Her nipples were already aroused and eager for his touch.

The storm still raged on, the wind howling, the lightning lighting up the bedroom window, the clap of thunder booming shortly after each lightning flash, setting the stage for what was to come.

She was wrapped up in the glorious moment with Paul—something she'd dreamed of forever. He kissed her mouth thoroughly, his hand still sweeping over her breasts and arousing the rest of her. He didn't seem to mind that she was in no hurry to remove her clothes either. She didn't want to rush through this in a desperate way—as if she wanted to claim him before he changed his mind.

The wine flavored their tongues and lips, and she enjoyed tasting him as she ran her hands down his muscled back, loving the feel of his naked body pressed against her.

Then he moved his head down, kissing her jaw, nuzzling her neck, and sweeping his warm mouth over her throat and lower. She was in heaven as her skin tingled with his touch. She raked her nails gently through his hair, loving every bit of this, just like she'd known she would. Only it was more real, more tactile. His tangled hair was soft, his mouth warm and well-versed in the art of seduction, and the heat of his body was making hers hot. He brushed his cheek against a breast, then turned his face to cover it with his mouth, licking through the fabric and getting her shirt and bra wet.

She watched him feast on her breast, still combing her fingers through his hair and taking in deep breaths of him. He smelled of the earth and pine and wolf, of delicious sexually aroused male.

He moved his hand up her shirt and unhooked her bra—she realized how convenient a front fastener could be—and he cupped her breast with his hand. That didn't last long before he pulled her shirt over her head and removed her bra.

So much for taking it nice and slow. He unzipped her jeans, but then concentrated on her breasts again, kissing and suckling now that they were bare. She smelled his excitement; it matched hers. The anticipation of this first time was overwhelming, combined with the joy of knowing it would be forever.

He slid his hand down her belly, his tongue artfully licking and encircling a rigid nipple. But his hand stole her attention as he slipped it under her panties and began to stroke her. She was already wet and aroused. His fingers stroking her made her want to yank off her jeans and her panties and slide against him, skin to skin.

She arched against his fingers, and then he paused, glancing at her as if looking for her approval. She started to jerk down her jeans impatiently, and he chuckled and began to help her. Her jeans tossed to the floor with the rest of their clothes, he slid his hand over her mound, still covered by the silky, black bikini panties.

He kissed her belly and then paused again, this time to look at her, his dark eyes filled with craving. "You're beautiful. I love you. And I want no other she-wolf to be my mate."

"I will always love you, Paul, and" — she smiled — "I have always wanted you to be my mate."

Then he slid her panties off and began to rub himself between her legs, hard and erect and very near to entering her.

She couldn't believe how hot he was, how sexy, how his touches could turn her on so fast. Yet she was almost there. Just a little bit further. She spread her legs farther apart, heady with the feel of his rigid cock stroking her until she felt the shattering high of the climax hit. She moaned her pleasure right before he captured her mouth with his.

He stroked her tongue with his, then pulled away and asked, "Are you ready?"

She treasured him for caring so much about her feelings that he wouldn't take it all the way until he was sure she was agreeable. His voice was drenched with lust, his body tense and eager for the mating, and she loved him for it.

"I've been ready forever."

"That's all I wanted to hear," he said wolfishly.

He didn't take it slowly then. He had held back as long as he could. He pushed into her tight sheath and then began to thrust, breathing in her aroused scent and loving the way she responded so eagerly to his touch. The way she fit around him like a snug wet suit, the way she kissed him and made him hard and aching for her.

All he could think about was how happy she had made him, how he was now regretting he hadn't done this sooner, and how much he wanted to do this over and over with her until they were tired, old wolves.

She was perfect for him. She completed him. And he hoped he'd always be that for her.

She was stroking his back and his sides, his buttocks, and he couldn't hold on any longer. She was just too arousing.

He spilled his seed deep inside her, thinking of how their pack would finally grow. It would be awesome to have little ones running around again, and he knew then just how right this was.

He collapsed on top of her, hugging her to the bed, still buried inside her, claiming her. She had her arms wrapped around him, holding him tight to her as if saying she wanted him just where he was.

"So beautiful," he said, then rolled off her anyway, not wanting to crush her, and pulled her into his arms. "And all mine."

She snuggled against him. "Ditto, mate of mine. Who's going to tell the rest of the pack?"

"Your grandma already knows," Paul said and closed his eyes.

"What?" Lori stiffened a little in his arms, but he held on tight before she moved away from him.

"I'm certain she's already told Catherine."

"Wait, when—"

"She assumed it when I was going to tell her I took over the pack. She cut me off before I could tell her we weren't there yet."

Lori relaxed against him, and he sighed with relief, loving the way she felt against him—soft, sexy, hot. He knew they were going to be like this from now on. Or…at least he'd sure planned it that way. He knew what he wanted when he wanted it, and he would have moved the proverbial mountains to come to this point in their relationship.

Lori didn't say anything for several minutes, then finally commented, "My grandma planned it this way all along."

He quirked his lips. "That makes her one of our most valuable pack members. Don't you agree?"

Lori chuckled. "She said she wasn't paying for you to take me on a date. That we'd have to figure it out for ourselves."

"She must have gotten tired of waiting."

"I would have waited forever," Lori said softly, stroking his chest.

"Not any longer." And then he kissed her, promising this was only the beginning.

The storm continued to rage, the wind and rain pounding the cabin. Lori's phone rang and she quickly climbed over Paul to get to her pants lying on the floor before he could wake enough to figure out what was going on.

She pulled the phone out of her pants pocket and checked her caller ID. Her grandma. "Are you okay, Grandma?"

"A tree crashed through the roof over the living room and took out the picture window." Emma sounded shaken up.

"We're coming. Are you all right?"

"Yes, dear. No rush."

"Several trees fell across the road down below the cabin, so it'll take us a little while to get back to the car."

"Okay, I'll see you when you get here. I've moved as many pieces of furniture away from the window and the rain as I can."

"Just *wait* for us. You don't need to be doing any heavy lifting. If you've got any plastic—a tarp, shower curtain, just anything—and can cover things to protect them from the rain, that would be the best thing to do for now. Did you need to talk to Paul?"

"No, dear. See you in a bit."

Paul was already dressed, looking worried as he shoved his phone in his pocket. "Is she okay?"

"Tree went through the roof over the living room and crashed through the big window. But, yeah, she's okay."

"I'll get the chain saw and call…well, hell, Allan doesn't have his car. We'll have to run by the cabin and pick him up first."

"All right." Lori hurried to get dressed while Paul headed out into the rain to grab the stuff they needed from the shed.

Dressed in jeans, T-shirts, hiking boots, and rain

jackets, they jogged down the gravel road in the rain and blowing wind to where the trees blocked their path. Paul climbed onto the tree trunk and gave her a hand up each time, then jumped down on the other side. They ran to get to the SUV and climbed inside.

"She's really okay, isn't she?" Paul asked as they buckled their seats, and he began to back down the road until he could find a place where he could turn around.

"She's fine as long as she doesn't lift a bunch of furniture. I tried to call Allan while you were gathering the equipment in case you didn't have a chance to, but I couldn't get hold of him. I hope he's okay."

"Uh, yeah, I tried too. Maybe he's occupied," Paul said.

"So do we bother him?" she asked as Paul found a side road to back into, then turned to drive the rest of the way to the main road.

"Yeah, we'll probably need him too, if the tree's very big. No matter what, it'll go quicker if there are more of us. We'll have to get a work crew out as soon as we can to repair the damage."

"I'll call Catherine to let them know what's going on." That was the thing with a pack. Everybody helped everyone. Plus, Lori wanted to make sure they were all right. Though she was certain Catherine would have called and let them know if she and Rose were having trouble.

"Good idea."

When Lori couldn't get hold of Catherine, she tried Rose. No one answering there either. "Okay, batting zero."

She didn't want to worry unnecessarily about them,

but she didn't think either Catherine or Rose would
have their phones turned off. Then again, if their phones
hadn't been charged sufficiently and the electricity had
been out all night, their batteries might have died. But
both of them at the same time? And they couldn't get
hold of Allan? That bothered her.

Because she was anxious, the drive to the Rappaports'
cabin seemed to take forever. Dark still claimed the area,
though the rain was letting up.

"Why don't you stay here and I'll roust Allan out of
bed. No sense in both of us getting wetter," Paul said as
he parked next to the steps.

"Okay. I'll keep trying to get hold of the others."

"All right. We make a good team."

She smiled at him. "We do."

Lori watched as he shut the door and ran up the steps
to the house, pausing to listen at the door. She wondered
if he was listening to make sure he didn't intrude on
something intimate. But there were no other vehicles at
the place, and Allan's car was in the shop.

Paul knocked, then unlocked the door and went inside.

Lori felt the skin prickle at the back of her neck. She
really didn't believe that Allan would be so sound asleep
that he wouldn't hear the phone, or that he'd gone out
in this weather without a car or in his wolf coat. She
called Catherine and then Rose again, but still only got
voice mail.

Paul hurried back out of the house, shaking his head.

"I'm calling Grandma to tell her that we're unable
to get hold of anyone. Maybe she's talked to someone.
I don't want to worry her, but she'd be upset with us if
we didn't let her know what was going on," Lori said.

"I agree."

While Paul left the mountain and they headed out toward the ranches, Lori called her grandma and was relieved to hear her answer. "It's just me. We tried to pick up Allan, but he wasn't at the cabin. His car is in the shop. We can't get hold of Catherine, Rose, or Allan."

"Why don't you run by their house before you come to mine," Emma said.

"Okay. Will you be all right?"

"Yes, of course. If you don't check on them, I'll have to run over there myself and get all wet."

"Okay. I'll call you as soon as we get there and let you know everything's all right." Lori prayed it was.

When they finally arrived at Catherine's house, they saw a pale glow of light inside.

"Candles," Lori said, feeling somewhat relieved.

As soon as Paul parked, Lori was out the door and Paul hurried to join her. He knocked at the door and Catherine called out, "Coming!"

Everything sounded fine.

Catherine opened the door and let them in. "What are you doing out in this weather?"

"We couldn't get hold of you," Lori said. "A tree came down on Grandma's house."

"Oh no. Let me get a tarp from the garage. What else do I need to bring?"

Allan stalked down the hall in a pair of jeans, no shirt, his hair wet.

"You've been here?" Paul asked.

"Yeah, I got worried about Mom and Rose during the storm. I called them and only got voice mail."

"Our batteries died," Catherine explained, dressed

in a fluffy white robe. "Normally one of us has a good charge, but we both charge them at night before we go to bed."

"I'm buying you one of those emergency phone chargers. You have to be prepared for these sorts of things," Allan said.

"You didn't have a car," Paul said to Allan.

"Yeah, I ran as a wolf. I didn't want to disturb the two of you in case you were…busy." Allan winked.

"We're mated." Lori clasped Paul's hand in hers.

He pulled free and wrapped his arm around her shoulder possessively.

"Ohmigod," Rose said, "finally." She slipped in to give Lori a hug.

"It's about time," Allan said.

Smiling broadly, Catherine gave Lori and Paul a hug. "I so agree."

"What's going on with your grandma?" Allan asked.

"Tree came down on the roof and went through her living room window. We've got a chain saw and need to clear it."

"Let me finish dressing." Allan stalked back down the hall.

"Me too." Rose hurried to her room.

"We're headed over there. You can catch up to us," Lori said.

"Sure thing." Catherine was still smiling at them, happy tears in her eyes.

Lori was glad everyone was happy for them as she and Paul took off for her grandma's place. She realized her heart was pounding way too fast when they reached Emma's house and saw the tree that had fallen during the storm. Fortunately, her grandma had probably been sleeping in her bedroom, far away from the catastrophe.

Emma opened the front door, but she wasn't frowning like Lori expected her to be. She was grinning, tears of joy misting her eyes.

Paul was anxious to get the equipment out of the SUV, but Lori pulled him to the porch so Emma could hug them both at one time. "You're mated."

"You already assumed so," Lori reminded her.

"Of course not. I was just giving Paul the added…push."

He chuckled. "Told you it all had to do with her animal guide."

Emma kissed Lori and Paul. "We have to celebrate."

"After we clean up your place." Lori took her grandma's arm and walked into the house.

"I'll have to stay with Catherine. Were the others okay?" Emma asked.

"Safely at home and Allan had joined them as a wolf, which is why he wasn't answering a phone. Catherine and Rose's phones had died." Lori walked into the living room and surveyed the damage.

It was a mess, glass and rainwater everywhere. The tree branches poking at the floor at least had kept the main part of the trunk from crashing through the maple coffee table.

Her grandma had moved a few things and had a broom out, as well as a dustpan and a tall kitchen trash container.

But it was still lightly raining and Lori prayed it would stop.

"What do you want me to do, Paul?" She would help him with the big stuff until Allan got there.

"I'm going to start sawing off some of the branches. Maybe you ladies can just wait until I cut off some of them and then you can haul out the smaller stuff. I'm not sure about *you*," he said, his gaze on Lori, "handling the broom."

Despite the seriousness of the situation, both Emma and Lori laughed.

They soon realized it would be an all-day affair. Firemen from the local fire department dropped by, and several other rescue workers combing through the area showed up to help remove the rest of the tree and cover the gaping hole where the window and part of the roof had been.

With so many men underfoot, the women had stopped helping. They were making sandwiches and coffee for everyone when they heard Dusty's and his brother's voices as they moved around the living room.

Rose shook her head. "They couldn't be here," she whispered under her breath.

Lori had to see for herself. Sure enough, the Cooper brothers and Jerome were here to help. Or to cause trouble.

Both Paul and Allan moved to intercept the men at once.

"We've got enough help for now. Thanks for offering," Paul said, not giving the men a chance to actually offer, if they intended to.

Dusty caught Lori's eye and smiled.

Paul glanced back at her. She moved forward then to show pack leader unity and wrapped her arm around

Paul's waist. He put an arm around her shoulders, show-ing they were together in much more of an intimate way than if they were just members of the same pack.

She wanted to tell the men they'd better watch out or they'd have to leave the area, but she was afraid that they'd be encouraged to take it further, so she just fol-lowed Paul's lead and gave them the wolf stare that told them to leave promptly.

Dusty's lips curled up in a small smirk and she knew them coming here was a challenge to the pack—maybe a way to see if Paul had taken over the pack and if Lori had become his mate.

"Come on, guys," Dusty said. "Seems we're not needed around here, though not by the looks of the place since it's in such shambles."

The other men glanced around and Howard said, "Their loss."

"Later," Dusty said, with a smug smile and a wink directed at Lori.

With a low growl, Paul immediately let go of Lori, grabbed Dusty's arm, and hauled him toward the door they'd come in, the same one that all the men were coming in and out of while transporting the tree and other debris.

Chapter 17

A FEW OF THE MEN HELPING TO CLEAR THE MESS stopped to see what was going on between Paul and Dusty. Paul just hoped no one would interfere in the wolf pack business. He had to set the ground rules with Dusty, his brother, and their friend...*now*.

In the light rain, Lori went outside with Paul as he continued to strong-arm Dusty. Dusty wasn't compliant, struggling to free himself, to prove he wasn't an omega wolf any longer. But he couldn't get loose from Paul's strong grip, no matter how hard he tried. Paul quickly yanked Dusty's arm behind his back and up, threatening to break it if Dusty didn't cooperate. Then he walked as far as he could go to the back of the brick house, away from the volunteers helping Emma, and shoved Dusty against the wall, plastering his face against the rough red brick.

Paul was beyond furious at the way the man continued to provoke a response from him regarding Lori. Even if she had not been his mate yet, Paul and Lori had made it clear that they were together; no other wolf need apply for the position. Humans would be clueless about what that meant. If a man thought he had a chance with Lori, he might try to get her attention away from her "boyfriend." But wolves knew better. Or at least they should.

"Our pack, our way. You will not cross me in this," Paul growled quietly for Dusty's hearing only, though the wolves standing nearby also heard. The humans couldn't hear because of the chain saws, but several watched, just the same. "If you or your cohorts ever touch Lori or any other members of my pack again, you'll be worse than sorry. Do you get me?"

"Yeah, man. We only came by to offer to help."

"We don't need your help," Paul said softly, his voice filled with threat.

"I got that."

"But you don't get the pack dynamics. Or you do, but you're ignoring them. You apparently don't get that you don't belong here. In our territory."

"All right. Let me go, will you?"

"No trouble," Paul said on another growl. "If I'd been there when you tore Lori's necklace from her neck and tossed it into the lake, or when your brother threw Rose into the lake, I would have killed the two of you. Just give me another reason…" Then Paul released him.

Pulling away from the wall, Dusty quickly rubbed his shoulder. He didn't eye Lori this time and didn't challenge Paul with a wolf stare. Instead, he quickly joined his brother and friend, and the three of them hurried out of there like beta wolves, well chastised.

But Paul suspected he hadn't seen the last of the men.

Not only had Lori followed the men outside, but Allan was also keeping an eye on them, ready to take down either of the other troublemakers.

Lori knew with all her heart that Dusty wasn't going to let go of the situation. The three omegas would just get sneakier and less bold about it. Had Dusty truly tried to offer just his help?

No. To humans, the men would look innocent. But the wolves knew better. Dusty's challenge to Paul—saying to Lori he'd see her later and not acknowledging that Lori and Paul were together—couldn't have been ignored. By allowing it, Paul would have signaled that he wasn't a strong leader. The three men had been pushing the wolf boundaries: the incident with the boat speeding in the water next to Lori's dock, the situation with the ladies, and even hooking up with a hunter who had been involved in illegal activities. They were headed down a path no *lupus garou* should take if he wanted to live long.

Red-faced and angry, Paul stared after the three men's backsides, ready to take this further if the situation warranted. He looked ferocious and endearing at the same time. And he was all hers.

Lori took him in her arms and tilted her face up to his. "I love you."

He pulled her tight against his body and kissed her like he was ready to take her to her bedroom. All of them were wet because of the rain, but she didn't care. A nice, warm shower with a hot SEAL wolf would be really appealing after they were done with this mess.

Allan cleared his throat and said, "I don't remember your parents ever ending a confrontation with other wolves in this manner. Seems to work for the two of you though. I'll make sure they've left the premises."

He stalked off after the men.

"Do you want to go with him?" Lori asked, concerned.

"Yeah, just to watch his back." Paul kissed her again, and then they parted and he hurried after Allan.

By nightfall, Emma's house was secure enough until they could get workmen out to rebuild the roof and replace the window. At least the rain had finally stopped.

"We're done here. Let's go to Catherine's house," Paul suggested.

"I'll fix us Cornish hens for dinner," Catherine said.

Rose quickly offered to help.

Emma was sitting on one of the only chairs in the living room that had escaped the rain and mess. She appeared absolutely exhausted, with dark shadows underneath her eyes, her hair wilted from the humidity, and her posture slumped. Lori was afraid that if they didn't move her to Catherine's home now, she'd be too tired to make the effort.

She helped Emma pack some things, while Paul and Allan loaded the chain saw and other equipment into the car.

Allan was smiling at Paul, arms folded across his chest, as they waited for Lori and her grandma to join them. "I thought it might take you longer."

Paul knew what he was referring to at once. "It all had to do with the storm," Paul said. "No electricity, nothing better to do."

"Says you," Lori contributed as she carried her grandma's bags to the car.

Paul chuckled and hurried to take the bags while Lori went back inside and fetched Emma.

"So that's all you needed to make it happen? An electrical outage?" Allan was still smirking.

"And love," Lori added while walking her grandma out to the car. Emma had definitely done way too much today.

"Are you okay, Emma?" Paul asked, his brow furrowing, worried about how tired she appeared.

"Grandma," Emma corrected, giving him a look like he'd better get with the program. "I'm fine."

He was all too happy to call her Grandma. He smiled at her, gave her a hug, and helped her into the car.

Everyone packed up, Lori locked the house, and they went to Catherine's. After they all cleaned up and changed into dry clothes, they had their first official mated pack-leader meeting.

"First order of business…" Paul said, taking a seat on one of the sofas next to Lori. "Do we all agree to continue with the name 'the Cunningham pack'?"

"It's only right," Emma said. "Your parents were good pack leaders."

Everyone agreed.

"And you're fine with Lori and me leading the pack?"

The others smiled.

"How does everyone feel about Widow Baxter and her daughter joining?" he asked.

Lori sat taller on the sofa. "They should join. They shouldn't be isolated from us if we're going to re-form the pack."

"Anyone want to volunteer to ask them?" Paul asked.

Emma raised her hand. "I'll do it. If you'd like, I'll be the greeter and check people out."

"Thank you, Emma. We need an emergency alert roster, though there aren't that many of us," Paul said.

"I'll do it," Catherine said.

Paul had thought he and Lori would ease into this business much more slowly, with Rose's babies coming first, and then maybe Lori's and his following some months later. But he never had considered having new pack members right away.

"What about the Cooper brothers and their sidekick?" Allan asked.

Concerning this issue, Paul addressed everyone in the pack. "If anyone has any trouble with them, let us know immediately. I don't believe that they're going to behave any differently. They were omega wolves with the Wolfgang pack, the scapegoats of the pack. They could have changed, but it appears they aren't about to. They're still challenging our pack authority. And even if they don't cause any more difficulties for our pack members, we're responsible for dealing with them as wolves if they do illegal stuff in the area."

"Agreed," Lori said.

"About a pack fund. We can put together money to use for things the pack will need, or leave things the way they are and just have everyone pitch in when we have a special pack need." Which was the way Paul's parents had handled the situation—just pitching in when they needed to.

"A pack fund," everyone said.

"We could set that up tomorrow," Lori said.

After discussing matters further, Catherine and Rose made dinner, and once everyone had eaten, Lori tucked her grandma away in Paul's bedroom, the one he always used when he stayed with Catherine.

As Paul waited for Lori in the doorway, Emma sighed peacefully. "I couldn't be happier with the way things turned out between you and my new grandson."

Lori stroked her grandma's arm. "I agree."

"I think it's worked out for the best," Paul said.

"You get some rest. We'll check on things tomorrow, and we'll be sure to get some workers out to fix up your place," Lori said.

She gave her grandmother a kiss, and then she and

Paul said their good nights and took off. It would be awhile before they actually got back to the cabin—they had to take Allan to his place and then cut up the trees on the road to the lake cabin.

After they dropped Allan off, they headed to the Greypaws' cabin. But when they came to the place where the trees had fallen, all they found was fresh, wet sawdust.

"What…?" Lori asked.

"I told some of the men we had trees down on our road, and they said they'd take care of it. I knew we'd be getting in late so we'd need help with it. I'm glad they managed to take care of it before we returned home."

"You know what that means, don't you?" Lori asked him as they entered the cabin.

"What's that?"

"We won't be too tired for what comes next."

He grinned down at her, and as soon as he shut and locked the door, he scooped her up in his arms and hauled her toward *his* room this time. "I like the way you think."

"*Your* room?"

"Hell, yeah. I kept thinking about what it would be like to roll around in the sheets with you. It about killed me to know you were so close that I could nearly taste you, yet not be able to have you."

"I love you," she said. "And, well, I won't deny it was the same for me."

"When you were rubbing up against me in the lake when I was wearing my wet suit and you were wearing that sexy wolf bathing suit, I wanted us to be like this."

"When it's not so stormy, that can be next on our agenda. Skinny-dipping in the lake."

"You got it. I love diving for treasure—*your* treasure."

In record time, they stripped off their clothes, dumping them on the floor in Paul's guest bedroom. Naked, standing next to the bed, he kissed her mouth, having wanted to do that since the beginning of the evening. They rubbed their naked skin against each other, wanting, needing the intimacy.

He was so glad they had reached this point in their relationship instead of waiting another year or more.

Her eyes were darkened with desire as he tilted her head back and kissed her mouth again. Her lips were hot and spicy, her tongue stroking his as her soft, pliable body pressed against him, enticing him to devour her. And he wanted to do so, to reach every wolfish, sexy part of her with his kisses. Her dusky, erect nipples brushed against his chest, and his cock was just as hard, stretching out to her, eager to feel her rubbing against him. She licked his nipple and he sucked in his breath, his body feverish for wanting.

She smelled of tangerines and the piney woods, of she-wolf and her own personal sweet and spicy scent. Their mouths fused as if he could never get enough. He'd never wanted to fight the attraction, not when he was young and wanted so much to prove he was the wolf she thought him to be. Even if he failed. She was always there for him, loving him just the way he was.

And she couldn't know how much that meant to him as he kissed her jaw, brushing his mouth against her throat. Her breathing was shallow, her pheromones hot with excitement, which helped kick his into a firestorm of desire. He was glad for his wolf senses because humans couldn't smell the stronger scents of arousal, the pheromones that triggered each of them into wanting and needing resolution. He stroked his mouth down her collarbone until he reached a breast, cupped both of them, and then licked each in turn.

She sank against the bed, and he smiled to see her so boneless.

"Sorry," she said.

"Works for me," he said, joining her. Leaning against her, he began kissing her breasts, licking the nipples while she swept her hands down his sides and buttocks, and growled softly.

He loved her growly nature, loved smelling the way she was so turned on. The dark, curly hairs between her legs were moist with her need, proving she loved what he did to her as much as he loved the way she made him feel—special, cared for, desirable.

He slid his hand down her smooth belly and stroked her between the legs, wanting to make her come as he listened to her tripled heartbeat.

Twisting underneath his sensual assault, she dug her fingernails into his sides and came unglued with a healthy cry.

She pulled at his muscled arms to join her, to enter her, to take his fill while she took hers of him. He rocked her world in a way that only he could, the way he touched her, kissed her, and molded to her. No one would ever be Paul—in his pink palm-tree shirt with the green flamingos and with his heart of gold—who wanted to save the world. A leader who loved his family and his pack, but most of all her.

He rubbed against her in a sweetly erotic way,

sliding his rigid cock against her slick folds, wanting her to take charge and slide him into her until she was full of him, eager to mate again and again. He was everything to her, their bodies on fire, her body needing him deep inside, softening for him, welcoming him.

And then he penetrated her tight sheath. Their breathing was ragged, their hearts beating in sync.

They rocked together, his kisses verging on desperate as he thrust into her hard, taking her, claiming her. He worked deep, satisfying her need to claim him for her own. He was dangerous to others but safe for her. She loved that about him.

His eyes were nearly black when he lifted his head, and she knew then that he was ready to come, but she hadn't expected his next move. He howled with his release—a robust, loving-her howl.

He continued to thrust into her until she had used him all up, and then he sank against her, one sexy, loving wolf. She wrapped her arms around him and sighed. "I loved your howl."

He kissed her cheek. "More where that came from."

"Good. I wouldn't expect anything less."

He chuckled and pulled her into his arms, and she knew the night had just begun.

Late the next morning, after they had been up half the night making love, they went to town to open a bank account. When Lori got a call in the SUV, Paul instantly assumed it was Emma and hoped the construction workers were there.

"Emma, what's up?" Lori asked. Neither Lori nor he had wanted to disturb her because they thought she might be sleeping late, as worn out as she had been the night before. "Really. Okay, thanks." Lori tucked her phone away.

Paul waited to hear what that was all about, and when Lori wouldn't say, he asked, "Good news?"

"Yeah. The workmen have started fixing her place. But…as you probably assumed, my assistant has been running my martial-arts center while I'm gone, and she said twin girls signed up."

"That's great." Paul pulled into the bank lot and cut the engine.

"They're wolves."

Paul glanced at her, not liking the sound of that. "Your assistant isn't a wolf. How would she know that the girls are?"

"Emma ran by there to check on the place, and she realized they were, and vice versa. She told them the owner was one too, and they said they already knew. Their momma wanted to join the Cunningham pack."

"How did they know about us? Wolf packs don't advertise."

"Word of mouth, I guess."

"What kind of jobs do they do?"

"The girls are six."

"The parents," he said, tilting his chin down.

"She lost her mate, so it's just the mom and her two girls."

"You can't be serious."

Lori smiled and reached over the console to curl her arms about his neck. "Except for Allan, you probably

have the only all-female wolf pack in the States, given
that females are fewer in number."

He wrapped his arms around her waist. "And that
could mean real trouble."

She frowned a little at him. "How's that?"

"Female wolves attract male wolves."

"And Allan and you can make them all behave."

Paul grunted.

She laughed, but before they entered the bank to set
up the pack's account, Paul noticed Howard Cooper sitting in his pickup truck outside. As soon as Howard saw
them, he called someone on his phone.

Trying not to wonder if something suspicious was
going on, Paul and Lori entered the bank. Lori really
would think he was crazy if he overreacted again.

Inside the bank, Paul saw a man wearing a motorcycle helmet approach the bank clerk. Then it dawned on
Paul. The guy might have hidden his face, but the clerk
would know him because he was withdrawing money
and had to have an ID.

Still, what if this was the bank robber? "Stay here,
Lori," Paul said, unable to help feeling something was
off with the guy.

This time she nodded and moved toward one of the
loan officers' desks.

"May I help you?" the woman asked Lori.

Paul could imagine Lori thinking she would have to
wait for her crazy mate to overcome his suspicion that
something was wrong every time he came home from
a mission.

"We're going to open a business account," Lori
said finally.

"New accounts is over there," the woman said.

"Thank you."

Paul cast Lori a look that said he didn't want her moving in that direction until he knew if everything was all right.

The man got his money, shoved it into his wallet, then headed out of the bank.

Hell, Paul thought. Lori was sure to think he was nuts.

She joined him, took his hand, and led him to the new accounts desk.

"We want to open a business account," Lori said and they took seats in front of the desk. "It will be the Cunningham Recovery Corporation."

Paul smiled at Lori. He loved his clever she-wolf.

It seemed more official today, maybe because setting up the account would acknowledge they had a viable pack.

After they finished at the bank, Paul wrapped his arm around Lori's shoulder and walked her outside. "I love the name of our corporation."

"Isn't it perfect? Between our pack recovering and the kind of work you and Allan do—recovering people, retrieving necklaces from the lake, and other really important things—it just seemed perfectly appropriate."

"It is."

Lori got another call and said, "Yes, Grandma?" She frowned. "I'll let him know. We're coming by to check on the work being done on your house."

When they ended the call, she said to Paul, "Well, not sure what's going on, but Widow Baxter said it's too dangerous for us to take her into the pack."

"What?"

"I don't know. Grandma figured we'd have to talk with her to learn the truth."

"You want to call her?"

"Sure." Lori had never expected that the Baxter mother and daughter *wouldn't* want to join their pack. She just figured for protection and camaraderie, they'd automatically want to be included. "Hi, Mrs. Baxter? This is Lori Greypaw-Cunningham," she said, smiling at Paul and glad she could say that now.

He looked just as pleased that she would.

"You can call me Jean," the woman corrected her. "If this is about joining the pack, we really can't."

"Can we come over and talk?"

"Do you want us to leave your territory?"

Lori was so surprised to hear her say it that she was taken aback for a second. Though normally she would discuss this with Paul and they'd both agree on it, given the facts, she said, "No. You've got our protection no matter what. Can we still talk about it?"

"I'd prefer not to. If that's all you wished to discuss?"

"Yes, but if you ever feel the need to talk, I'm a good listener."

"Thanks." Then the woman hung up on her.

Stunned at this turn of events, Lori said, "Well, they won't be joining, but they want to stay here as long as it's all right with us."

"As long as it doesn't have a negative impact on the pack."

"Agreed."

When they arrived at Emma's house, they were glad to see all the men working away.

"How are you doing?" Paul asked as he gave Emma a hug.

"Oh, just fine. What do you think about the Baxters?"

"Not sure," Paul said. "But we'll have to keep an eye on the situation." His phone rang and he answered it. "Yeah, Allan?"

"I got a doctor's appointment for Rose to see Hunter's doctor on the Oregon coast in a couple of weeks."

"Nothing closer than that?"

"Everyone's still looking. Mom said she'd take care of the shop while we're out there."

"All right. They're doing a great job on repairing Emma's house." Paul walked into the living room and nodded to the workmen.

Lori and her grandma had gone off to talk in private, away from all the noise, but he swore he heard Lori say something about a Facebook party and inviting wolves to join. And something about papers needing Paul's approval that were sitting on the kitchen table.

"Have you told Hunter you've taken over the pack and mated with Lori?" Allan asked.

"Not yet. I guess I'll give him a call and let him know the good news."

"Hunter said he might have a lead on this Everett Johnston, the guy who got Rose pregnant, but he wanted to make sure before he shared the information."

"Good. Maybe we're getting somewhere with this then."

Paul glanced back down the hall and tried to listen to what was being said between Lori and her grandma. "Two more, yes!" Lori said.

"Do you need me to come over there?" Allan asked Paul.

"The workmen have got it well in hand."

"Okay. Did you hear about that motorcycle-helmet bandit getting away with another thirty-one thousand dollars? He hit the same bank twice. You'd think they'd learn."

"Sounds like the police need some help with this one."

"That's what I was thinking. Maybe you and I could run over there later and check out the bank, see if we recognize anyone's scent. I've got some work to do on this place. I'll talk to you later."

"All right. Out here." Paul tucked his phone away and watched the men, but he was still trying to hear what the ladies were up to.

Lori joined him while her grandma was starting a load of wash after using so many towels to mop up the water last night and this morning.

"What's going on?" he asked as Lori slipped her arms around his waist.

He really liked the way they were leading the pack if it meant having Lori close like this.

"Well, Emma asked two of the women in her quilting group if they'd join our pack."

"They're…wolves?"

"Of course. They live two hours away, widowed like her, and are sisters, no pack. So they want to move here. What do you think?"

Even if he didn't want any more females in the pack, looking down into Lori's enthusiastic, smiling face, there was no way he could say no. "You're not putting out the word somewhere that all female wolves who need a pack can join ours, are you?"

He was thinking of the comment he'd heard them make about Facebook.

"Emma's excited about having a larger pack. Now that I'm going to be even busier with helping to run it and still offering my martial-arts classes and spending time with you, she wants to have some friends in the area to go to the movies with, have more frequent quilting bees, or have lunch dates, play cards, whatever," Lori said. "I'm going to fix spicy beef enchiladas and fried rice for lunch. Does that sound good?"

"Delicious. You know I mated you because you're a great cook."

She grinned at him as she took his hand and they walked into the kitchen. "Among *other* things."

"Hmm, the *other* things too. What's this?" Paul asked as he spied the papers on the kitchen table. "Four more single female wolves who want to join our pack? They know we have no mates for them here, right?"

"Allan will be in seventh heaven since he's at least one eligible bachelor here."

Paul leaned his back against the counter as she made the enchiladas. Once she placed them in the oven, he pulled her into his arms. "Are you sure someone isn't putting out the word somehow to open up the pack to a whole lot of stray females? On average, there are more male *lupus garous* than there are females. So I don't understand how we're getting so many new unattached females."

Lori sighed. "All right. Here's the thing. Emma and Catherine are spreading the word that we have a safe pack here, a good leader—"

"Leaders. There are two of us."

"Well, three, since Allan's our sub-leader." Lori kissed him. "I have nothing to do with this."

"Why only females?" he asked, sensing there was more to it than helping out some single women, widows, and single moms raising kids. He could handle a larger pack, and women and kids were fine, but he could envision a big hassle with a bunch of footloose males if they learned about all the single women in the pack with only Allan and him there to offer protection. Not that the ladies probably couldn't fend for themselves, but it was a pack thing. Still, he could see all the trouble that would bring.

She pointed at the papers. "I thought they were fine. What do you think?"

"I think I'm bound to be in real trouble."

She chuckled. "But you handle trouble so well."

After the meal was cooked, he helped her set the table and Emma joined them.

"He said yes, didn't he?" Emma asked, all smiles.

Just like with Lori, there was no way he could say no to Emma, and he was thrilled they were so happy.

He started eating the enchiladas, then paused. "You and Catherine don't think that if we had other males in the pack, one of them might try to take over, do you?" he asked Emma.

When Lori and Emma shrugged, Paul shook his head. "Over my dead body."

They smiled.

After two days of finishing several more projects at the lakeside cabin, while Lori taught more of her

martial-arts classes, Paul and Allan took a drive into the
next county to check out the bank that had been robbed.
They smelled no one they recognized, though Paul was
still suspicious of the guy who'd worn a helmet into the
local bank twice.

"Did they ever say what was wrong with your car?"
Paul asked Allan as they returned home.

"Sugar in the tank."

Paul glanced at Allan. He shrugged. "Your guess is
as good as mine."

"The Cooper brothers or Jerome, or all three did it
while you were watching the movie and I was taking
Rose home," Paul said.

"I didn't smell any sign of them. Did you?"

"No, but they could have been wearing hunter's
spray. It had to be a wolf; no one else would know not
to leave a scent."

"My thought also. But we don't have any proof."

Paul wasn't going to threaten someone with bodily
harm when he didn't have proof that the man had done
something wrong. Though if Paul talked to them, he
might be able to smell their anxiousness while questioning them. "Let's go have a talk with them."

Allan nodded. "I'm all for it."

On the way home, they detoured to the ranch where
the men worked. From another ranch hand, they learned
that the Cooper brothers were mending fences somewhere out on the 150-acre property. Jerome was mucking out one of the horse stalls, so they went to question
him. When he saw Paul and Allan walk in, he immediately straightened and his knuckles whitened as he held
the shovel tight in his fisted grasp. "What do you want?"

"Know anything about the sugar in Allan's gas tank?"

Jerome's eyes widened. "Hell, no. Why would I do something like that?"

"What about your friends?"

"They wouldn't have."

But he didn't sound too sure of himself.

"Tell them if it happens again, you can all find someplace else to live." Paul turned and Allan followed him out.

"He didn't know anything about it," Allan said.

"Yeah, I know. I suspect it was one of the brothers, probably pissed that we're here telling them what to do. And maybe because we called the cops on that hunter friend of theirs."

Allan and Paul climbed into the vehicle. "I doubt they're going to stop causing trouble."

Paul was sure they wouldn't. But he and Allan would have to catch them in the act next time.

For now, he was busy meeting with female wolves wanting to join the pack as news of the new leadership spread by word of mouth. And he was spending a good deal of every night and some afternoon delight making love to Lori, working around the classes she was giving at the dojo. He couldn't have been happier with his new settled life. Not once had he given the SEAL missions any thought.

Until he got a call from Hunter in the middle of the night.

Chapter 18

WHEN PAUL HEARD FROM HUNTER AT THREE IN THE morning, he knew something bad was up. No way would Hunter call with another mission again so soon unless it was vitally important that Paul and Allan be there. Especially after he'd informed Hunter that he and Lori were now mated and he was sticking closer to home for a good long while. It was unlikely someone on their team was dying or had died. As far as he knew, nobody was on a mission. Finn, Bjornolf, and Hunter were still home with their mates.

Paul quickly said in a hushed voice, "Yeah, just a sec." He climbed out from underneath Lori, trying not to disturb her, grabbed a pair of boxers, and left the bedroom. The adrenaline was already rushing through his veins, preparing him for the worst. He was trying not to think of what it would mean if he had to leave Lori behind after promising her he would be here for the next ten months.

He pulled on the boxers in the living room and took a seat on the couch. "Yeah, Hunter, what's up?"

"Michael's in trouble. He was at his art exhibit in São Paulo, Brazil, and was taken hostage."

Immediately, a cold sweat broke out on Paul's skin. Tessa adored her brother, and if anything happened to him, Paul knew she'd be devastated—and Hunter along with her. Even Paul's family would be shattered if Michael was a casualty.

"Tessa's in a panic," Hunter continued, his voice strained and growly. "Wes Caruthers in my pack, the police officer, went with him to watch over him. But Wes ended up with a bad case of dysentery and was too sick to go with Michael to his art exhibit. When Michael didn't return to the hotel within a reasonable time after the gallery closed, Wes dragged himself out of the hotel and went looking for him.

"Then Tessa got a call from her brother. Some rebels picked him up, figuring Michael was rich and famous, and have taken him into the jungle. They're looking for a ransom. Wes was ready to go into the jungle after him, but I told him to sit tight. He doesn't know his way around the place like we do, and he's still not a hundred percent. We're looking to free Michael with whatever force we have to use as long as we can return him home safely."

Everyone on the SEAL team and Anna, their unofficial member as an undercover operative, was family. And their families were family. Michael might not be part of Paul's official wolf pack, but that wouldn't keep them from saving one of their own wolves.

"I'll get hold of Allan. We'll meet up with you at the São Paulo-Guarulhos International Airport," Paul said, not hesitating to take part in the mission.

"Finn, Bjornolf, and I have the first flight out of Portland. See you in Brazil."

After they ended the conversation, Paul called Allan, and before he could even tell him what was going on, the first thing Allan said was, "Where are we going now?"

Paul hated that they'd agreed to take over the pack, that Rose was in a bind, that they hadn't located the father of her baby, and that now he and Allan would be leaving them all behind. He didn't even want to see how disappointed Lori was sure to be. But Michael was like family. If Paul and the rest of the team didn't attempt to bring him home and they lost him for good, Paul would never forgive himself.

"I'll arrange for the flight. You haven't told Lori yet?" Allan asked.

"No. I'll need to let the rest of our pack know also."

"All right. I'll take care of everything else."

Lori cleared her throat and Paul looked over the back of the couch to see her watching him, wearing a long T-shirt, arms folded over her chest, brows raised.

He said to Allan, "Got to go. See you in a few."

"Good luck."

Paul ended the call and rose from the couch.

"I'll let the pack know that you're both leaving." Lori was trying hard to look like it didn't bother her, but he knew her better.

He stalked across the floor, placed his hands on her shoulders, and pulled her close, kissing her. "Tessa's brother has been taken hostage in Brazil. Hunter needs our help to bring him home."

Lori's eyes misted and Paul held her tight.

"I'm sorry. I know I said I'd stay…"

"Oh, Paul. You couldn't. He's just like family. Tessa would be shattered if she lost him. And we would be too. If you didn't go and Michael didn't make it out, I would feel it was all my fault. Knowing you, you would feel it was all yours too. I'll drive you and Allan to the airport. I'll let the others know what has happened when it's a more decent hour."

Trying to lighten the mood, he said, "I trust you in everything you do. Just don't make any wild changes while I'm gone."

She smiled so wickedly that he wasn't sure what she might have in mind.

———

This was why Lori had such a difficult time with the kind of work Paul and Allan did. Before, she'd put her heart on hold. Now, she'd given it to him, and for however long it took for him to come home, she'd be worrying about him and the rest of the team. Not that she hadn't always been concerned about them when they were gone on assignments. But now that she and Paul were mated, it was more personal. They had declared they'd run the pack, and now it was strictly her responsibility. But she knew he had to do this. She loved him whether he was here with her or not. And she would run the pack whenever he was away.

Yet when she kissed and hugged him, trying so hard not to get all misty-eyed, she knew it wasn't going to be as easy as all that. Then, she checked with Emma to see if she was up to taking the trip with Rose to see the wolf doctor in Oregon about Rose's pregnancy.

———

As soon as Allan and Paul had taken their seats on the plane, Allan said, "Was Lori upset about us leaving?"

"No. I mean, yeah, of course she's upset. Lori and the rest of our pack took Michael in like he was one of our own, partly because he's Hunter's brother-in-law and partly because they love Tessa. But the guy is plain likable on his own. So it's personal. She's as concerned about him as she is about the rest of us. She also knew neither of us would have forgiven ourselves if we hadn't gone with Hunter and the rest of our team to free Michael. Lori's running the pack while we're gone."

"So things will be as they usually are," Allan said. "Except for the nine new females in the pack."

"And your sister's pregnant."

"And we haven't located the dad. But nothing life-threatening."

"Right." Paul knew that during any mission they undertook, they had to remain focused or risk getting their team members or themselves killed. Simple as that. Yet he couldn't help remembering the tearful expression on Lori's face and how hard it had been for her to keep her feelings in check. He hoped that everything would be all right while she was in charge of the pack, and he felt bad that he had left her with all the responsibilities.

And he worried that if the Cooper brothers and their friend learned Paul and Allan were away, the women would have trouble.

—◦◦◦—

One thing Lori, her grandma, Catherine, and Rose wanted more than anything was a real pack. A real backup for each other in case they needed it. More family. More wolf friends.

In the four and a half weeks the SEAL team had been gone, Lori and the others did get some new males in the pack, but they were mated. So no worry about them. Lori and the other original members of the pack ensured the men were beta wolves and wouldn't try to take over.

Trying not to worry about Paul and Allan going back into the Amazon this soon, the ladies continued to chat with other female *lupus garous*, offering them a safe haven with the Cunningham pack.

When a female wolf doctor contacted Lori, she was ecstatic. She knew Paul would be pleased with the news that Rose wouldn't have to continue to fly anywhere to see another pack's doctor.

The only problem was the Cooper brothers and their friend Jerome. Once they'd caught scent of the female wolves joining the pack and found out that Allan and Paul were gone, they'd begun causing trouble.

"Well," Emma said as she and Rose, Catherine, and Lori sat down to coffee and chocolate cake, "now that we've got our doctor, EMTs, and a nurse, we're all set for Rose's babies."

Rose groaned. "I can't believe I'm having triplets."

Lori patted her hand. "I'm so excited for you."

"Yeah, but what will Paul and Allan think about Everett?" Rose asked, looking worried.

"They'll be fine," Catherine said. "I'm glad Everett finally returned to see you and told us what was going on, that he'd only been afraid to involve his family and the rest of us in his situation. Paul and Allan will look into this bank robbery business and clear Everett's name. Then his sister, Tara, and widowed mother will join the pack. No wonder we didn't make the connection between mother, daughter, and son, since Jean was using her maiden name. We'll be one happy family."

"Right," Emma said. "We'll make sure that if their former pack comes looking for them, Everett will be like Bjornolf, a ghost SEAL. No one will ever know he's here."

They all looked at Lori.

"Well?" Emma said. "Do you have anything you want to share with us? Rose waited far too long to tell us about her pregnancy."

Lori hesitated. "I should tell Paul first, but I haven't been able to reach them since they went into silent mode in the jungle. He was able to get a message to me daily for a while, but then said they had to go silent."

"Well, he's not here, so we need to be here for you," Emma said, smiling. She had already started making baby moccasins for Rose's babies, and Lori knew she was dying to make some for hers as well.

"Oh, all right. Don't let on that I told everyone before I told him."

"*Ohmigod!*" Rose screeched and threw her arms around Lori. "They'll be born only a few months after mine. How many?"

"Too early to tell. When I have my first ultrasound, I'll know for sure."

"This is too exciting," Rose said, beaming.

All grins, Catherine and Emma gave her huge hugs.

Lori just hoped Paul was ready for it. And…all the other changes she'd made while he was gone.

"You're not going to keep training students at the dojo, are you?" Emma asked.

"I will for a while. In fact, I've got to get going. I'll see you all later. Things are really looking great with the pack."

One thing Lori wouldn't give up was jogging around

the park near her dojo. She might be walking later, but until she was too far along, she was keeping in shape.

As soon as she was on the walking trail, she breathed in the pine fragrance and was enjoying the cool afternoon air when she heard someone jogging behind her. She moved farther over on the path so the man—she could tell it was a man from his heavier step and longer stride on the footpath—could pass her.

When he pulled in beside her and smirked, she felt a chill slip up her spine. Dusty Cooper.

They hadn't had any trouble with them while Paul and Allan were away...well, not too much. She had taken Dusty to task for bothering three of the females in the pack, and he'd thrown up his hands, sneering, and left.

"The SEALs are gone. You're here, all alone, running things. What if they don't ever come back? It's been...what, nearly five weeks already?"

She didn't respond.

"I've only been interested in you, you know. What if we got together just for a drink at the—"

"No. Having you and your brother up at the lake was a mistake. I'm a mated wolf and pack leader here. You're not welcome. Quit hassling me." She continued to jog at her regular pace, but she felt wary, smelling the aggression rolling off the cowboy in waves. He hadn't liked it when she'd rejected him the first time and then taken up with Paul. She supposed the human women didn't often turn down his advances. Why couldn't he just let it be? She was a mated wolf and that meant forever.

"Hey, I wanted to..." He paused. "Well, I wanted to

say sorry about the necklace. I just felt you led me on and then I got mad."

He wasn't sorry and she suspected he'd always behave in such a manner when he was turned down.

"Thanks for the apology." Then she turned down the trail that would take her back to her dojo.

When he followed her, she felt like shifting and taking a bite out of him.

He grabbed her arm and pulled her to a stop. Furious, she immediately twisted away from him, and before he knew what hit him, she kneed him in the jewels.

He roared as he clutched his crotch and fell to his knees. She ran full out then, figuring he wasn't going to chase after her, but not wanting to risk it.

When she reached the parking lot, she heard heavy footfalls behind her on the trail and she turned, expecting to face a pissed-off Dusty. Instead, she saw his brother and Jerome, but they still had a ways to go. She sprinted for her dojo and saw four of her students getting out of their cars to join her at the class. She hurried to get her keys out and unlocked the door, just as Howard Cooper came around the corner of the building.

She ushered her students in as the two men reached the door.

"What do you want?" she growled.

"We want to sign up for classes," Howard said.

So they could learn how to counter her devastating moves? She didn't believe they really wanted to sign up to learn anything.

"I'm sorry. This is strictly a women-only class and my others are all full."

They exchanged glances and she prepared to take them both on, calculating how hard it would be. If she took Howard down, she figured Jerome might leave on his own accord.

Howard said, "If a wolf appeals to us, she's ours. You're not going to be able to do anything about it."

Meeting his challenge to her authority, Lori kicked her foot out and slammed it into Howard's chest, knocking him flat on his back on the concrete.

Jerome looked so startled as he turned his attention from Howard to her that she didn't believe he'd try to retaliate.

"What Paul said stands for me and our pack. Stay out of our business."

Howard got up and brushed himself off, scowling, but he didn't look her directly in the eyes to challenge her. "You can't fight all three of us off. And you have no say in what we do with the other women in your pack," Howard said.

"They've been forewarned about you. They know any who form ties with any of you will be cut loose from the pack."

Howard stared at her, then slapped Jerome on the shoulder. "Come on. We'll see about all that." He motioned with his head to leave and they took off.

She knew she'd have more trouble with them later.

—⁓—

For five weeks, Paul and the rest of the SEAL team followed the rebels' and Michael's trail through the jungle.

"You know the full moon is out tonight," Bjornolf warned.

Everyone knew it. But they'd been born *lupus garous*. All of them had several generations of wolf blood.

A wolf who had only been turned for about a year, like Michael, could have trouble with feeling the urge to shift during the full moon. He could control the shifting at other times, but during the full moon, that was a different story.

If Michael was bound, which undoubtedly he would be, Paul wasn't sure what he could do. Shift while still dressed and bound? And then they'd probably shoot him.

Hunter and his team couldn't think about that. All they could do was pray that Michael could hold out.

"I still smell the scent of the female wolf," Paul said. That added a complication to the rescue mission. Not only did Michael need rescuing, but a female might also need their help.

But was she a hostage? Or one of the rebels?

Twice, they'd encountered armed men who had quickly found themselves outmatched. No matter how good these criminals were at hiding like chameleons in the jungle, the SEAL team was just as familiar with the terrain and camouflage—and had the added advantages of their wolf sense of smell and their night vision.

When they came upon a lightly guarded camp at dusk, they smelled Michael's and the she-wolf's scent. Still crouched in the dense foliage, they considered the guards: four on the perimeter and three more sitting in front of a campfire. A large tent was behind them with no telling how many guards inside.

Hunter signaled to each of the SEAL team members about who would take out which of the perimeter guards.

Paul and the rest of his team members quietly made their way to their targets, and without alerting anyone, Paul took out his guard, then waited for Hunter's signal to go after the ones sitting around the campfire.

As soon as Hunter motioned to the team, Finn, Allan, and Paul moved simultaneously into position to take down their new targets, while Bjornolf stayed on perimeter watch. The others threw daggers, and each of the men targeted slumped over, no one having made a peep.

While Allan stayed on perimeter watch, Paul and the others rushed to reach the tent before anyone else arrived. Carefully, Paul pulled the tent flap aside. Inside, it was dark, but with the glow of the campfire nearby and their wolf night vision, they found three kidnappers inside, sleeping on mats. Michael and a dark-haired woman were tied up to the center tent pole. The team quickly took care of the remaining guards. Thank God, Michael hadn't shifted into a wolf.

Paul hurried to untie Michael, who was scowling, while Finn removed the woman's bonds. Her face was flushed and she appeared to be in pain, from the way she was grimacing. Her dark brown hair framed her face in damp curls, and her dark brown eyes were heavily lidded. She was barefoot, wearing a torn linen skirt and silk blouse, and had numerous scratches on her arms, legs, and face.

"They broke her leg," Michael growled. "This is Cora Smith from San Antonio, Texas."

"Are you all right?" Paul asked, considering both of their appearances. They looked starved and dehydrated.

"Yeah." Michael was wearing a nice pair of dress pants, or had been. They were grungy and torn, and his cotton shirt was stained and exhibiting fresh tears. He was wearing sneakers at least, not dress shoes. But boots would have been better.

Paul had envisioned a similar scenario to the hostage situation on his and Allan's last mission—the captives malnourished and dehydrated. He hadn't expected the woman to be so injured.

"Were the two of you together when they grabbed you?" Hunter asked, and Paul knew he was trying to learn if Michael had made friends with her, or if it was just a random kidnapping.

"Yes," Michael said.

"No," Cora growled.

The guys smiled.

Their injuries healed more quickly than humans, so hers had to be very recent. "I'll get something to splint her leg."

Hunter was already pulling out his med pack. When Paul returned, Hunter had finished taking care of Michael's and Cora's cuts. They had to keep her quiet on the trek, so Hunter gave her a shot for the pain.

Paul had found a couple of straight and sturdy tree branches to splint her leg, while Allan got Cora to drink and eat a little. Hunter shared his extra rations with Michael.

"So what happened?" Hunter asked as he helped Bjornolf hold Cora still while Paul and Finn started to set her leg.

Michael ran a wet cloth over her face to cool her down. "She came to the art gallery to check out her competition."

"I did not," she gritted out, scowling.

"Okay, so she says she stepped into the gallery to talk

to the owner about carrying her work. Then when it was closing time, we headed out at the same time, and we were both grabbed," Michael said. "They thought I was famous and she was my girlfriend."

She rolled her eyes.

"So you're a painter too?" Hunter asked, and Paul knew the ploy. Hunter was trying to get her mind off her leg.

"Landscapes."

"Wolves," Michael said. "I know *my* competition."

Her eyes widened a bit, then she narrowed them. "And landscapes."

"With wolves."

Despite the dire situation, the guys were smiling.

"How are you doing as a wolf?" Hunter asked Michael.

"I'm fighting it."

"Maybe he should run as a wolf," Paul suggested. "We'll carry his clothes."

"He's newly turned?" Cora managed to get out, looking aghast.

Paul assumed she wasn't then. Which was a good thing.

"What about you?" Hunter asked.

"Royal."

Which meant her *lupus garou* ancestry went so far back that she could control when she shifted any time of the year.

"Good," Hunter said.

When Paul and Finn tightened the splint, her cheeks drained of color, her eyes rolled into the back of her head, and she was out.

Everyone was silent while Paul and Finn finished strapping her into the makeshift splint.

"She's okay, isn't she?" Michael asked, concerned.

"Yeah, just passed out. Better for her until the pain-killer kicks in," Paul said. "Maybe you should run as a wolf. You can use my field pack for your clothes." He wasn't used to being around newly turned wolves, so he waited for Hunter's take on it.

"Yeah, Michael, why don't you do that?" Hunter asked.

Michael looked down at Cora, then acquiesced, quickly stripping and shoving his clothes into Paul's bag. "Be careful with her, will you?"

"Yeah, you know we will." Bjornolf gathered her in his arms.

Michael shifted into his gray wolf form and they headed out.

The trek was hot, buggy, and humid, and tropical birds sang in the jungle high above in the canopy as the team made their way to the quickest point where they could be helicoptered out.

They remained quiet, Paul and the others providing protection as they made their way through the jungle. They took turns carrying Cora and stopped to rest a few hours from the kidnappers' campsite. Even Michael had shifted after hours of hiking, dressed, and carried her for a couple of hours. Cora had woken a few times, gritted her teeth, and passed out again, but despite the pain medication, she moaned from time to time. And had been irritated at herself for doing so.

Paul and the others were dying to know more about

the woman, but for now, they had to keep quiet and keep moving.

They'd avoided any jungle villages, trying to keep from attracting anyone's attention, afraid word would get back to someone that the hostages had escaped and were headed this way. They hadn't encountered any predators of the two-legged variety, but when they crossed a stream and saw cliffs ahead, Paul felt an eerie chill sweep up his spine. He knew if Hunter had led them here, it was the quickest way to the landing site. They had no choice but to make the climb.

Since everyone had recently taken a turn carrying Cora but Paul, he would carry her on his back. Michael would be beside him on the climb, and the rest of the team would hurry to the top and provide cover. Not that anyone was able to hurry in this heat and humidity.

As soon as they started the climb, Paul felt this was too much like the last time. He fought replaying the last scenario, telling himself he'd be to the top in no time, that no one would see them or begin shooting at them.

It was different this time, he reminded himself. They had a hell of a lot more firepower than when he and Allan had freed the college students. And all of the team members were trained in combat, unlike the students.

Yet, because Cora was injured and unable to climb out on her own, the scenario was too similar to the last time. Michael was right beside him if he needed to grab Cora. Paul's skin was sweaty, but despite the heat and humidity of the jungle, and the heat of Cora's body, Paul felt ice-cold.

Then from the jungle across the stream, shouts ripped

through the thick, humid air, sounds he'd hoped he wouldn't hear on this trip. He was maybe fifteen feet from the top of the cliff, but no matter how much he told himself he had to move faster, with Cora's weight and the fear of making a fatal misstep while climbing, he couldn't ascend any quicker.

As soon as the deadly pops of gunfire filled the air, sounding like firecrackers, Paul knew he was once again in a bad place. "Go," Paul gritted out. "Get up top and find cover."

Michael wasn't really helping, and with him hanging on the cliff beside Paul, he was every bit as much of a target as Paul and Cora were. Paul's mission was to get Cora to the top, not to worry about anything else. If he worried about Michael…

He couldn't help thinking how this could end badly though. And he couldn't help thinking about Lori and how she'd tried so valiantly to be brave for him when she felt anything but.

Michael was near the top when Bjornolf and Allan helped pull him to safety, pushing him behind them while they continued to shoot at the rebels.

Rounds were pinging off the cliff face all around Paul, way too damned close. One nicked his cheek. He growled and looked up, realizing he was about to reach the cliff's edge and praying Cora hadn't been hit. He wouldn't know until they made it to the top whether she was all right or had been injured.

Then strong arms, Bjornolf's and Allan's, were pulling him up and over the cliff's edge, out of the gunfire's path.

Bjornolf quickly untied Cora from Paul's back and

cursed. Paul felt cold all over as he turned, fearing the worst—Cora had been shot and was dead.

The men weren't looking at her. They were crouched around him, appearing concerned.

"Why don't you roll over and lie on your belly," Hunter said. "You'll be all right, Paul. You've got a pack to lead now and a wolf mate to get back to."

"Cora," Paul said, not understanding what the trouble was.

"She's fine," Bjornolf said, sounding relieved to an extent, but he was still tense. "They didn't hit her."

"*You've* been hit, Paul. Minor scratch." Hunter pulled out his med pack, while Finn sliced open the back leg of Paul's pants.

Then Hunter hurried to dress and bandage Paul's leg wound while Bjornolf and Allan watched for any more surprise attacks. Michael was seeing to Cora, who was still passed out.

Paul hadn't even felt the bullet hit him, which wasn't all that unusual. The shock, adrenaline, nerves severed, all of that could numb the feeling. At least he hadn't felt anything until he saw the bloody mess, and Hunter poured antiseptic on the wound, which stung to hell and back. Minor scratch, his ass. But he appreciated the guys acting like it was no big deal.

Even though he knew that they realized it was a big deal. Not only had he suffered some blood loss, but any open wound in the jungle, no matter how minor, could become infected. At least with Cora's injury, the broken bone in her leg hadn't torn through the skin.

"So you think there's something there for you to

build on with Cora?" Paul asked, trying to get *his* mind off his injury.

Michael frowned as he cradled her in his arms. "She was pissed to high heaven that the rebels took her hostage too, thinking she was my girlfriend." Then he smiled a little. "I wouldn't mind, really."

The guys chuckled.

"I've seen her artwork. And she's really good. But I don't think she likes that I'm so newly turned."

Paul glanced at Hunter. He saw the look of speculation on his face. If he could encourage the two wolves to hook up, he'd have a problem solved. Watching out for a newly turned wolf was a job. Someone in the pack always had to do it.

After they finished bandaging Paul, who was feeling the burning pain now, they headed out again.

They had two days of vigorous hiking left to reach the pick-up zone, but Paul was slowing the team down. Carrying Cora out was one thing. Michael couldn't help. He had to run as a wolf all day because he was having trouble with the pull of the full moon. And two of the men had to assist Paul.

"Leave me behind," Paul said as they had to take another damnable break because of him. "Get her out of here and come back for me later."

The guys frowned at him. Cora was sleeping again, which was the best thing for her. Paul was in agony, every step killing him, and they only had one teammate ready for an attack. It was a recipe for a disaster, and more than anything, Paul wanted Cora evacuated to get medical treatment pronto.

"Are you kidding?" Allan said. "My mother and

sister would never speak to me again. Lori would kill me. Emma would put a curse on me. If you stay, I stay. Lot safer that way. And you're not talking me out of it."

"We stay together," Hunter said, glancing at the rest of the team.

That was what Paul loved about Hunter's way of doing business. He ultimately made the decisions, but he was always open to everyone's suggestions. That's just how he wanted to lead the pack with Lori.

"Hunter and Allan are damn right, Paul. You saved the woman's life. We're not leaving you," Bjornolf said.

Finn agreed. "We leave no one behind."

Still a wolf, Michael growled and shook his head.

Paul was glad they hadn't wanted to, in truth, but he hated how much he was holding up the mission. They took turns getting some sleep and pulling guard duty, then headed out again.

The men had been worried about Cora. She had been running a fever, but Paul heard the relief in their voices when it abated on the last day of their journey. Michael had been able to stay in his human form the whole day too. They'd only had one further skirmish—no injuries on their side—before they reached the landing zone, called in the helicopter, and all made it out of there in one piece.

Paul heard Hunter telling Wes Caruthers, his police officer who'd stayed in São Paulo, that they'd rescued Michael and to go home.

Now *Paul* was fighting a fever, and he felt disoriented and sicker than a wolf.

Allan finally got a call through to Lori as he cast a

worried look at Paul, though he smiled at him when he caught his eye. "We're all fine. Michael's got a few cuts and bruises and such, but he's healing on his own. His"—he paused and glanced at Cora, who was bundled up in blankets—"his friend, Cora Smith, also was taken hostage, and she has a broken leg. They'll have to re-break it to set it right if the bone has started to knit together.

"Paul has a bullet in his leg and it needs to come out, but otherwise, he's fine. Paul said to tell you he loves you. He'll be home soon. We'll be home after Hunter's doctor sees to him." He paused, raised his brows, and then grinned at Paul. "Hot damn. You go, girl. I'll let him know."

Paul was having a hell of a time following the gist of the conversation with the way he was burning up and chilled to the bone at the same time.

"Um," Allan said, "he's unable to talk right now. But we'll get on a flight for home as soon as we can. Call you later to let you know when we're coming in."

Chapter 19

LORI KNEW SOMETHING HAD GONE WRONG WHEN Allan called her instead of Paul. She let her grandma know to alert the rest of the pack. When she called Catherine to let her know her son—well, both sons—were coming home, Catherine said Allan had already called.

Together, the pack had bought a used ambulance at an affordable price. They thought it might come in handy if Rose needed a ride to the new clinic that Dr. Christine Holt had set up and outfitted. Or any other pack emergencies. Like this one. The ambulance was already stocked with all the first-aid equipment they should need. The vehicle had a lot of mileage, but when the pack brought in more money, they could eventually replace it. It was good having their own clinic for pack members.

Paul would probably kill her when they arrived at the airport to pick him up in an ambulance, but having an open wound in the jungle, she assumed he'd need quick medical attention—from their kind.

Their new doctor was so eager to have her first real, important medical case—wolf type, not strictly human, not to mention the prestige of working on one of their pack leaders—that she couldn't wait to get Paul to her clinic.

It was ten in the morning when Paul and Allan arrived

at Glacier Park International Airport. Emma was holding up a sign that said: Cunningham Pack. Lori was holding two dozen roses, one from each member of the pack.

When she saw Paul in the wheelchair, his face flushed with fever, she fought tears and rushed forward to greet him. Hopefully, Paul wouldn't be too upset with her for all the changes to the pack in the month and half that he'd been gone. But that was the way it would be, she decided, whenever he was away. Her pack. Her way.

When he was home, it was *their* pack.

"I missed you so much," he said and wrapped his arms around her, giving her a SEAL wolf's hearty hug.

"Oh, Paul, you're so hot," she said, worried about his fever and kissing his forehead, his cheeks, and then his lips.

He gave her the devilish smirk that said he hadn't lost his sense of humor. "I'm so glad you think so."

She chuckled. "Always." She held his hand while Allan pushed the wheelchair to the door.

All the members of their pack, new and old, were smiling at them. She suspected Paul didn't realize they were all wolves and part of their pack now.

"Welcome home," Catherine said with tears in her eyes, giving him a hug and kiss on the cheek, Rose and Emma doing the same afterward.

Paul was still fighting a fever but no longer feeling disoriented. He hated that he had to be pushed out in a wheelchair and couldn't walk under his own power. He could have, but he was still a little tipsy. The wound was infected and hurt like the devil. Lori was holding his hand with a firm grasp, as if she thought he might try to slip away. He loved the contact and

wished he could pull her into his lap and really kiss
her like he wanted.

When he had seen Lori with roses in hand—along
with Emma, Catherine, Rose, and maybe twenty other
people waiting for others to get off the plane—he was
so grateful to be home again. He realized then that this
really was home. Not just a place to drop by for a visit
to recuperate from a mission. It felt good, and he understood now how important Hunter's pack had become
for him, once he'd found a mate and truly settled down.

Paul and Lori's pack might even expand a bit more
if they found other wolves that would like to join. With
a *lupus garou* pack, all members would be family. It
wasn't just a community of them living in the same territory. So each had to fit in and contribute to the well-
being of the whole pack.

Lori leaned down and handed the flowers to Paul,
which made him smile. He loved her, the roses, everything. Her hugging and kissing had made him hard for
her. Even feeling like hell, he wanted to take her to bed
and renew their mated vows.

When he saw the ambulance parked just outside the
doors, he frowned.

Two EMTs quickly brought the ambulance gurney
out and Paul said, "What—"

"We're taking you to our new pack clinic. This is
Dr. Christine Holt, and her registered nurse, Allie
Wertheimer. They'll take care of you," Lori said, intro-
ducing them.

"This isn't necessary," Paul said, but Allan helped
them load him into the ambulance. That's when Paul
noticed that many of the people he'd seen waiting for

family or friends in the airport were standing around watching him. What the hell?

Didn't anyone have flights to catch, others to greet? He guessed it was like the scene of a crime or injury— there would always be onlookers who wanted to see what was going on. He just hoped no one would take a picture of him like this.

When he'd seen Emma proudly showing off the Cunningham pack sign and smiling warmly at him, he couldn't have been more touched. Of any of the members of his small pack, he believed she was the most pleased that he had taken it over. Maybe because he was mated to Lori, and now Emma didn't have to worry about putting curses on any wolf sniffing around Lori with interest.

A little girl came up and gave Lori a pink carnation, and then Lori climbed into the ambulance and gave the carnation to Paul. "From your pack members, the youngest to the oldest."

The doors were closed and the ambulance drove to the clinic.

Paul eyed the roses, his vision blurring a little with the fever. And his head was pounding. "What?" He knew he wasn't hearing her right.

"Twenty-four pack members. Teach you to leave me alone and in charge of the pack." She grinned and leaned down for another kiss.

Before Paul knew what had happened, he was in a room recovering from the surgery to remove the bullet and on antibiotics for the infection. Because of *lupus garous*' faster healing genetics, he would recover quicker than a human would, but even so, wolves didn't heal instanta-neously. What he hadn't expected, but should have, was that when he fully woke, he would have an audience of Lori, Emma, Catherine, Rose, and Allan.

They all smiled at him. He realized he had a ton of new houseplants in the room, and one vase holding a couple of dozen red roses and the one pink carnation. When he'd half awakened, he thought about what Lori had said to him before he was out. She'd commented about the pack members.

"How long has it been since the surgery?" He'd lost track of time, though he'd been up and about, limping, wanting to prove he was ready to go home, but the doctor had wanted to keep him there just a little bit longer.

"Five days," Lori said.

"I wasn't quite certain if I heard right. You said…we have a couple of new pack members?" Paul asked.

Everyone but Allan laughed.

Allan folded his arms. "This has to be a record for the fastest-growing *lupus garou* pack in the West. One little pack of six has increased to twenty-four."

"They're good people," Lori said. "They were tired of being lone wolves or small families without a pack."

"How did you solicit so many so quickly?" Paul couldn't believe it.

"We started a Facebook page for wolves only. Well, our kind only, not as in wolf lovers. It's a private group, by invitation only. We were looking for special skills, com-patibility with a pack, that sort of thing. All of us," Lori said, motioning to the rest of their original pack members, "interviewed them while you were in the jungle, and we said their membership was contingent on the alpha male leader's approval. But if you want to delegate that job to Allan since you're still under the weather…"

Paul looked at Allan to see if he wanted the job. As far as Paul was concerned, all he wanted to do was spend some quality time with Lori. He was all too happy to give Allan the opportunity to make a difference with the pack. Paul would always treasure the small core of family and friends that had made up the Cunningham pack for so many years. As to the rest, he knew, given time, he'd be just as pleased to have them here.

"You got it," Allan said, sounding a little more enthusiastic than Paul thought he would. He was relieved that Allan was eager to take on the job.

"I'll be glad to talk to our new pack members, welcome them, and get to know them." He smiled broadly. Paul hadn't even thought of it, but several of the ones standing around watching them at the airport were women who looked about Allan and Paul's age. Allan was going to really enjoy this "getting to know the pack members better" business.

Rose was looking so anxious to talk with him that Lori shooed the others out, saying Paul was going home today and should be ready to see everyone in a couple days.

Rose held back while Emma and Catherine kissed Paul.

Allan shook his hand, and then they all left.

Paul eyed Rose, who looked rather grim-faced.

"You found the father of the baby, and it's not good news, I take it," Paul guessed. "Have a seat, Rose, before you fall down. Everything is going to be all right."

Both Lori and Rose took seats.

"He's here. With the pack now," Rose said. "We learned he's...well, he's the brother to Tara, Widow Jean Baxter's son."

"So he wasn't just a loner. He must have come here to visit them." Which Paul gave him points for. "What is the trouble they're in?"

"There was a bank robbery—"

Paul narrowed his eyes.

"He didn't do it. He was framed. He rides a motor-cycle and someone stole his helmet when he was at a grocery store in the vicinity of the bank that was robbed. The pack he was with didn't believe he didn't do it. They said it was too much of coincidence that he suddenly came into money at the same time the bank was robbed."

"The bank robberies in western Montana."

"No, it was in Seattle. That's where they're from. As to the two bank robberies here, he was home with his mother and sister when the one occurred."

"So he could have been a copycat. Or someone else could have copied him."

Rose ground her teeth and looked furious with Paul.

"It could be everything you say it is," Paul said, not wanting to be bamboozled by some slick-talking wolf, "but I'm trying to look at this in a more objective way. He could have copied what the other man had done. And beyond that, his mother and sister could have vouched for him if his other pack wants his head and they're trying to save him. He didn't tell you what he'd done before he slept with you, did he?"

When she looked away from Paul, he frowned, suspecting the worst. "Did he?"

"I believe him when he says he's innocent!"

Paul couldn't believe it. He glanced at Lori to see her take on it.

"I didn't know anything about it until he returned, and Rose finally told me. He should be her mate if they can agree on it."

Paul glanced back at Rose, surprised she wouldn't agree to it. Or maybe Everett had refused.

Lori sighed. "Everett Johnston wants to be part of the pack, but he said he wouldn't stay if it caused you any trouble with the law or with his previous wolf pack."

Paul hadn't given any thought to how much trouble running a pack could be. The original members of their own small pack had been fine together all these years, and they'd never had this kind of difficulty before. He understood now what Hunter had to deal with in managing his own pack and respected him all the more.

"I'm leaving with him if he goes," Rose said, looking as though it was tearing her up inside to say so.

Hell, Paul only had her best interests at heart. No way could she be out on her own if Everett's former wolf pack wanted to terminate him, and Rose was left all alone with babies—

The doctor. They had a doctor. He had to thank Lori for having done such a great job with that. He asked Rose, "Did the doctor check you out?"

Rose nodded, tears welling up in her eyes, her lower lip trembling. She started to cry. "I'm going to have triplets."

Paul felt like a real heel. "Ahh, come here, Rose."

She joined him at the bed and he lifted his arms to give her a hug. She melted against him, her hot tears

soaking the front of his hospital gown. He would do anything for her, but he wouldn't risk her life or her babies'.

"If he's innocent of the bank robbery charges, we'll
prove who actually did it. Does your mother like him?"
It shouldn't matter, but Paul trusted Catherine's opinion because she was a lot more levelheaded than Rose
right now.

She nodded against his chest, still sniffling.

He'd never seen Rose so emotional. Was it due to the
pregnancy? He glanced at Lori as she smiled brightly
at him.

"Good. We'll...work it all out somehow," he reas-
sured Rose.

He wondered if he was in for the same emotional
turmoil when Lori got pregnant. Speaking of which, he
was ready to go home with his mate.

Lori said, "Come on, Rose. Your mom will be waiting for you."

"Thank you, Paul," Rose said, wiping her tears away.

He smiled at her. "You're my sister. I only want
what's best for you." He was afraid to mention the
triplets, in case that was what had upset her so much.
But he wanted her to know he was happy for her.
"Congratulations on the triplets. They'll be the first ones
born to the Cunningham pack in years. It's a real cause
to celebrate."

She swallowed hard and kissed him on the cheek.
Then Lori said, "I'll be right back." She wrapped her
arm around Rose's shoulders and walked her out of the
room, closing the door behind her.

Paul took the opportunity to get dressed. He felt much
better. His leg would be sore for a few days, and he

probably couldn't go running for that time, but he was ready for another form of exercise. Fully dressed in a fresh set of clothes—jean shorts, his palm-tree shirt that made him smile, and a pair of sandals—he was about ready to limp out of the room. He was trying hard not to show he was limping when Lori returned, pushing a wheelchair.

"I don't need that," he said with conviction.

"Doctor's orders. Now that we have one, we *all* have to listen to her."

He grunted and let Lori push him in the wheelchair out to his SUV.

"So I asked about what physical activity you can do—"

"No running, right?" he asked.

Lori helped him into the vehicle. He didn't need her help, but he'd humor his mate. Then the nurse joined them to take the wheelchair back inside.

"That's all I'm agreeing to," he said as he fastened his seat belt. "No running for a couple of days."

She laughed as she climbed into her seat, shut the door, and pulled out of the parking lot. "Grandma gave us the lake cottage as a wedding gift. It's ours. *All* ours."

"That's great news." He loved the lakeside cottage. "Good thing we like the colors we chose for the furniture and paint." Now he knew for certain Emma had been trying to get him and Lori together. He had to show his appreciation to her later. "I've got to get the painting Michael did of you from the Rappaports' cabin and hang it over the fireplace."

Lori shook her head. "While you were gone, we moved all your clothes over to the cabin and everyone said the painting had to hang over the mantel. Though I was thinking we should commission one of the two of us for that special spot."

"We could do that later. But for now, I'll enjoy seeing you sitting by the river as a wolf."

"Grandma said the reason she didn't answer my text about the furniture was that she wanted it to be our decision, if you had any decorating sense. Otherwise, she hoped I would prevail on what I wanted the most. Are you really all right after this last mission?"

"Yeah. We all got out safely this time." He rubbed Lori's back. "I missed you though."

She humphed. "As busy as you were, having the adventure of a lifetime?"

He smiled. "Yeah, I did. Every time we took a break, I thought of you."

"Allan told me you offered to stay behind. You felt you were holding the rest of them back because of your injury, and you wanted to make sure that they got Cora out all right," Lori said softly.

"We had to get her out."

She frowned at him. "And you! I told Allan that if he had come back without you..."

Paul chuckled. "Did he tell you he was going to stay with me and let the others get her to safety?"

"No. He just said if he'd left you behind, I would have killed him." Then she glanced at Paul and sighed. "And he was right. I've always wondered why you took off on your own when he was shot in Florida."

"To give the assassin someone else to track, in case he realized Allan had survived. Then I thought the assassin was headed for the Oregon coast. Just a hunch."

"You're good at that." She chewed her bottom lip, then asked, "You're not upset with having so many new pack members, are you? Not feeling a little overwhelmed?"

"Why? Are you?"

She shook her head. "I hoped you weren't just taking over because you thought there were so few of us."

He laughed.

"What about Rose's mate? What do you think we should do about him?"

"You've met him. What does your gut instinct tell you?"

"I think he's telling the truth. Catherine does too."

"Good. I respect your opinion and Catherine's. Both of you would only want the best for Rose. I'll make every effort to learn the truth and prove his innocence."

Lori breathed a sigh of relief. "Good."

"Anything else happen while I was gone that we need to discuss about the pack or otherwise?"

"Nothing else that needs your attention."

"Okay, good." He figured Rose's situation with Everett was enough of a problem for now. "I guess I need to get back to working on that list."

"Forget that!"

Paul eyed her with curiosity. "It's our place now, so if we still need to do some work around the cabin…"

Lori shook her head.

"I'll be perfectly fine in a couple of days." He wasn't about to be babied when he was healing just fine.

"We have a wolf pack now."

"I'm not asking the wolves in the pack to do work for—"

"You don't have to. They were so excited to be part

of the pack, wanting you to approve them, that we had picnics and swimming and work parties the first week you were gone." She parked at the cabin.

He couldn't believe it.

"See? Having a bigger pack was worth it."

"Hell, Lori," he said, getting out of the car. "You should have taken over the pack years ago."

She laughed, took his hand, and led him up to the deck. "Then I would have been fighting off all the hot male wolves who wanted to mate with me and help run the pack."

He smiled down at her. "I would have been fighting them all off."

Despite her objection, as soon as she unlocked the door, he swept her up in his arms, bumped the door closed with his hip, and turned to let her lock the door. Then he carried her into the bedroom, trying damn hard not to limp. He wanted her to believe he was completely healed and nothing was stopping him from the next thing on *his* list.

Oh my God, Lori loved Paul. He was the only wolf for her. No matter how much she hadn't wanted him to go, she'd made the most of her time and had actually loved being the pack leader while he was gone. Now she was even more thrilled for him to be home. She knew he was the right wolf for her because he seemed to admire everything she had done while he'd been away.

She'd told Allan about all the new pack members, but Allan had said she had to tell Paul all the good news on her own. She suspected Allan had worried a little that Paul wouldn't be happy about it. Or maybe he just thought that since she was the alpha she-wolf leader of the pack, it was her responsibility to tell her mate.

But now that they were in the privacy of their home, she had to tell Paul the news and hope he was happy with it.

"You know if we keep doing much more of this," he said as he carried her down the hall to her bedroom, "we could end up with some pups of our own."

"Well, um, it already has…happened. I think it was the storm that did it."

Paul stared at Lori and she hoped it was good news for him, because she was thrilled.

"You're saying…?"

She grinned. "You're going to be an old papa wolf."

"Hell, Lori, when did you know?"

"When you were on the mission. I couldn't get hold of you. Then I couldn't talk to you right afterward because you'd been injured and were so out of it. And well, I wasn't sure about doing it even now because I wanted to really celebrate that you're home, more than anything."

Grinning, he kissed her soundly. "The storm had *nothing* to do with it."

She laughed.

Paul had reacted just the way she had hoped he would—accepting, admiring, and accommodating.

He dumped her on the bed, and she thought it was because it hurt too much for him to bend down, but she had every intention of riding him so he wouldn't have to put pressure on his injured leg. He yanked off his shirt, and she kicked off her sandals. Then she was on her knees on the bed, unfastening his belt and unzipping his zipper. He was already full to bursting.

She glanced up at him. "It looks like you're eager to see me."

"Hell, yeah."

She loved his enthusiasm and intended to help him off with his pants, forgetting about his sandals. "Sit," she said, and he gave her a cute raised-brow look. But she wasn't having him make love to her while he was silently suffering. She wanted to make this as easy for him as possible so they could both enjoy the connection between them again.

He sat down on the bed and she pulled one sandal off, then the other, then his jeans shorts and boxers.

"Just the way I like you," she said when he was completely naked. Then she encouraged him to lie down.

"Ditto here," he said, eyeing her tank top and shorts.

She moved his legs apart, careful not to hurt his wounded leg, and took a moment to admire his whole, hot, naked body.

He grinned at her as his erection jerked from her perusal.

"Hmm," she said, then slid her body over his, rubbing her soft shirt against his hard erection. He ran his fingers through her hair. She wanted to smell him, feel every bit of him, and taste him as she licked a nipple, then kissed his mouth.

She pressed her breasts against his chest while she slipped her hands between them and unzipped her shorts, the whole time rubbing against him. His eyes had taken on a lustful cast.

She loved when he looked at her like that, the way his body smelled so sexy, a wolf's way of ensuring that her own pheromones were kick-started. Not that she hadn't been wanting this from the moment she had seen him and his wolfish smile at the airport.

"Lori," he said, her name sounding like he was both in agony and in ecstasy.

She was afraid he was in pain, so she was ready to make love to him in more of a rush and then let him rest. But he reached up and tugged at her shirt. She pulled it over her head, and then she slipped off her panties. In a hurry, she unfastened her bra and threw it aside. She was going to line herself up and ride him, but he pulled her closer and began stroking her between the legs as if it didn't matter that he was hurting, as long as she was pleasured.

She arched back as his fingers connected with her nub, his other hand on her thigh, keeping her in place. He continued to stroke her as she closed her eyes and savored the feel of his touch on her aroused flesh.

She groaned and spread herself further, wanting him inside her now, but when he pushed a finger between her feminine folds, she about came unglued. She rode on top of his finger, wanting more, wanting to find the peak. He began to stroke her harder, then softer and faster, watching the way she reacted, moving slower, then faster, then nearly there, slowing down and...

Crying out, she exclaimed, "Holy cow, Paul!" as the need and pure enjoyment rushed through her—her mate's gift to her.

"Wolf," he said.

She laughed.

He quickly seated her on his rigid cock, and she began to rock against him, wanting him so badly, as she had every minute of every day that he'd been gone. She hoped he wouldn't tire of making love to her because she had every intention of doing this every chance they got.

"Beautiful," he said as she rose up on his cock and slid back down it, her body soft, tan, and stunning. He'd had to keep his mind on business while he was in the jungle, but on the way home, all he'd thought of was making love to his mate.

He loved her.

She rode him, clenching her inner muscles around him, her heart pounding, her skin lightly moist with perspiration, her nipples dark and rigid, just beautiful.

He slid his hand between her legs as she rose again and coaxed another climax out of her. She looked wrung out, like she could collapse on top of him and cuddle for hours, but he wasn't finished with her yet. He wanted her to know nothing would stop him from pleasuring her, so he turned her over on her back, careful to remain seated deep inside her, and continued to pump into her. Her hands slid up his chest, her thumbs caressing his sensitive nipples, and he moaned with her touch.

How he'd missed this—breathing in her sweet, feminine, wolfish, and very sexy scent, touching her soft body, and feeling them joined. He leaned down and took one of her nipples in his mouth, tugging gently with his lips, rolling his tongue around one nipple and then the other. Her hands combed through his hair, and then he began to thrust harder, feeling the end coming, and wanting it to last forever.

With a final push to reach that end, he came deep inside her. He was completely sated, and yet not. He had every intention of waking her for more after they slept for a while.

Curled up around her, his loving and lovely wolf mate, he couldn't imagine why he had waited this long. He realized then he should never have let her avoid him when he'd returned home for the last couple of years.

"Do you have any regrets?" Paul asked her as they cuddled together.

"Only that I didn't insist we do this years ago," she said.

He loved the way she'd taken over the pack and increased their numbers, and he knew without a doubt they were going to be better off for it.

But then she said, "Be nice to Everett Johnston, by the way. Rose needs him for her mate."

Paul grunted. Being nice to the man wasn't on the agenda.

Chapter 20

TWO WEEKS LATER, WHEN PAUL WAS FEELING A HUN-
dred percent, Lori and he got out of bed and dressed
late in the morning. Lori's eyes sparkled with impish
delight, and Paul knew she had some kind of scheme
in mind. "I've been waiting for things to settle down a
bit, but I have to take you out for your bachelor lunch
or dinner. We sort of forgot that part of the honey-do
bachelor auction."

"I'm no longer a bachelor," Paul said, interested, "but
what did you have in mind?" This was so different from
when he usually came home from a mission. He loved
being with Lori, with a pack.

"Well, how would you like something Italian?"

"The Italian restaurant, Fame del Lupo, owned by our
own pack members?" He'd heard about it when he was
waiting to be released from the clinic.

"That's the one. We're all eating there from time to
time to get their business off to a good start."

"Good food?"

"The best. We'll have a late lunch there and then I
need to teach some classes."

"I'm ready."

"Do you know what their name means?"

"*Lupo*, something to do with wolf?"

"'Wolfish appetite' in Italian."

"Love it."

—◠◠◠—

When they walked into the brand-new restaurant, Italian songs of *amore* were playing overhead. Statues of curly-headed angels and paintings of the Leaning Tower of Pisa, the Pantheon, Pompeii, the canals of Venice, and the vineyards of Italy decorated the walls. The aroma of Italian seasonings, wines, and spicy sausage scented the air.

The couple that owned the place were so pleased to have the pack leaders eat there that they greeted them personally. Fred Garafalo and his wife, Ginny, gave them the special table that would be reserved for them anytime they wished to eat there, overlooking a small patio garden.

Two of the waitresses serving at other tables smiled at Paul and Lori, and he realized that pack-run businesses would help to provide employment for their pack members. Something that Lori could also use in her dojo and Rose in her shop. Lori had done a super job while he'd been gone.

Paul felt like royalty as the Garafalos fawned over them while he and Lori took their seats, then hurried off to fetch Italian rolls, wine, and salad.

Nearly everyone eating there was a wolf. A woman and her twin girls were eating pizza with a lone male wolf who was checking out the pack. He bowed his head a little at Paul and Lori to acknowledge them. Even Emma was sitting with a couple of friends at a booth.

The Garafalos set a basket of buttered rolls and a large glass bowl filled with salad on the table, then returned with wine for Paul and glasses of water and left them in peace.

Paul switched his attention to Lori. "I can't believe how much you have done for the pack while I was away."

"Teach you to leave me in charge of it in your absence. But I think everyone's happy. Oh, there will be some discontent. There always is. But generally speaking, everyone's thrilled to be here."

They ordered, finished their rolls and salad, and before long, the lasagna was served.

"I thought we'd go to the movies tonight. I know you want to speak with Everett Johnston first. Then when you're done with that business, we could have a movie date."

"The last time I had a movie date with you, I learned Rose was pregnant."

"Right. So we'll have a nice movie this time, no interruptions, and cuddle. That will be your bachelor auction date. After that, no more bachelor stuff."

"I was truly through with the bachelor business years ago. All I ever needed was you."

She drank some of her water. "You need to go away more so you'll return and keep saying such nice things to me."

"I have no intention of going anywhere else anytime soon. If I did, our pack could explode until it was as big as the population of the state of Montana."

She laughed.

They finished their plates of lasagna, and Lori knew she'd eaten way too much.

"Cuddling at the movie might even lead to something more tonight," Paul said, setting his plate aside.

"I'm counting on it."

When they went to pay for the meal, the owners held

up their hands, saying no. "Our treat. We are happy to be here."

"Okay this time, but next time we pay," Paul said. He escorted Lori outside and gave her another hug. "I can't believe it. We're going to have our own pup or more."

"Are you happy about it?"

"Sure as hell am. Couldn't be happier." He gave her another hug and kiss. "The pack is going to be too big before long."

"Never."

"So what's playing at the theater tonight?" Paul asked as he drove them back to the cabin.

"Action, adventure, fighting, car chases, killing, that sort of thing. Strictly silly humor. An animated feature. Or a romance."

"What do you want to watch?"

"The romance. You've had enough violence to deal with lately."

"Sounds good to me. Have you got any more classes to give today?"

"I do. So I'll meet you at the cabin in a couple of hours."

"All right."

When they reached the cabin, before she left in her car, with one last parting kiss, she reminded him, "Be nice to Everett. I like him. And Rose loves him."

"We'll see." Paul kissed her, wanting to forgo meeting with Everett and the movie, and take her back to bed with him.

Instead, he headed inside while she drove off. Everett was there promptly at three, which immediately made a good impression on Paul.

He had to learn what he could about Everett and the bind he was in. Paul sure hoped that Catherine, Lori, and Rose's faith in the man was warranted.

He was blond, tall, and muscular, and Paul could see how the man could have appealed to Rose. He wondered what kind of work Everett did.

"You want a cup of coffee?" Paul asked, motioning with a mug.

"No, thanks." Everett took a seat in one of the chairs while Paul got a cup of coffee and rejoined him. He hadn't cared about the coffee as much as he wanted to put Everett at ease. He didn't want to give the man the impression he was out for blood. Not when Rose seemed to really care about him.

"First, what do you do for a living?"

"Build log cabins. I was building them in Seattle. I... was with a gray wolf pack there."

"Okay, so what's the deal with the bank robbery?"

"Well...like I told Rose, I didn't do it. I have some extra money, sure, because I've been doing some honey-do projects on my own. Lots of older women need some trim work or repairs done that are too small for most builders. But the women and sometimes older couples, or really just anyone who doesn't have the skills, need the help. Like I told Rose and the others, I was at the wrong place at the wrong time. My motorcycle helmet was stolen, used in the bank robbery, and then tossed later."

"How did anyone know it was yours?"

"My helmet had a picture of a gray wolf baring its teeth on it. One of my pack members works at that bank and saw it and knew it was mine. Why in the hell would

I wear a helmet that was so recognizable to commit a bank robbery?"

Paul sipped some of his coffee. "Would-be robbers can pull some pretty stupid stunts. The police caught a guy pulling a ski mask over his face before he held up a convenience store. Only the camera caught him on film while he was in one of the aisles *before* he put on the ski mask. Another case was a man trying to rob the money from an electronics store that had more than ten security cameras going. They had his picture from every angle. In another case, a man tried to steal from a mirror store."

"Mirror store?"

"Yeah. He thought there would be money left overnight in the store. The only things there, other than mirrors, were two Doberman pinschers. He was terrified of dogs and ended up calling the police from inside the store to come and rescue him."

Everett smiled.

"The police, thinking that the man was dangerous, sent in a SWAT team, but when they realized he was just an idiot, they laughed as they rescued him and hauled him off for booking."

Everett laughed. "Yeah, I get your point."

"I'll have some men look into this. About the time you came here and were seeing Rose, there was a bank robbery."

Everett's eyes widened.

"He was wearing a motorcycle helmet."

"Not me. After that happened, I stopped riding my bike. At least for the time being."

"You don't have to ride a bike to have a helmet with you." Which made Paul wonder if the motorcycle bandit even rode a bike. "If someone was using that MO and it was successful, they'd continue to use it. Were you the same build as the robber?"

"You know how it is. If you always wear something and others saw that identifier from a distance, they'd think it was you. Doesn't matter if they don't see the face, or the person doesn't have the same build as you. Anyway, this guy wore blue jeans, like I always wear. He wore work boots like I always wear—the protective steel-toe kind while I'm working on the job. A lot of men wear jeans and heavy boots out there. So, no, it wasn't me, but it could have 'looked' like me."

Paul could see the logic in that. "So one of your wolf pack members, the one working at the bank, believed it was you?"

"I'd been in the bank earlier. My scent was recent. She didn't get close to the guy when he was armed and potentially dangerous. I leaned on that same counter. Saw the same clerk. So it was a given. Circumstantial. She was wrong."

"No coincidence that you were at a bank that had been robbed, and then another was robbed where the guy used the same MO?"

"Copycat? Hell, I don't know. The other man had robbed six banks in the Seattle area."

"Do you have alibis for them? Any of them?"

"For four of them."

"Witnesses?"

"I was up working on a log cabin three of the times. So it couldn't have been me. I was visiting my mother and sister another time. But you probably won't believe anything they say."

Paul nodded. "I'll have it looked into. What about this situation with Rose? You know she's pregnant, right? And she's having triplets?"

Everett looked a little pale. "Triplets?"

"And that you had sex with her."

"Not all the way."

"Well, here's the thing. Your 'almost sex' with Rose produced triplets. Rose is like a sister to me. I don't want to force her into anything she doesn't want. But if the two of you care for each other enough, we can clear your name with regard to the bank robbery here in town, and if you're both willing, you can stay with the pack. I'll settle things with your last pack. As long as I know you're innocent. So that brings us back to Rose. What are your intentions toward her?"

"I wouldn't have done that with her, given my current situation. I wanted to see more of her. I wanted to make sure my mother and sister were all right. But I couldn't quit thinking about Rose."

"That's a good start."

"I only left because I knew the other wolf pack would be looking for me. I was trying to clear my name. I had to talk to the crew I was working with, to ensure they could vouch for the times I was working with them on the job sites when the bank robberies went down. I didn't want Rose involved in this. She didn't tell me we were having triplets."

No wonder the guy looked pale. Paul almost felt sympathetic for him. Except that Everett had left Rose in a bind. And she really seemed hung up on the guy. Paul just hoped he truly felt the same way about her.

"I have an obligation to Rose," Everett said. "I don't shirk my responsibilities."

"There's got to be a hell of a lot more to it than just an obligation." Paul's phone vibrated again. Rose. "Do you mind if I take this?"

"Go ahead." Everett rose to leave.

"You can stay. This will only take a second." Paul said, "Yeah, Rose?" He watched as Everett's worried expression brightened a little, and he realized just how much the guy did care for her.

"You're not killing him, are you?"

Paul smiled. "No, he's allowed to live for now."

She sighed audibly. "Well, when you're through with him, he needs to take me to see the doctor."

"Are you all right?"

"Yes, it's just the usual visit."

"Okay. You should have told him about the triplets. It was a good thing he was sitting down when I gave him the news. I thought he already knew." Another call was coming through. "I've got another call. I'll tell him to head on over there."

"How was he about the news?"

"He won't shirk his responsibilities—"

"Tell her I love her and I'm thrilled we're having… uh, triplets."

Paul smiled. Everett didn't look thrilled, rather a little panicked. "Did you hear that, Rose? He's thrilled."

She started crying again. "Okay. Thanks, Paul. You're the best."

"Talk to you later." He picked up the other call. "Yeah, Allan, what's—"

"I've been shot," Allan gritted out.

Chapter 21

ALLAN FELT LIKE SHIT. HIS SIDE WAS HURTING LIKE hell, and he couldn't believe he'd fallen into the trap, which was plain stupid after all the training he'd had. Go to the jungle, return unscathed, and get shot by a damned bank robber. Or…a man who was an accessory to the crime.

"Hunter," he said, trying to catch his breath. He was afraid he was dying.

"What? Wait, where the hell are you?" Paul asked.

"Near the jumping cliffs on Flathead," Allan croaked out.

"On my way."

"He's still…out there, well, gone, but afraid might return."

"The shooter?"

"Bank robber," Allan said, stumbling away from the place he'd been shot. The guy had driven off on his motorcycle in a panic, and the hunter had left in his pickup.

"Everett's with me. We're coming. Just grabbing my Glock, a couple of throwing knives, and the medical kit."

Allan heard the SUV doors open and shut, and the engine roar to life. "He drove off but might return. To finish…me. The hunter." He didn't think the motorcycle guy had it in him. Which is why the hunter ambushed him as Allan followed the bank robber into the woods.

"We're on our way. Twenty minutes, max." Paul sounded like he was ready to kill the bastards.

Allan wished *he* could. "Wolves."

"What? Damn it. Not the Cooper brothers."

"Jerome was with him. I always…thought he was the sneaky one. Quiet."

"Allan's been shot," Everett said to someone. "Where?"

Allan listened to the conversation, glad wolves had such good hearing.

Paul gave Everett the location.

"The EMTs are new to town. They don't know where it is. I'll call Lori," Everett said.

Allan didn't like hearing that bit of news.

"She'll know the location." Paul said to Allan, "Everett's sending the EMTs, and I've got my medical field pack and weapons as we speak."

"Can't call police."

"No, not if they're wolves. Hang in there, buddy."

"Moving. In case they come back." The pain was so bad that Allan felt his vision blackening twice before he moved away from the place near his vehicle where he'd collapsed.

Everett said to Paul, "Got hold of Lori. She's going with them to show them where Allan is."

Paul repeated the information to Allan.

"'K."

"Don't you dare die on me, Allan, damn it."

Allan smiled.

"You hear me?"

"Pack leader order?"

"It sure as hell is."

"'K."

—⁓—

Paul was sick with worry over Allan's condition. He'd
never heard him sound so bad. Normally it would have
taken Paul forty-five minutes to an hour to get there,
but he was moving like a wolf on a hunt and hoped the
police wouldn't stop him. In a case like this, had it been
a human, Paul would have reported it to the police and
tried to get there first, but a wolf?

"Don't hang up on me," he told Allan.

"Won't."

Everett wisely didn't say anything, but Paul knew he
wanted to prove himself, to show he could be a valuable
member of the pack. Which meant if he wasn't trained
like they were, he could get himself killed. And with
Rose having triplets?

"No heroics," Paul said to Everett.

"I know how to shoot a gun and use a knife. I wasn't
born yesterday."

"Good. I'm serious though. No heroics. I need you
and Allan alive."

Everett was already a valuable attribute, not waiting
for direction and figuring out Lori needed to be there
to guide the EMTs to the location since she had lived
in the area all her life. And he'd called Rose to let her
know he couldn't get her to her doctor's appointment.
He'd even called Catherine to let her know about her
son's emergency.

"How bad is it?" Everett asked.

"Not good. Allan would say it was a flesh wound if it
was." Paul turned onto a dirt road. "Almost there. Allan,
you still with me?"

"Yeah," he grunted out. "But I heard a vehicle returning."

"Mine?"

"Hunter's."

"The hunter? You mean the guy we had arrested for illegally shooting the elk?"

"Yeah."

"He's not a wolf."

"Hunter's spray, probably. Jerome's with him at least. Heard voices. All four doors opened, slammed shut."

Hell, more than just the hunter and Jerome then. "What happened?"

"I was at the bank." Allan's voice was weaker than Paul would have liked.

"Bank robbery?"

"Yeah. Couldn't call police. Jerome involved."

"Okay, gotcha."

"Followed him. Robber. Didn't…think he saw me."

"But he did?" Paul wished to hell Allan hadn't gone after the guy on his own.

"Must have. Set trap."

"We're here, Allan. You should have called me."

"Wasn't planning to get…caught."

"I smell your vehicle and the hunter's."

"I'm…to the southeast of my car."

Paul parked his vehicle and got out while Everett grabbed the med pack. Paul gave him a spare Glock he had in his glove compartment. Then the two headed for the vehicles, saw Allan's window shot out and blood on the seat, and found a blood trail that turned Paul's stomach.

"Jerome was the bank robber?"

"Diversion. Lookout."

The other men could follow Allan's blood trail and scent just as easily.

"Hell," Allan said.

His heart drumming, Paul feared the worst.

Shots suddenly fired. A wolf howled and snarled.

Hell and damnation! Lori?

Paul raced toward the sound of the shots and the growling. "Allan, if you can hear me, I'm sending Everett your way." He motioned for Everett to follow the blood trail to see to Allan and protect him. Everett gave a slight nod in acknowledgment, and Paul raced after the man who intended to shoot Lori.

"Shoot her!" a man yelled out. The hunter?

Paul's damn heart was already beating so fast he thought it would explode.

"She bit my damned arm!"

"Go after her!" Dusty yelled out.

Glad she was biting and not injured yet, Paul listened for signs of where everyone was.

Damn, how many of them were here? The whole lot of them, he assumed. They were headed for the cliffs next to Flathead Lake. There was a lower ledge, about a thirty-five-foot drop into the water, where locals and visitors liked to jump. But higher up, it could be dangerous if Lori were pushed and fell onto the rocks instead.

Paul heard her growling in the trees up ahead. She was close to the cliffs.

Then he saw Jerome taking aim, and Paul aimed his own weapon and fired. The guy ducked or fell, Paul couldn't be sure. But at the same instant, another shot rang out, and that one clipped his arm. What the hell?

He swung around but didn't see anyone through the trees. As he dove for cover, he couldn't see Lori either. He moved at a crouch through the underbrush, trying to get closer to where the hunter had been.

A gunshot sounded off in the distance. And then another. Near Allan, Paul assumed. He sure as hell hoped Everett had killed someone and not the other way around.

And then he heard low growling. Lori.

He raced to the location, saw a wolf, and recognized Dusty backing her up against the edge of the cliffs. Paul aimed to shoot Dusty, but another wolf slammed into him from the side, and he dropped the gun.

Damn it! With snarling teeth bared at him, Paul was having a devil of a time keeping the dark brown wolf from taking a bite out of him. He could smell Howard's scent and recognized him like he did the others from years earlier.

With a tight grip on the wolf's head, Paul rolled with him until they were at the cliff's edge. Figuring out what was next, Howard tried to get free, but Paul was determined to end this now with the brothers. He swung his leg and kicked the wolf in the side as hard as he could. Howard yelped as he fell over the edge of the cliff. If he was lucky, he'd only break a few bones.

But Paul's concern was Dusty and Lori for now.

Paul had lost his Glock, but rather than go back for it, he stripped and shifted, right as Dusty charged Lori. To avoid his snapping jaws, she backed up too far, too quickly, and slipped off the edge of the cliff.

Paul's heart nearly stopped beating. If he had been in his human form, he would have cried out her name. Instead, he growled so ferociously as he dove for Dusty

that the other wolf panicked, head down, tail tucked
between his legs.

It was too late for Dusty to respond. Paul tackled him
and tore into him viciously, killing him within seconds.
Paul had no time to lose. He released the dead wolf and
hurried to the cliff's edge.

Lori was lying on the ledge used for jumping into the
lake, not moving. But she was still in her wolf form. She
wasn't dead. Stunned maybe. Hurt.

Howard was floating in the water below, facedown,
human now. Dead.

Paul couldn't climb down to reach her without
being in his human form. He shifted and threw on his
clothes. Trying not to kill himself in his rush to get to
Lori, he finally reached her and felt for a pulse at her
neck. "Lori…"

She shifted, her eyelids fluttering. Then they opened
quickly. "Allan."

"I don't know his condition. I've got to get you out of
here. What hurts?" Paul tugged off his shirt.

"Bruised. I think the fall knocked me out, but I don't
feel like anything's broken."

"The baby?" he asked, helping her into his shirt.

She smiled. "I think it's too little to have
been affected."

But he wasn't smiling. If the brothers hadn't been
dead already…

"Hey!" Everett called from up above. His right
arm was bloodied and dangling at his side. "Are you
all right?"

"We're okay. Allan?" Paul asked, his heart
still thundering.

"EMTs have got him."

"What about you?"

"I had to check on you first. Is Lori all right?"

"Yeah," Lori said, and Paul helped her to stand, then lifted her in his arms.

"Are you sure you're all right?" Paul asked, concerned about the way his mate was trembling.

"Shaken."

"We're coming. What happened to the other guys? Jerome, was he with them? They better look worse than you," Paul growled.

Everett smiled a little. "Yeah. Allan said the two I killed were Jerome and the hunter you turned in for illegally hunting elk."

"Somebody call the police?" Paul asked.

"Just waiting for you to give the go-ahead."

Paul really liked Everett. He was a team player. "Enough of us have been shot to prove they were the bad guys and, well, the bank money is in their vehicle, right?"

"Hopefully. Unless the motorcycle guy took off with it."

"Hell." Paul shook his head. "Where are your clothes?" he asked Lori, needing to get her back to the SUV.

Everett walked with them until they reached her clothes. "I'll head down to the ambulance. Feeling a little woozy," he said.

"Be there in a minute." Paul helped Lori dress. "Are you sure you're all right?"

"Yeah, I am. But you've been wounded."

"Nicked. Flesh wound." He helped her stand and they headed for the vehicles.

The EMTs were taking care of Everett when they
reached the ambulance. Allan was already inside.

"How's Allan?"

"He's going to be fine. Vitals are good."

"Good. Meet you at the clinic in a bit."

"Yes, sir."

Paul called the police, and then he and Lori waited
for them to arrive. He held Lori tight in his arms as
they sat on a log, taking in the scent of pine and listening to the wind blowing through the trees. It was so
peaceful, beautiful, home. To think only moments ago,
they were having a wolf fight with the remnants of the
Wolfgang pack.

"Still want to see the movie tonight?" Lori hugged
Paul to her, thankful he was their leader. That she was
his mate and running the pack too. And that Allan,
Everett, and Rose would be all right.

"You bet. No violence or anything. Just romance."

Paul wanted to take her right back home, but he realized she was like him—the movie was part of her list.
Afterward, they would spend the rest of the night naked
at home, enjoying each other to the max.

Catherine called to tell them that Allan would be
fine. "Everett said the men are all dead. And it's a good
thing too. After they hassled Lori while she was jogging
before her martial-arts classes, I knew they would never
stop causing real trouble for us and for others."

Paul felt Lori stiffen a little in his arms.

"I agree. Glad to hear Allan is going to be all right.
We'll be there in a few minutes. Police are just pulling
up. Got to go."

"See you in a bit."

Paul ended the call and looked down at Lori. "Want to explain?"

"Nope. I handled it. We won't have any more trouble with the likes of them."

"Lori…" Paul wanted to kill the bastards all over again.

She smiled up at him. "I love you."

He shook his head and hugged her tight.

Before long, they were explaining to the police and sheriff's department about the bank robbery and Allan getting ambushed after he followed the robber into the woods. Paul didn't have any explanation for the deflated tires on Dusty's truck, but Lori knew how that had happened. She had bitten them in case any of the men tried to make a fast getaway.

Paul and Lori told the police where the bodies would be found but couldn't give any reason for why the two brothers were naked. They'd let the police figure that out for themselves. As to the animal that had bitten into Dusty's neck and killed him, they hadn't seen anything.

"Gonna get that taken care of?" the police officer asked Paul, looking at his arm.

"Yeah, got a movie to go see. Did you get the bank money?"

"Half of it," the officer said.

"What? Hell, the guy who was wearing the motorcycle helmet. He had to have run off with the rest. Maybe the other men hadn't been called to take out Allan, but were just meeting the bank robber to divide up the money in the woods," Paul said, furious they didn't know who the robber was by name and hoping the police didn't think Paul and their pack had anything to do with the missing money. But he and Lori did know the motorcycle guy by scent and by sight, and if they caught sight of him, they'd notify the police and he would be picked up.

"Hey, I gave you his license plate number. Remember? That first time we saw him going into the bank wearing the helmet, and you were suspicious then," Lori said.

"You sure did. SEAL material." Paul opened his vehicle, pulled the slip of paper out of his console, and handed the note to the police.

"Great work. You ever need a job on the force..." the officer said.

"Diving," Paul said. "Allan and I are settling down here and we'd love to be on the diving team."

"I'll put in a good word for you. You folks are free to go."

"You want me to drive?" she asked Paul.

"How are you feeling?"

"I'm fine now. I'll drive."

When they reached the clinic, they found Allan in a hospital bed surrounded by Catherine, Emma, and four pretty she-wolves, newly joined. Allan was groggy but looking like he was in heaven. Paul was glad for that. After giving him their well-wishes, they stopped by to see Everett recovering in another room, Rose holding his good hand, all teary-eyed.

"Thanks for everything," Everett said.

"Hell, we owe you our thanks," Paul said, meaning it.

"Are your mother and sister ready to join the pack?" Lori asked.

"Hell, yeah," Everett said smiling.

"Good," Lori said.

Before they could leave, Dr. Christine Holt pulled Paul aside and insisted on looking at his flesh wound. But that wasn't all. She checked on Lori too, after the fall she'd had. "If you don't mind," the doc said to Paul, "that geneticist is here to take your and Allan's blood samples. Dr. Aidan Denali is doing gene mutation analysis and more, trying to determine why our longevity changed from a shifter's to a human's life span. And if there's anything he can do about it."

"Sure. I'm game." The worry among the shifters was that they'd suddenly begin aging more quickly than humans.

She called the other doctor into the exam room, introduced Paul and Lori as the pack leaders, and then made her excuses and left. The man was tall, wearing a white lab coat, his hair a dark, wavy brown, his eyes just as dark brown. He appeared about thirty with a rugged build, like he worked out. But Paul couldn't figure why the doctor was wearing glasses.

"Thank you for allowing me to take a sample of your blood," Dr. Denali said as he prepared Paul's arm for the needle.

"Are you learning anything?"

"Discovering why something like this happens can often take years. But I'm hoping to learn something sooner than later. One thing I will say, in the very early years, we lived much longer lives. Over the last hundred or so years, our prolonged endurance has been shortening, but so subtly that we didn't realize a change had been occurring until the last decade or so.

"For one thing, we've had a significant number of

older members die earlier than we anticipated based on the earlier life spans of our kind, a year for every thirty of theirs—all of natural causes. I don't have figures on all the *lupus garous* that exist here or in the world, but from those that I've learned of, our life span appears to have changed significantly."

The doctor took the blood sample, then said, "If you or any of your pack experience aging that's more rapid than a human's, let me know, will you? Or anything else that concerns you about this matter." He handed both Lori and Paul business cards.

Paul had to ask because at first he'd thought the doctor wasn't a wolf, and that had him worried. *Lupus garous* didn't have vision problems unless they had an eye injury. "What's up with the glasses?"

Lori looked as eager to learn, though her cheeks turned a little red, and he guessed he'd embarrassed her by asking the personal question of the doc.

Dr. Denali readjusted his glasses. "So that no one confuses me with my younger twin brother. And people, both in the field and laymen, take me more seriously."

Paul wondered why the doc wouldn't want to be mistaken for his brother, but figured he'd asked enough. He could understand why some might not take the doctor seriously since he looked to be only thirty.

After Paul and Lori were finished, they said their good-byes to everyone and headed to the theater.

"They caught the bank robbers in Seattle. I saw it on the news while I was at the dojo teaching a lesson. Then Everett called about Allan's emergency. Did you know that Everett intends to build a log cabin for Rose and himself on Catherine's property? She gave them five acres to build on," Lori said. "Catherine's so excited about her triplet grandchildren and about our wolf pup or pups. She's never talked about it before, but she's just over the moon about being a grandmother."

"That's great to hear." Paul had never thought about how Catherine would react now that she was going to be a grandmother. He was glad she was thrilled. "I like Everett. In a pinch, he was there for us, and he took a bullet for Allan. He respects pack laws too. He'll be a good mate for Rose, I think."

"I agree. I believe she really lucked out. Um, also I got a call from Cora, the she-wolf artist you helped rescue. She said she wanted to thank you and Allan personally for helping to save her. She's flying out in about a week. She said she was in so much pain that she didn't remember what she'd said on the trek through the jungle or in the helicopter. We talked and, well…"

"Don't tell me."

"Yeah, she wants to join the pack. I knew you'd be agreeable."

Then his phone rang and he recognized the policeman's name. "Yeah, this is Paul Cunningham."

"I just thought you'd like to know we caught the man who owned the bike that you had the license plate number for. Rhett Scott was holding on to the rest of the bank money. It was hidden in his boat."

"What did the boat look like?"

"It's an inboard bow-rider runabout. Blue stripe on white."

So now Paul and Lori knew where the Cooper brothers and Jerome had gotten the boat for their drive-by of Lori's dock. "Good deal. And he lives in the area?"

"One of our residents. He never robbed the local bank. But he has robbed four others. He confessed that he and the other men canvassed the banks, drove the getaway truck after he hid his motorcycle, and helped plan the next operation. And you were right in your assumption. He met the others in the woods to split the money, but they heard Allan close by and panicked."

"Good to know they've been stopped."

They ended the call and Paul felt good. Bad guys had gone down. Pack was safe. And he was home again with Lori.

When they arrived at the theater, they saw a couple of wolves who had just joined the pack. They smiled and greeted them. Paul hadn't considered this added benefit of having more wolves in the pack again.

The camaraderie, the secret they all shared, their common heritage.

"They love you." Lori preceded Paul into the row of seats.

Four more single female wolves in their pack sat as close to them as they could get. The pack was gathering.

It was a good feeling. "I love you, Lori Lee Greypaw."

"Cunningham," she reminded him.

And they kissed, missing the opening of the movie— boy meets girl, and all the rest. The wolves had found what was most important to them: each other, the family, and the pack.

"And I love you." Lori cuddled against her mate, glad for all the adventures they'd shared over the years and looking forward to so many more. Their pack. Their territory. Their home.

READ ON FOR A SNEAK PEEK FROM

A Silver Wolf Christmas

CONNOR JAMES SILVER, BETTER KNOWN AS CJ, couldn't believe it had been a whole year since he and his brothers rejoined their cousin Darien Silver's wolf pack. He was glad they had made amends, though his oldest brother was still butting heads with Darien. But the rest of them were happy to be home. Silver Town, Colorado, mostly gray wolf run, would always be home. It had been built by their ancestors, and he envisioned staying here forever.

Especially now that three lovely sister she-wolves had joined the pack and were remodeling the old Silver Town Hotel. In two days' time, they would have hotel guests. CJ smiled as he strode up the covered wooden walkway in front of the tavern and glanced in the direction of what had been the haunted, neglected hotel across the street, which was now showing off its former glory. The windows were no longer boarded up, the picket fence and the fretwork had been repaired, and a fresh coat of white paint made the whole place gleam.

"CJ!" Tom Silver called out as he hurried to join him. Tom, the youngest of Darien's triplet brothers, was CJ's best friend.

He turned to watch Tom crunch through the piled-up snow, then stalk up the covered walkway. He had the same dark hair as CJ, although his eyes were a little darker brown. Tom was wearing his usual: an ecru wool sweater and blue jeans. The toes of his snow boots were now sporting a coating of fresh snow.

Tom pointed at the hotel, evidently having observed CJ looking that way. "Don't *even* think about going over there to help with the final preparations before their grand opening."

CJ shook his head. "I know when I'm not wanted." But he damn well wasn't giving up on seeing the women—well, one in particular.

Tom smiled a little evilly at him. "Come on. I'll buy you lunch. Darien has a job for you."

Even though CJ was a deputy sheriff and took his lead from the sheriff, everyone stopped what they were doing when the pack leader needed something done. Pack took priority.

He and Tom headed inside the tavern, where the fire was burning in a brand-new woodstove in the corner, keeping the room warm. The Christmas tree in front of one of the windows was decorated with white lights, big red bows, and hand-painted ornaments featuring wolves. The aroma of hot roast beef scented the air, making CJ's stomach rumble. Sam, the black-bearded bartender—and now sandwich maker—was serving lunch without Silva, his waitress-turned-mate. She was now down the street running her own tearoom, where the women ate when they wanted lunch out. The men all continued to congregate at Sam's.

The tavern usually looked a lot more rustic, less... Christmassy. Sam loved Silva and tolerated her need to see that everyone enjoyed the spirit of Christmas either at her place or his, though he grumbled about it like an old grizzly bear.

CJ glanced at the red, green, and silver foil-covered chocolates in wooden Christmas-tree-shaped dishes on the center of each table. Those were new. Silva had also draped spruce garlands along the bar and over the long, rectangular mirror that had hung there since the place opened centuries earlier. She'd added lights and Christmas wreaths to the windows and had put up the tree, though Sam had helped. He looked rough and gruff, and was protective of anyone close to him, but he was a big teddy bear. Though CJ would never voice his opinion about that.

"We'll have the usual," Tom called out to Sam.

He nodded and began to fix roast beef sandwiches for them.

"Staying out of trouble?" Tom sat in his regular chair at the pack leaders' table in the corner of the tavern. This spot had a view of the whole place, except for the area by the restrooms.

"I haven't been near there." CJ glanced around the room, nodding a greeting to Mason, owner of the bank; John Hastings, owner of the local hardware store and bed and breakfast; Jacob Summers, their local electrician; and even Mervin, the barber—all gray wolves who were sharing conversations and eating and drinking. It was an exclusive club, membership strictly reserved for wolves.

CJ looked out the new windows of the tavern—also Silva's doing, now that the hotel was quite an attraction instead of detracting from the view. The new sign proclaimed Silver Town Hotel, just like in the old days, as it rocked a little in the breeze. Only this time, the sign featured a howling wolf carved into one corner. CJ loved it, just like everyone else did.

The pack members couldn't have been more pleased with the way the sisters had renovated the place, keeping the old Victorian look but adding special touches. Like the two wrought iron and wood-slat benches in a parklike setting out front, with the bench seats held up by wrought iron bears.

Tom turned back to CJ. "Darien said—"

"I know what Darien said. My brothers and I were getting under the women's feet. They didn't want or need our help. Don't tell me we can't participate in the grand opening." Even though CJ would be busy directing traffic for a little while, he intended to stop in and check on the crowd inside the hotel to ensure everyone was behaving themselves.

Sam delivered their beers in new steins, featuring wolves in a winter scene etched in the glass, along with sandwiches and chips on wooden Christmas tree plates. He gave CJ a look that told him he'd better not make a comment about the plates or steins. CJ was dying to ask Sam how domesticated life was, but he bit his tongue.

"I'll be setting up the bar for the festivities," Sam said. "Silva is bringing her special petit fours, and she's serving finger sandwiches. The hotel had better be ready to open on schedule."

"Do you think any of the guests will run out of there screaming in the middle of the night, claiming the place is haunted?" CJ asked. It was something he'd worried about. He wanted to see the sisters do well so they could stay here forever.

Sam shook his head. "Blamed foolishness, if you ask me."

Sam didn't believe in anything paranormal. Some might ask how he could feel that way when they were *lupus garous*—wolf shifters. But then again, their kind believed they were perfectly normal. Nothing paranormal about them.

Someone called for another beer, and Sam left their table to take care of it.

"When you were over there getting underfoot, did you see anything?" Tom asked, keeping his voice low.

Even though they'd been best friends forever, this was one thing CJ really didn't want to discuss with Tom. Neither of them had, not once over all those years. "Darien said he and Jake were just playing tricks on us, making us believe the place was haunted so we'd race out of there like our lives depended on it. We were what…seven? Pretty gullible. Just your brothers having some fun at our expense—like usual."

CJ took another bite of his sandwich, hoping now that the hotel was opening, he could finally start seeing Laurel MacTire in more of a courtship way. He would never again make the mistake of mispronouncing her name. Who would ever have thought that a name that looked like "tire" was pronounced like "fear" with a *T*? He couldn't know every foreign word meaning "wolf." But he did love that she was a pretty redheaded, green-eyed lass. She had been born in America, but she still had a little Irish accent, courtesy of her Irish-born parents. He loved to listen to her talk.

The problem was that she and her sisters, Meghan and Ellie, acted wary around him and everyone else in the pack. In fact, they didn't seem like the type of proprietors that should manage a hotel, since they were more reserved than friendly or welcoming. He wasn't sure what was wrong. Maybe they'd never lived with a pack before. He had to admit that everyone had been eager to greet them, so maybe they felt a bit overwhelmed.

The pack members were so welcoming because fewer she-wolves were born among *lupus garous* than males, and many of the bachelors were interested. The women in the pack were also grateful that they had more women to visit with. Besides that, the wolf pack's collective nature was such that its members openly received new wolves.

After eating the rest of his sandwich, Tom leaned back in his chair. "The two painters working on the main lobby left prematurely yesterday after demanding their pay for what they'd finished. They said that when they returned from a lunch break, their paint cans had been moved across the room, their plastic sheeting was balled up in a corner, and an *X* was painted across the ceiling in the study. And that was only the half of it."

CJ frowned. "None of the sisters saw or heard anything?"

"The sisters had returned to their house behind the hotel to have lunch."

"Could it have been kids? Vandals?" CJ figured that what had happened wasn't the result of anything supernatural.

"Who knows? If we discount the ghostly angle, could have been."

"Did the women smell the scent of anyone who had been in there earlier?"

"Not that they could say. So many people have been traipsing through the hotel, finishing up renovations, that maybe somebody else just moved the stuff. The electrician and a plumber were in earlier."

"About that...I've seen that they've hired humans for a number of the jobs. Except for Jacob, the electrician. I would think everyone, even if they're new to the pack, would hire wolves."

Tom shrugged. "They've never been in a pack before. It'll take a little getting used to. Maybe no one gave them a list of who could do the jobs for them. We all know who does what in the vicinity. The sisters wouldn't have a clue."

CJ nodded, but he was already thinking about how the painters had left the work unfinished. Maybe the women could use his help in painting the rest of the place. As long as the town or surrounding area didn't require him to get involved in any law enforcement business, he was free to help out. And eager to do so.

"Of course, that doesn't explain the *X* on the ceiling," Tom said.

"Most likely vandals."

CJ wasn't afraid of any old ghost in the hotel. He hadn't been since that day when Darien and Jake had tried to scare him and Tom when they were all kids. CJ told himself it had just been them. But neither of the Silver brothers had said anything about what CJ had witnessed, and he was certain they had nothing to do with it. He was still telling himself the apparition he'd seen was only a figment of his imagination. That, as a kid, he'd been so scared, he could have imagined anything. That the darkened shadow of a woman was nothing more than dust particles highlighted by moonlight shining through the basement door's window.

Tom sat taller in his chair. "If visitors ask about the hauntings, Darien wants everyone in the pack to tell them the stories are just rumors."

"Right. Ghosts don't exist."

Tom let out his breath. "But you know differently. We both know differently."

That made CJ wonder what Tom had experienced. But if CJ admitted to even one soul that he believed the hotel was haunted, there would go his best-kept secret of all time. Besides, Tom had never shared what he'd experienced either.

Tom straightened a bit. "Okay. Well, as I said, Darien has a job for you."

If it had to do with helping Laurel MacTire— "MacTear" as in "fear," CJ kept reminding himself—he would jump right on it. He was certain that she *really* didn't mind that he'd been so in the way when she was trying to get the place fixed up. She was just overcautious about everyone in the wolf pack.

"Hang some Christmas lights on the hotel?" Then again, the job could have nothing to do with Laurel, her sisters, or the hotel.

Tom tilted his chin down. "*No* helping the women with the hotel. Unless they change their minds and ask you to."

"All right," CJ said. "What then?"

"We have some ghost busters in town."

"That's just what we need." CJ was ready to protect the three sisters from anyone who might try to ruin things for them.

"For now, they're staying in the Hastingses' bed and breakfast, both tonight and tomorrow. But they have reservations at the hotel, and they will be moving over there as soon as it opens. They've been grilling Bertha Hastings and everyone else about the hauntings."

"That's not good."

"Of course, we're worried they might stir up trouble for the ladies by reporting the place is haunted to discourage people from staying there. But what we're really concerned about is that they'll learn that something a lot more serious than ghosts exists in the area."

"*Lupus garous.*"

"Yes. Us."

"You want me to get rid of them?" CJ asked, surprised. Not that he thought Darien wanted him to kill anyone, but keeping their wolf halves secret was paramount to their well-being.

Tom chuckled. "No. But you're assigned to watch over them. If they see anyone shift when they shouldn't, then we'll have to take care of it."

CJ's whole outlook brightened. "Right. They're staying at the hotel." And if he had to really watch them, he'd have to stay there too! That meant he could see Laurel more.

"Can you handle it?"

"Hell yeah."

"I mean…" Tom glanced around the tavern where pack members filled nearly every chair at the wooden tables. The room was humming with conversation. He leaned forward. "Because of the ghosts."

"That don't exist."

"Right."

"Yeah, I can handle it." CJ smiled. He would do any-thing to be able to spend more time with that wickedly intriguing she-wolf. Though he hoped he wouldn't be the one running out of the hotel and breaking out into a cold sweat—again.

More than that, he knew something else was going on. The women didn't just buy the hotel because it was a beautiful building or a great investment opportunity, or because they desperately wanted to join a pack. They'd been reservedly friendly. Like they didn't trust anyone. And they hadn't joined in any pack functions during the six months they'd been renovating the hotel. Not once.

Of course, they said it all had to do with getting the place ready, and they were too busy or too tired after-ward to participate. But he'd noticed the looks between the three sisters when he'd asked them why they chose this hotel to buy. It was as if they had some deep, dark secret, and they had to keep it that way.

So yeah, he was definitely interested in Laurel, but not just because she was a hot she-wolf. He wanted to know what she and her sisters were *really* doing here.

Laurel MacTire's luck hadn't been so hot lately. Tomorrow, both her sisters had to go out of state to ensure the shipment of furniture had arrived from Paris and then was safely transported here. When she and her sisters had tracked down the auctioned highboy and blanket chest that had belonged to their aunt Clarinda, they were afraid something bad had happened to her. In her will, their aunt had promised the furniture to their mother, her twin sister, Sadie.

But they'd learned from their mother six months earlier that Clarinda had vanished fifty years ago. Someone had auctioned off the furniture around that same time. It had taken the sisters all this time to finally locate the pieces and buy them back.

Clarinda had said in a letter to their mother that the furniture was unique, with an added feature. Their mother thought one or both of the pieces might contain a secret compartment. Maybe a clue hidden in a secret panel in a drawer would help them learn what had become of their aunt. Pictures documenting the initials of the furniture designer, *ELS*, and the fact that each piece had been made specifically for its owner, had helped the sisters to prove the items had belonged to their aunt.

No matter what else happened, the sisters wanted to keep the furniture in memory of their aunt.

That meant Laurel had to manage everything on her own for a couple of days, starting early tomorrow morning—and including the grand opening ceremony and the first hotel guests' arrival. What made it worse was that, according to Darien Silver, three of the men who had booked rooms for a week were supposedly ghost busters. That was *all* they needed!

What if the three men told the whole world the hotel was haunted? There would go the business. They'd either not get any guests, or they'd have a bunch of paranormal thrill seekers wanting to stay there. Maybe even a well-known author like Stephen King, staying there to gain information and planning to use the setting for a new book. Well, on second thought, she supposed that could be a boon.

She opened the buffet drawer in the lobby and pulled

out the fifty-year-old postcard, the last communication that her missing aunt had sent to Laurel's mother. Laurel reread the note for the millionth time, as if she'd miraculously get more clues from it.

Silver Town Hotel. Miss you. Falling in love. Kiss girls for me. See you at Christmas. Love, C

Ellie was headed for the stairs, a box of blinds in hand, when she saw Laurel reading the postcard again. "Hey, no matter how many times we look at it, it's not revealing anything new. We know for sure these were our aunt's last words to our mother—that she was staying at the Silver Town Hotel. And she sounded like she was involved in a romance. When she failed to show up at Christmastime, Mom got worried. But though she investigated, she didn't find any sign of her sister. We were too little to really understand what was going on. Just that our aunt wasn't coming to play with us. She was always so much fun."

"Right." Laurel tucked the card back in the drawer. "I wish Mom hadn't waited until she was dying to tell us this about Aunt Clarinda."

Meghan came around the banister with a drill and a couple more boxes of blinds. "Are we talking about the postcard again? Mom was worried that something sinister might have happened to her sister—and that we'd learn about it and go looking for her, which could get us in trouble. But in the end, Mom wanted us to discover what happened to her sister. It was her last dying request. You know it had to have weighed heavily on her mind all these years. I think she figured her sister had been murdered, but it had been so long ago that we were safe now."

Laurel agreed. "I hope we can learn the truth sooner

than later." She closed the buffet drawer as her sisters headed up the stairs to hang the faux wooden blinds in the windows.

So far they didn't have anything to go on but the postcard and a lot of supposition. What if one of the Silver Town pack members had something to do with Aunt Laurel's disappearance? He could still be here. That was one of the things about the wolves' longevity. Their aging process was so much slower, or at least it had been. Recently, something had changed the dynamics and now their life spans were closer to humans'.

That meant anyone could be suspect—even CJ Silver, who was so eager to please her in his own way. She'd caught herself a ton of times letting down her guard with him. She needed to remember that she couldn't trust anyone but her sisters.

Now Darien was assigning CJ to watch the ghost busters? She'd never expected that to happen.

As soon as CJ walked in the door, all six feet of him, his amber eyes immediately sought her out as she worked on varnishing the countertop of the check-in desk. His sable hair complemented his tan face, and his muscular but wiry build had definitely turned the head of more than one she-wolf. She reminded herself that getting involved with any of the wolf pack members could be a bad idea.

"Did Darien tell you that I'll need to stay here when that ghost-busting crew arrives?"

"Yes."

"I heard you had trouble with the painters. Do you want me to finish the painting for you?" CJ looked perfectly willing.

Against her best judgment—because she was feeling a bit overwhelmed with all that still needed to be done— she nodded. "Thanks. You're...not afraid of ghosts?"

CJ smiled. "They don't exist. I'm ready to paint when you are. Just let me know what I need to do."

"The painters left the paint, brushes, plastic, everything, and won't return. So it's all over there." She pointed to the corner of the lobby.

"Great. I'll get right on it."

He was cute, but he looked so restrainedly pleased, she smiled. Until she saw her sister Meghan walking down the curved stairs and staring at CJ. Meghan shot her a look, as if to say she shouldn't have invited him to paint. Laurel hadn't had a chance to tell her sisters that Darien wanted CJ staying with them to watch over the ghost busters.

"What's Ellie doing?" Laurel asked.

"She's finishing up the blue room, still hanging the new blinds in there. *We* were going to finish the painting down here, I thought."

"We have to decorate the whole place for Christmas next. We don't have time to finish the painting too. Not with the two of you leaving tomorrow to take care of other business. Plus, we sort of have an issue."

Meghan narrowed her green eyes at her sister. "What *sort* of an issue?"

"You know the three men who were the first to rent rooms?"

Folding her arms, Meghan nodded.

"Darien learned they're self-professed ghost busters. They even have a TV show."

"*Great.*" As if they hadn't had enough problems.

A frozen, then broken water pipe that flooded the basement, the painters getting spooked by ghosts, and half of the windows arriving in the wrong size were only a few of the minor disasters they'd had to deal with.

CJ had already started painting one wall. It was white, but the pictures that had hung there had left rectangular shadows on the walls. Even with the start of a fresh coat of paint, it looked better. "Darien is checking our guest list to make sure we're not going to have any other trouble. That's how he discovered who these men are and why they wanted rooms. He's concerned about them."

Meghan frowned. "Darien isn't doing background checks on all our guests forever, is he?"

As if Laurel and her sisters were staying in Silver Town forever. This was their business—buying, renovating, and selling hotels. They never stayed long. "He's the pack leader. If he thinks we might have any trouble, or that the rest of his pack might, he'll keep a close eye on the hotel. So with regard to that, he wants CJ to stay with us until the men leave."

Openmouthed, Meghan stared at her. Her gaze switched from her to CJ to Laurel again. "*You're...kidding.* Stay with *us*?"

"Yep. Darien gave him the job of watching the ghost busters to ensure they don't see anyone shifting. If they do, then the pack will handle it."

"*Just great.*"

"Yeah, I know. Tell Ellie, will you?"

"Sure. So which room is he staying in?" Meghan smiled a little evilly. "The maids' quarters?"

"No way. He can have the attic room. Hopefully nothing will bother him up there." Laurel frowned as she stared at the center of the wall that CJ had already painted over. "Do you see a letter in the center of the wall?"

Meghan studied the wall. "I was hoping I was just imagining it."

They moved closer as CJ considered the section he'd just painted.

"Okay, so your name is CJ and you're being cute by painting a *C* on the wall?" Meghan asked, her voice sharp and on edge.

Laurel knew very well CJ hadn't done it. Not considering how much he seemed to want to please her and her sisters. If he was going to initial his paint job, why not make it *CJ*? The letter was a foot and a half tall, maybe a foot wide, about six inches thick, and whiter than the white wall he was painting. It hadn't been there before he started painting, and he was using a paint roller. It would have been impossible for him to paint the letter without using a paintbrush and a guideline, a stencil, or something, considering how crisp and clean the lines were.

CJ stepped back from the wall and stared at it. "If the letter is still there after I paint the wall and it dries, I'll us some special paint that covers water stains and the like."

Laurel pointed to the corner. "A can of that kind of paint is over there."

"Okay, I'll take care of it."

Meghan headed for the stairs. "I'll tell Ellie about the trouble we might have with the ghost-hunter TV personalities." She glanced warily at CJ.

Laurel went back to work varnishing the old oak countertop while her sisters put the finishing touches on the rooms. The Silver pack had planned a grand opening ceremony, and all eight rooms were booked, now including the attic room. It only had a small table, a chair, a three-drawer bachelor chest, and a twin-size bed. They'd fixed it up but hadn't really thought they'd have anyone staying there—unless someone desperately needed the lodging, was single, and wasn't overly tall. Which made her realize that CJ would be too tall for the bed.

Where else could they put him? The basement had four rooms and a shared bathroom for the maids' quarters, but Laurel and her sisters had put off renovating those until later because of all the other plumbing, painting, and electrical problems they'd had to deal with. They lived in the guesthouse out back, a lovely four-bedroom home with gingerbread trim to match the hotel. The nearby gazebo, fountain, and gardens were perfect for guests during any season, though the fountain couldn't run until spring now. For winter, they were decorating everything for Christmas. That way the rooms that had a garden view would see festive touches everywhere.

"*What?*" Ellie said, her voice elevated as Meghan talked with her upstairs in the blue bedroom.

Laurel didn't know if Ellie was outraged about the ghost busters staying with them or one of the members of the Silver pack lodging here, or maybe a little of both. In any event, they had to deal with it.

She and her sisters felt like they were walking on the edge of a cliff. One wrong turn and they would fall off, without a safety net to catch them. She was certain the pack wouldn't be happy if she and her sisters discovered that one of its members was involved in her aunt's disappearance.

Laurel looked up from her varnishing work and saw that CJ had started painting over the *C* with the stain-killing paint—three feet out in every direction to hide the letter.

Morbidly fascinated, she watched as the whole area became one block of white. As the paint began to dry, the letter reappeared as bold as day—white on white, as if it was meant to be there. Or Clarinda MacTire was trying to tell her nieces she had been here.

Maybe she still was here.

Acknowledgments

Lanny Wilkinson, for advice on removing a skeleton from the lake. Also, Alaina Armbruster, Tori Scott, Stephanie Shaw, Barbara Wilt Gerber, Carolyn Wain McCanna, and Donna Fournier, who all helped me with diving and skeleton questions. As always, my beta readers are the best! To Loretta Melvin, Bonnie Gill, and Dottie Jones, a big thanks! And to Deb Werksman, my editor, and the cover artists who do such a beautiful job!

A Silver Wolf Christmas

by Terry Spear

USA Today Bestselling Author

—∿∿—

Wolf-shifter CJ Silver is more than happy to help the new female shifters in town renovate an old hotel for the holidays— especially if it means opportunities under the mistletoe with the tempting Laurel MacTire.

But renovations become a lot more difficult when the hotel attracts the attention of human ghost hunters. Determined to keep their visitors from discovering that werewolves live in town, CJ and Laurel have to work together to protect their community. As they sneak around the old hotel to keep an eye on the ghost hunters, CJ and Laurel are in for a much hotter holiday treat than they expected…

—∿∿—

SEAL Wolf
Diving for Trouble

by Terry Spear

USA Today Bestselling Author

———❧———

Debbie Renaud is a police diver working on criminal cases with SEAL Allan Rappaport. She admires him greatly for his missions in the navy, plus he's just plain HOT. Allan seems to share her attraction, but what she doesn't know is that her partner is wolf shifter.

Allan is really hung up on his smart, beautiful dive partner, but he can't get involved with a human outside dive duty. Yet when she gets between a werewolf hunter and his intended victim, one of the members of Allan's pack, they run into real trouble, and their lives are altered forever.

———❧———

Praise for Terry Spear:

For more Terry Spear, visit:

www.sourcebooks.com

Her Wild Hero

X-Ops

by Paige Tyler

USA Today Bestselling Author

The third book in the hot, pulse-pounding paranormal romantic suspense X-Ops series from *USA Today* bestselling author Paige Tyler.

Department of Covert Operations training officer Kendra Carlsen has been begging her boss to let her go into the field for years. When he finally agrees to send her along on a training exercise in Costa Rica, she's thrilled.

Bear-shifter Declan MacBride, on the other hand, is anything but pleased. He's been crushing on Kendra since he started working at the DCO seven years ago. Spending two weeks in the same jungle with her is putting a serious strain on him.

When the team gets ambushed, Kendra and Declan are forced to depend on each other. But the bear-shifter soon discovers that bloodthirsty enemies aren't nearly as hard to fight off as his attraction to the beautiful woman he'll do anything to protect.

Praise for *Her Perfect Mate*:

"Absolutely perfect. One of the best books I've read in years." —Kate Douglas, bestselling author of the Wolf Tales and Spirit Wild series

For more Paige Tyler, visit:

www.sourcebooks.com